GLIMPSES
of the
UNKNOWN

GLIMPSES
of the
UNKNOWN

Lost Ghost Stories

edited by

MIKE ASHLEY

This collection first published in 2018 by
The British Library
96 Euston Road
London NW1 2DB

Introduction © Mike Ashley 2018

Dates attributed to each story relate to first publication.

Cataloguing in Publication Data
A catalogue record for this publication is available from the British Library

ISBN 978 0 7123 5266 6

Frontispiece, 'Photograph of a psychic and spirit', from the Society
for the Study of Supernormal Pictures, 1870 © British Library Board

Text design and typesetting by Tetragon, London
Printed and bound by CPI Group (UK) Ltd, Croydon, CR0 4YY

CONTENTS

INTRODUCTION

There have been anthologies of ghost and supernatural stories for over two hundred years. An anthology is a collection of stories or poems by more than one author. In that sense Antoine Galland's translation of the *Arabian Nights*, *Les milles et une nuits*, published between 1704 and 1717, may be classified as one of the earliest anthologies, though the idea of an author translating and adapting stories to fit into a cohesive volume goes back many years and includes the *Decameron* of Giovanni Boccaccio, completed in 1353, and as far back as the *Garland* of Meleager who lived in the Middle East in the first century BCE. So it certainly has an ancient tradition.

The earliest "modern" anthology concentrating on ghost stories and strange tales was almost certainly the French compilation *Fantasmagoriana* published in 1812. It was translated into English the following year as *Tales of the Dead* and it was this book that Lord Byron and his friends, Percy Shelley, Mary Shelley and Dr. Polidori read at the Villa Diodati near Lake Geneva in June 1816 and gave rise to the contest between them to each write a ghost story. The most memorable result was Mary's novel *Frankenstein*.

Since then there must have been around 3,000 such anthologies published in the English language—I recorded 2,100 when I compiled an index to them, *The Supernatural Index*, in 1994. Whilst few of them have been as influential as that initial *Tales of the Dead*, there's little doubt that there's always been a place for the ghost story anthology, bringing together some of the best and most memorable supernatural stories. However, what also became evident when I compiled my index was how often anthologists fell back on the same stories. "The

Signalman" by Charles Dickens, "The Haunted and the Haunters" by Edward Bulwer-Lytton, "The Upper Berth" by F. Marion Crawford and "The Monkey's Paw" by W. W. Jacobs headed the list of the most reprinted ghost stories. If you were to bundle together a handful of reprint anthologies, I'd be very surprised if at least one of these wasn't amongst them. They are, of course, excellent stories. Don't get me wrong. Each new generation of readers needs to discover these stories for themselves, but there is a danger that we fall back on tried and tested stories without searching for those lesser known but equally good tales.

Over the years there have been those anthologists that went out of their way to track down little known authors and their works and thus broaden our understanding of the field and of the depth of material available. Of course, one way to do this is to assemble an anthology of all-new, original stories, which is always a treat. But this provides a contemporary outlook and interpretation of weird fiction and even if an author chooses to set their story in the Victorian or Edwardian periods, it will still be through modern eyes.

What I wanted to do in this anthology is track down stories that have never been reprinted before but which date from that Golden Age of the supernatural story, the 1890s to the 1920s. I feel as certain as I can that all of these stories will be new to, hopefully, all readers, though there may just be a chance someone has come across one or two of them before. I sincerely hope, though, that my belief that not one has been reprinted since its first (and therefore, only) publication, holds good.

The result is not only stories that will be new and original to everyone, but will introduce a wave of writers hitherto forgotten or only known for a few weird tales. I did not expect to find lost stories by writers well known in the field, and was thus delighted to find a previously unreprinted story by E. F. Benson, one of the greats of the supernatural. Some may also recognise the names of F. Britten Austin and Guy Thorne, popular in their day for their unusual and often daring fiction. But most of these writers have been unjustly forgotten even though some, such as Elsie Norris, Huan Mee, James Barr, Lumley Deakin and Philippa Forest, wrote quite a few weird tales—and, in the case of Jack Edwards, many.

I've tried to find out what I can about each writer and have provided a preface to each story to add some flesh on to the bones, so to speak, but I believe the stories speak for themselves. Whether or not you know the author, I am sure you will find the stories memorable for their own sake. Not all of them evoke horror or fear. I believe a ghost story can work on several levels ranging from the unnerving tingle of the unknown, to that hauntingly evocative atmosphere of something strange or uncertain. That whole spectrum of the supernatural will be found here and I hope that each story leaves its imprint in your memory, so that these ghosts are no longer lost.

MIKE ASHLEY
January 2018

ON THE EMBANKMENT

Hugh E. Wright

Hugh Esterel Wright (1879–1940) was an actor, song writer and music-hall entertainer. He came from a well-to-do family whose ancestors had been bankers and owners of the Butterley Iron Works in Derbyshire. He had followed his elder brother, Philip, into the Royal Navy in 1893 as a midshipman and was invalided out in 1902. Hugh turned to the stage, working in concert parties and variety before graduating to the theatre, establishing himself in Seymour Hicks's 1910 play, Captain Kidd. *From then on he was never out of work, usually in comedy roles. When not acting he was performing his nonsense songs, accompanying himself on the piano, and was a regular in revues, pantomime and end-of-the-pier summer shows. He also became a regular in films and, in the 1930s, on radio, for which he also wrote children's stories.*

His reputation as a comic actor did not prepare his followers for a sudden change when, starting in 1919, he wrote a few horror stories, culminating in the one-act, grand guignol play Ha-Ha!, *performed in 1923. The play, which showed how a séance goes horribly wrong, was not a critical success and Wright did not repeat the experiment. Perhaps because of that his few weird tales have been forgotten. Most appeared in* The Blue Magazine, *a small circulation fiction monthly which ran many off-trail stories and mysteries. The following was one of his earliest, from 1919.*

I

DO YOU KNOW THE EMBANKMENT? I DON'T MEAN THE
Embankment you can see through the windows of your
hurrying taxi, as you drive into the City to see your most respect-
able solicitor about that matter of the drains at Hampstead; I don't
mean the row of flaring lights, each reflected in the blackness of
the sloppy pavement, as you see it from the windows of the Savoy,
when you are having supper after the theatre, on a wet night; I
mean the Embankment at two o'clock in the morning, in a driving
November drizzle, when the tide of London's gaiety has ebbed, and
left its residue of London driftwood high—and wishing to God it
were dry—littered about under bridges, on seats, and in unexpected
crannies and corners, which even the most optimistic would hardly
call sheltered. Stark and ugly the wreckage is; battered by many winds
and tides; broken and twisted by storm and stress; grim caricatures
of the past! Do you know the Embankment? Think yourself lucky
if you do not!

Possibly it has changed now. I am thinking of fifteen years ago,
before the electric trams buzzed angrily up and down it at half-hour
intervals, and shattered its silence and solitude, with their clanging
bells, and flashing lights. They sleep lightly, those London derelicts,
and are easily disturbed; possibly they have drifted to quieter quarters.

Midway between the Avenue and Westminster Bridge, there
is a seat that has a story, and a peculiarity. Its peculiarity is this: no
matter at what time of night you pass it, no matter how crowded
with dilapidated humanity the seats next to it may be, that seat is
always empty. Fifteen years ago it was empty; each night, for twenty

odd years before that it had been empty; and unless the hand of time or the L.C.C. has removed it, I am willing to gamble that it is empty now. That's queer, isn't it? And the story about it is queerer still. But it's not my story, so before I tell it you, I'd better explain how I got it.

It happened about fifteen years ago. I was doing a spell of night-work at the office, and my road home took me along the Embankment there, at three-fifteen every morning. Every morning for a week or more, I passed that empty seat, and wondered why it was empty. Once I stopped a policeman and asked him. He admitted that it seemed funny, but—like the noble six hundred—"his not to reason why," and he "reckoned it was just fancy."

I wasn't satisfied with that, and a week or so later, Fate sent me to the one man in London who knew the story. I was introduced to him at a club dinner; he was twenty years my senior, I should think, and—as I knew—had the reputation of knowing more about odd corners of London than any other man living.

He had left successful journalism for successful literature, and I was a little in awe of him. However, he sat next to me at dinner, and was great enough to bring me into the conversation, and take a real interest in what little I had to contribute towards it.

During dinner the idea flashed through my mind, "I wonder if he knows anything about that empty seat? I've a good mind to ask him." But it wasn't till the coffee and cigars, that I found courage enough to say: "There's a little bit of London I know that I feel sure must have some story connected with it. I wonder if you could help me?"

"London's a biggish village," he answered pleasantly, "but if I know it, I will. What place is it?"

"Strictly speaking, it isn't even a place, within the meaning of the Act," I said, hesitatingly. "Now I'm asking you, I'm afraid it sounds unutterably silly. It's only an empty seat on the Embankment."

He was raising his coffee-cup to his lips, but he put it down again, untouched. "Between the Avenue and Westminster Bridge?" he said slowly.

"You know it, then?" I asked, with some relief.

"Yes, I know it!" he said, and looked at me queerly. "So it's still empty," he added, half to himself.

"It was all last week," I replied, and explained how I knew.

The man on the other side of him dragged him into some argument, and for some time I didn't get a chance of getting another word in. In fact, he was just rising to go home before I found my opportunity.

"Excuse me," I said quickly. "About that story."

"Still want it?" he said, smiling.

"Rather! If you don't mind," I replied eagerly.

"Come and have dinner at my place Thursday week, then. You know my address?"

You can easily understand that I didn't take long accepting his invitation.

"And, by the way," he added, ignoring my thanks, "if we get a dry night between now and then, have another look at that seat at about seven or eight in the morning. If you notice anything else odd about it, you can tell me, and you shall have the story in exchange. Good night!"

Three nights later it was bone-dry, and about seven-thirty next morning I strolled down the Embankment to have another look at the seat, as he had suggested. I wasn't going to run any risk of losing the story if I could help it.

The seat looked ordinary enough in the early daylight; the only thing that I noticed at all was that there was a little puddle of water at one end of it—as if someone had been wringing out a wet towel.

It couldn't have been rain; the night, as I said, had been fine, and, besides, the other end of the bench was quite dry. I looked over it minutely, but could find nothing out of the ordinary, and eventually tore myself away, very much disappointed.

Thursday night arrived, and with it my dinner with the great man. He was most affable. During dinner he asked me if I had been to see the seat any morning, and if I had found anything.

"I went and looked on Saturday morning," I replied, "but I couldn't find anything out of the ordinary."

"No little detail at all?" he asked.

"One thing I noticed," I said doubtfully, "but it seems hardly worth mentioning."

"What was that?"

"One end of the seat was quite wet, and there'd been no rain in the night, you know."

My host didn't say anything, but I fancied he grew thoughtful. After dinner he told me the story. I asked him why he didn't write it himself.

"I was a bit too close to it to get the proper perspective," he said. "But if you want it for copy, use it by all means. Don't mention my name, that's all. You won't do anything with it, though. Nobody will believe it; and if they did, they wouldn't like it. It isn't funny, and it isn't pretty. Take my advice and leave it alone!"

I haven't taken his advice, and here it is. I've tried to tell it as nearly as possible the way he told it to me. But he's quite right about one thing—it isn't pretty!

II

It's a funny coincidence that you should ask me the story of the empty seat, because, I suppose, barring one other, I'm the only man who knows it, began my host. I haven't told it to anyone else either. For one thing, I have to confess to two crimes against society—poverty and cowardice. I started by being very poor, and ended by being very frightened. I suppose the former matters most, but perhaps even that may be forgiven me after over twenty years.

(He puffed lazily at his cigar for a minute or two, and then resumed his story.)

Yes, it's well over twenty years ago; but I haven't forgotten that seat, and I don't think I ever shall.

Have you ever been very poor? I don't mean just hard up; but absolutely "broke to the wide," "on your uppers"? I was then, and it's not pleasant, I assure you.

And even I wasn't absolutely destitute like most of those poor beggars down there. I had a job to go to in a fortnight's time, a fairly decent suit of clothes on my back, shoes that kept the wet out, and exactly two and fourpence in my pocket. I had a portmanteau in the cloak-room at Charing Cross, too; but, on the other hand, I didn't know a soul in London who'd trust me with board and lodging, so I had to leave it there, eating up a penny a day out of my modest savings, or else carry it about with me wherever I went.

I soon made up my mind to reserve my two and fourpence for food. I thought I could just manage to keep body and soul together on that, but I couldn't see any margin for sleeping accommodation. I'd read about people who'd "started on the Embankment," and I thought I'd try that. It sounded rather romantic, somehow. It would be fine to look back on, and say one had been through it. After all, it was only for a fortnight. One is several different kinds of a fool at twenty-two!

I won't weary you by telling you how I got through that first day. It was pretty deadly, though! Still, London was new to me, there were shops to look at, and people to watch; and it kept dry—that was one comfort.

I know that by midnight I was dog-tired. Half-an-hour later the crowds began to thin, and I made my way slowly towards the Embankment—the goal of all my hopes.

My idea was that I should find a seat, stretch myself out as comfortably as might be, and fall asleep. You can judge my surprise and annoyance to find that each seat I came to was packed with bundles of rags, which, on closer inspection, proved to be human beings. And not only the seats; every possible corner that promised any sort of shelter had its human occupant. I was a good half-hour too late.

I slopped along despondently; to make matters worse, a thin drizzle had started, and I wondered vaguely where on earth I was going to rest that night. That the Embankment should be full up seemed to me to be the last straw.

About half-way between the Avenue and Westminster Bridge, I suddenly saw a ray of hope. To my surprise I spotted a vacant seat on one of the benches. It was the end seat, too, though the rest of the bench was crowded with five or six ragamuffins huddled together in grotesque heaps.

They looked up incuriously as I approached, and I was about to sit down, when something at the end of the bench said, in a hoarse voice: "The stalls is hall reserved, cully; try 'igher up in the gallery."

There was a "tee-hee" of feminine laughter, and another voice squeaked: "Garn! Corn't yer see 'e's a-lookin' fur the r'yal box!" A third voice grumbled wrathfully: "Any'ow,'e can't set 'ere! Blarsted torf! 'Op it, see!"

Then the man next to the vacant seat spoke. He was a ferrety individual, with a pale face and watery, redrimmed eyes; a bowler hat, several sizes too large, was pushed down over his ears, and his only clothing appeared to be an enormous, dirty, yellow overcoat, tied round the middle with a bit of cord.

"Shut up!" he snarled. Then, peering up at me, with shifty eyes, he whined: "Sit dahn, mite! Never you mind them; swine they are—bloomin' swine—and be'ave as such!"

There was an indistinct muttering along the bench. I thought I caught the words: "Wot abaht Squinty?"

"Got a bit o' baccy?" whined the ferrety man as I sank down into the seat with a sigh of relief. I told him I hadn't.

"Got a copper?" he whined again.

"No! Stony!" I explained.

He spat accurately into the gutter, and looked up at me venomously. "Thort you was a bloomin' torf," he snarled, turning his back on me, and digging a particularly sharp elbow into my ribs.

"'E corn't sit 'ere, yer know, torf or no torf," grumbled the voice at the end of the seat.

"Blarst yer! I know, don' I?" snarled my next door neighbour. "Shet yer fice! Wan' 'er spile a bit o' sport?"

"Tee-hee," cackled the draggled female of the party. "There'll be a bit o' fun when Squinty comes along." She gave another rusty cackle of laughter, which merged into a horrible, hacking cough, and died away in a spluttering gurgle.

I wondered hazily who Squinty was, and why there should be "fun" when he arrived. I was too dead-tired to think connectedly, I fancy, or I should have understood. An old saying floated through my mind, "It's the poor who help the poor"; they seemed a nice hospitable bunch I'd drifted amongst. I tried to squeeze myself more into the corner out of the way of that infernal elbow. I distrusted that filthy yellow coat, too; it looked verminous, and stank abominably.

There was silence for a bit, save for a muttered curse occasionally, and another fit of coughing from the old woman. Then I heard the sound of shuffling footsteps, a ripple ran along the line, and heads were raised. I looked up too and saw a man standing over me.

I wish I could describe him to you properly. His age might have been anything between forty and seventy; he was tall, six foot at least, I should say, but he stooped a good deal, so he may have been more; he had a huge, flabby, greyish-white face, half-hidden in a tangle of grey-black hair and beard; and abnormally long arms, ending in the most enormous hands I have ever seen. He wasn't so much clothed as wrapped in the sweepings of a fifth-rate old clo' shop; I counted the remnants of at least three overcoats, I know. He peered closely into my face, and I noticed that he had a most repulsive cast in his left eye. Needless to say, I guessed at once that he was the redoubtable "Squinty" of whom I had already heard. He looked at me in silence for a minute.

"Did anyone inform you that you were occupying my seat?" he said at last, in a hoarse, wheezy whisper. It was a horrible voice; it creaked and grated like a rusty hinge; and, in spite of its harshness, it was an educated voice; that made it worse, I think.

"I admit I wasn't made particularly welcome," I answered. "It was even suggested I should 'hop it,' I believe. But I was certainly given no definite reason why I should do so."

"A neophyte of the Ancient Order of Tatterdemalions, I fancy," said he, peering into my face once more.

"If you mean this is my first night out here, yes!" I answered shortly.

"Don't be ashamed of it, laddie," he croaked. "Don't be ashamed of it! Everything must have a beginning. Even I had a beginning—a wonderful thought that, for anyone of a philosophical turn."

He seemed to think for a moment. He was right, you know—it was a wonderful thought. It seemed impossible to realise that that frowsy, unclean abomination had once been a pink and white baby gurgling in its bath.

"Don' stan' harguin' wiv the swine, guv'nor," pleaded my ferrety friend, suddenly. "'Oof 'im aht! 'Ave a bit o' your fun wiv 'im."

"Gently, Ginger, gently," wheezed the old ruffian. "Why so impetuous? Justice shall be done, don't be afraid. But let us be as gods to-night, Ginger, and temper justice with mercy."

"I don' unnerstan' all that tork," grumbled Ginger. "'Oof 'im aht! Give 'im 'ell!... You can!"

"Don't let's argue about it," I said.

"If I've got your seat, I'll clear out." And I rose to go.

Immediately a huge hand gripped me by the shoulder and forced me into the seat again.

"Not so fast, young sir!" whispered Squinty. Then, turning to Ginger: "Did you tell this gentleman that seat is the one that I invariably use?"

"Course I did," whined Ginger. "'E would take it."

"You infernal liar!" I turned on him angrily. "It was you asked me to sit down! For the sake of the copper and baccy you thought you were going to get and didn't," I added, suddenly realising the reason for his hospitality.

"You oughtn't to lie, Ginger!" Squinty shook his head sadly.

"S'welp me Gawd!" began Ginger.

"To lie once is a mistake," said Squinty. "To lie twice is very nearly an offence, Ginger!"

"I thort 'e might as well stop. I thort yer'd like yer bit o' fun, guv'nor," muttered Ginger, shifting in his seat.

"I do like my bit o' fun, Ginger," wheezed Squinty, monotonously, "but I like to find it for myself." He bent down suddenly and seized the unfortunate Ginger by the arm, just above the elbows. Lifting him sheer off his seat, he stood him up in front of him, and bent forward until he almost touched his face. "Have I found my bit o' fun Ginger? Have I?" he whispered softly.

"Gawd!—my arms!—Gawd!" moaned Ginger, writhing. "Gawd! Ye're brikin' 'em! Leggo, guv'nor! Oh, leggo, carn't yer!"

The big man turned to me. "Ginger's seat is at your service, young man. Bear with an old man's fancy, if I tell you that I prefer the corner."

I shifted into Ginger's seat. The other occupants of the bench looked on apathetically; only the drab old woman gave her little cackling laugh, and creaked out, "'E's a one is Squinty," and collapsed into another fit of coughing.

Squinty must have been enormously powerful. Taking Ginger with him, he sat down in his corner. Forcing his victim down upon his knees on the pavement, he coiled his legs round him, and slowly altered his grip on Ginger's arms till both wrists were held firmly in one sinewy hand.

"If you yell, Ginger, one day I'll kill you slowly!" he wheezed gently. "So don't yell!" And he proceeded to smack his face.

It sounds funny, I know, but I think it was very nearly the most horrible thing I've ever seen. He did it in dead silence, monotonously, like a machine, with his open hand. And he kept on. Ginger moaned, squirmed, cursed—all quite quietly, too—and ended in an incessant, snivelling whimper, which was simply beastly. At last Squinty had enough of it, and pushed Ginger down on the pavement at his feet. He lay there for two or three minutes, too dazed to move; but at last he scrambled up, blundered into the wall, and, laying his head on his arm, cried like a small schoolboy. Eventually he shambled off—still whimpering—in the direction of the Avenue, and so vanished into the night.

I know what you're going to say: why didn't I stop it? I ought to have, I suppose. But I'm not the stuff martyrs are made of; I wasn't at twenty-two, anyway. Besides it was two o'clock in the morning—a drizzly, beastly morning—I was miserable, cold, wet, and all-in, physically as well as mentally. Oh, it's no excuse I know! I did venture a feeble, "I say, that's enough!" after a minute or so, but he took absolutely no notice of me. After all, it was only what Ginger had hoped was going to happen to me. And that extraordinary man could have done it, too—I should have been a helpless kid in those infernal hands of his.

When Ginger had disappeared, Squinty turned his regard on me.

"A little lesson in elementary justice," he whispered, softly.

"I didn't notice that it was tempered with much mercy," said I.

"It might have been you, you know," he retorted.

"Still, I hardly think he deserved all that," I ventured.

"I don't know that he did," he replied, reflectively. "I overdid it perhaps. But I enjoyed it—that's the main thing. A bit brutal, of course—bullying is brutal—but it's a rough school, the gutter. Bully or be bullied—that's the rule. I bully; I like it! By means of judicious bullying I retain a vestige of self-respect. If you get through your novitiate with us successfully, you will realise the truth of what I am saying. But I should say that you were 'amongst us, but not of us,' if I may put it in that way."

"I certainly don't intend to stay here all my life; I've got a job to go to in a fortnight's time, only I'm absolutely broke now."

"We must try and make your stay amongst us pleasant," he murmured, politely; then he leant forward, and addressed the rest of the bench: "This gentleman will have Ginger's place during his short stay with us. I hope I shall always find my seat vacant for me," he added, turning to me again.

"I may consider that I have received the freedom of the Embankment then," I said, smiling a little.

"Under those conditions, yes," he replied, gravely.

"I shall do my best not to be bullied," I assured him.

"It would annoy me to be compelled to bully you," he admitted. "This riffraff do not shine in the give-and-take of conversation. I waste my breath on them. Now you appear to have a certain amount of Intelligence. Callow, of course, but intelligent."

I bowed my thanks. He grew thoughtful for a few minutes.

"And to think," he murmured, after a long silence, "to think that in a fortnight's time you go to swell the ranks of the world's workers! Every day you go and do your little best; every week, with a grateful heart, you go up and draw your little stipend; week after week, year after year. You get married, you beget children—proud moment—and eventually you cease to be a world's worker; they give you a small imitation marble tombstone, with 'Sacred to the Memory of, etc.,' carved on it, and the village boys play leap-frog over it when the sexton isn't looking. It's a fatuous life!"

"It's better than the Embankment, anyhow," I said.

"That, of course, is purely a matter of temperament," he answered. "Outside that there is no arbitrary better, or worse."

"Some of the world's workers do work that lives after them," I suggested.

"I wonder if they sleep any the sounder, because their tombstone is real marble, with railings put round it to stop the small boys' innocent amusement," he said thoughtfully. He crossed his legs, and, putting his arm along the back of the bench, gazed down upon me benevolently. "If I were ever asked for my advice—which God forbid!—but if I had to advise a young man—such as yourself—about to start on the Journey of Life, I fancy I should say: 'Make no habits!' Yes, I think I should say that"; he repeated it slowly, "Make no habits!"

"Not even good ones," I protested.

"There are no good ones! They're all bad. Damn bad! Believe me, the lowest hell on earth, is to have a habit that you can't break." He looked hard at me with one eye the other appeared to be gazing out over the river. "The lowest hell!" he repeated gloomily, and was silent for a space.

Presently he began again: "You'd hardly believe that I was comparatively a rich man, would you?" he said surprisingly.

"I must say—" I began.

"Of course you wouldn't," he interrupted; "you're not a fool! But I am, all the same. I've got thirty shillings a week coming in regularly. It goes to a little eating-house I know; the landlady takes it, and gives me twenty-six shillings of it; the other four shillings I take out of her in food."

"Then why on earth d'you sleep out here?" I asked. "Surely, you could get a decent room."

"Just what I've been telling you," he wheezed. "Habit! Brandy, as it happens. I've tried to make it beer, but I can't—I could get more beer, too—. I always make up my mind to be careful—spend three and nine a day on it, and make it last the week—but it's no good, it always goes in the first twelve hours."

"Twenty-six shillingsworth of brandy in twelve hours!" I cried, incredulously.

"Habit," he croaked, "habit! And the hell of it is, I've lost the zest for it. It doesn't even make me drunk! This seat here," he patted it, "that's another habit. Close on forty years I've had this seat. Forty years!"

"Good God!" I said, involuntarily. "How awful!"

"There's no hell lower than the habit you can't break," he croaked.

He muttered to himself for some time. I thought he was going to sleep, but suddenly he said fiercely: "Who says I can't break it?" Then more quietly he muttered, "I could if—" and turned to me. "There's a way of breaking all habits, isn't there, eh?" His one sound eye glared at me.

"It's a matter of strength of will," I ventured.

"Ah, that's it," he muttered. "The will… and the way! There's the way all right, if you've got the will!" He got up and lurched over to the wall of the Embankment; he leant his arms on it, and looked out over the river for a minute or two—God knows what he saw—then he turned half round towards me. "Never make habits," he wheezed across to me; and before I had any idea of what he meant to do, he was over.

Well, there isn't much more to tell. You can guess the scene that followed. The usual crowd, which sprang up from nowhere apparently; the usual rather officious policeman—they got the police-boat round too, I fancy—I cleared out of it as soon as I could, but not before I'd heard the draggle-tailed old woman pronounce his epitaph.

"Tee-hee!" she cackled. "Tee-hee. 'E was allus a one, was Squinty!"

I needn't weary you with the rest of that weary night, nor with the equally weary day which followed it. I got through it somehow. What it was dragged my footsteps back to that damnable seat shortly after midnight is more than I can tell you. I didn't know where else to go, for one thing, I suppose; perhaps it had a queer, morbid fascination for me; anyhow, I went.

Ginger's seat was waiting for me; some of the others were there already; that drab old woman was one of them, and greeted me with that creaky laugh of hers. I sat down; then suddenly realising that poor Squinty would not want his corner any more, I moved up and made myself more comfortable.

I don't think I slept at all, but I may have dozed off for an odd minute, now and then. I was just utterly listless, weary and dispirited.

I had heard Big Ben strike two some minutes before, when I fancied I saw something moving on the wall of the Embankment. I watched curiously. Yes, there was something! A man was scrambling over from the river side; he flopped down on the pavement in an ungainly heap. He struggled to his feet again, and I saw that he was very tall. It was a man, of course... It must be. Only—if it was—what was it that was wrong with his face? I clutched my next-door neighbour by the arm; he looked up. I shall never forget the white terror on his face.

"Christ!" he sobbed. "Christ!... It's Squinty!" and faded into the night.

One by one they got up and shambled off, in utter silence—even the old woman forgot to cackle. And I? Have you ever been frightened?—frightened, to the very soul of you? It's not worth it as an experience; avoid it if you can. I sat still; I couldn't have moved for a thousand pounds! I couldn't even call out! And the thing shuffled over to me, and peered into my face. I won't try and tell you what it looked like—I don't want to spoil your night's rest—but the eyes that glared into mine, with a sort of smouldering fire at the back of them, squinted horribly.

Then a wheezy, bubbling whisper came to me. "Damn you! You've got my seat again." I hadn't strength enough to get up, but somehow I managed to scrabble along the seat, out of its way, as it sat down. My hand just touched it for a second, and it was slimy, sodden, and icy cold.

"Forty years," it wheezed. "Forty years o' habit! You can't break it so easy as all that! I had to come back, you see! I had to come back!"

Somehow I managed to find my feet, and ran—babbling incoherent nonsense—right into the arms of a burly policeman.

"'Ere! Wot's yer little game?" he said gruffly.

I could only stutter out: "The seat! My God! The thing on the seat!... It's Squinty! God! God!" and point to the empty seat a few yards away.

The policeman held me up; I was nearly falling, I trembled so.

"Nightmare's the matter with you, my lad," he said, not unkindly. "There's nothing on the seat!"

I looked, trembling; the seat was empty. "But I saw him," I stammered, "I saw him!"

"Come on," said he, "look for yourself." He walked with me to the back of the now empty bench. "Nothing there," he said again, and swept his hand along the back of it to prove it to me. His hand stopped suddenly, and he looked at me oddly. "Which end was it?" he asked.

"That end—where you're standing now," I answered. He turned his bull's-eye on that end of the bench; there was nothing—only a little puddle of water.

"Nothing at all," he said, half to himself. Again he swept his hand across, and stopped, drawing it away quickly. He turned to me with a queer look of disgust on his face. "I believe you're right, lad," he said slowly. "There's something there that I ain't anxious to move on. I can feel it; it's cold and wet! Ugh! Come along o' me to the station; a cup of 'ot cawfy 'ull do us both good."

On the way to the station I told him the whole story. When we got there, he had a word or two with the sergeant, and eventually I was installed in front of a big fire, with a cup of steaming coffee and a thick slice of bread and butter.

Nobody worried me for the rest of the night, though I didn't sleep much, as you can guess. At six o'clock my policeman returned and told me I was to go with him; I was too listless to wonder why. We were just moving off, when we were stopped by the sergeant and another policeman.

"They've just got a body in from the river," said the sergeant. "I was wondering if this young chap could identify."

"Precious little chance, I should think, sir," said the other policeman. "He must a' been in for a goodish bit; and, besides, the screw of some steamer got 'im, poor beggar; it's took one arm and 'alf 'is face off."

"But his eyes aren't touched," I whispered, "and he squints horribly."

"By Gawd, 'e's right," said the policeman. "'Ow the 'ell did you know that?"

"That's why it's really a mistake to call it the 'empty seat,'" concluded my host, rising; "it isn't empty. Squinty couldn't break the habit so easily."

THE MYSTERY OF THE GABLES

Elsie Norris

The name Elsie Norris appeared on over a hundred short stories during the years 1906 to 1914, yet I can find nothing certain about her. Almost all of these stories appeared in the weekly story magazines Yes or No *and* The Weekly Tale-Teller *published by the London firm of Harry Shurey, who also produced many romance novelettes primarily for a readership of young women. She also wrote a few stories for the* Theosophical Review *so may well have been a convert to theosophy.*

My search for her identity is hampered partly because it's a fairly common name—although only two can be found in the 1911 UK Census, neither a likely candidate. It's possible that "Elsie Norris" was a pseudonym, in which case all hope of identifying her is gone. But she wrote plenty of ghost stories and strange tales for the penny magazines including this one, which was part of a series which appeared under the heading, "Glimpses of the Unknown" in 1908.

C ARSTONE PULLED ASIDE THE BILLIARD-ROOM CURTAIN AND peered out into the darkness.

"It is strange that a fine old place like The Gables should remain empty," he said. "Gray is the landlord, isn't he? I wonder he does not live there himself sooner than let it go to ruin. Should think it would worry him to see everything going to waste."

"Five years ago, after Dr. Vivian died and the next tenant had left hurriedly, Gray did come down for two days," a voice answered from an armchair in the shadow, where Brendon lounged and smoked. "But he only remained for the two days, and then back he went to town. Something or other made him uneasy, and he has never been near the place since."

"And no one else will go near it, either," another voice chimed in. "My gamekeeper, who fears nothing in the shape of man or beast, told me a queer tale one morning. He says that he arrived home late one night and found his better half had locked him out. So he entered The Gables through the door, which is broken, and went to sleep. But he was soon out again. He says he awoke out of a horrible dream to find a dog sniffing at him, but when he put his hand out to drive the thing away there was nothing there."

"Who was this Dr. Vivian?" Carstone asked, still by the window.

"Nobody knew much about him," Brendon answered. "He was supposed to be interested in some special branch of medical research, and wrote sundry learned articles in papers much too dull for me ever to read, and I believe spent all the rest of his time in experiment. But what his particular line was I do not know."

Carstone drew the curtains together again and pulled his chair up to the fire.

"I should hate to be baffled by a thing like that, right at my very door," he said.

"I also hate it, dear boy," Brendon agreed cheerfully. "It's deuced awkward to have a haunted house almost next door. If I want a letter posted in the village after dark both the maids have to go together, accompanied by both the gardeners, and even with the four of them they sometimes return scared almost out of their senses. They say there's a light in the top window sometimes."

"I wasn't alluding to that sort of inconvenience," Carstone said. "I meant the annoyance from a psychological point of view, the feeling that there is something you cannot fathom. Haven't you ever wanted to go and find out?"

"Divil a bit," Brendon answered, with a fervour that made his guests laugh. "I'm a good Catholic, and if there are any works of the Unholy One going round I prefer to leave them well alone."

"But surely you do not believe there is anything there?" Carstone asked. "I've been in a dozen or so haunted houses and have never been able to find anything. It's only superstition."

"Very likely; but I don't see why I should do any detective business. It's Gray's affair."

Jordan—he who had told the gamekeeper incident—chuckled.

"I say, Brendon," he said, "let's make a bet that Carstone will not stay a night over at The Gables."

"Certainly not," was the prompt answer. "I wouldn't go myself, and I would not like a guest of mine to go."

"I would very much like to," Carstone said. "If there is any mystery I should like to find it out. I'll go this very night."

For some time Brendon demurred, but seeing that his old friend was bent on going, he gave in.

"I'll lend you a couple of rugs," he said, "and you're to come back to breakfast at eight o'clock to-morrow, or as soon after as you feel inclined. I don't mind telling you, though, that I think it's a harebrained scheme with no sense in it."

"I shall not rest till I know what really is wrong with the place," Carstone declared.

"You always were a pig-headed brute," Brendon retorted, but he went in search of the rugs.

They walked with Carstone as far as the gate, where Brendon stopped and said he would not go a step farther.

"Not another inch do I go," he declared; "and you to want to go into that dismal hole when there's a fire in your room and an eider-down bed waiting for you—to go gallivanting after ghosts. Thank heaven, I'm an Irishman and sensible."

"I'll come over for you in the morning, old man," Jordan said, "and I must say I admire your nerve."

"Good-night, and heaven protect ye," the Irishman said, half laughing, and then they turned back, leaving Carstone to enter the gloomy house.

It was not an enticing prospect.

It looked as neglected as most houses do when they have been ignored by their owners for several years. The path that led up to the door was thick with weeds, and the shrubs had spread almost across it. The door was open, the lock evidently having been broken.

He lighted his lamp (an acetylene cycle lamp, that he had filled with carbide to last six hours) and entered.

The house looked as other empty houses. Cobwebs hung from the ceilings and banisters and dust was everywhere, and his footsteps echoed drearily on the bare boards. Most of the rooms were large, with nothing remarkable about them save that one on the basement had a concrete floor (he supposed it had been used as an engine-room of some sort), and that one large room at the top was lined with shelves. He further noticed that all the walls were very thick and most of the doors padded with baize.

He went all through the house and opened every cupboard, examined the chimneys for traces of any bats or birds that might cause disturbing sounds, and stopped up every keyhole that the wind might not whistle through, then he settled himself in a room on the ground-floor and waited.

It was deadly still. The district was a lonely one, and the house lay off the main road. Not a sound came from outside, and the only sound from inside was an occasional faint crackle from the lamp, or a creak from the door as the wind came in from the open hall door adjacent.

An hour passed. Carstone finished his third cigar and began to feel rather chilly. Through the unshuttered window he could see the lights of Brendon's house still gleaming, showing that his friends were not yet abed.

Another hour. Nothing had happened yet, and he was beginning to think that nothing would happen when suddenly he got up and went to the door, feeling the revolver in his pocket to make sure it was there. He had heard no noise, yet for some unexplainable reason he was alert.

He had had the same feeling once before, when he had awakened in the middle of the night from a heavy sleep.

There was not a sound, not a movement, but in a flash he had switched on the electric light and his hands were at the burglar's throat. And he felt it again now, that instinct of a lurking enemy, inherited from some ancestor of the forests.

For several minutes he waited at the door, the lamp in one hand, the revolver in the other. The air seemed electric, thrilling with something that was disturbing, painful. He shivered with a feeling that was new to him. Every room on the basement and ground floor he explored, then went upstairs, having discovered nothing.

Of the upper rooms he searched every one, till the only one left was the room with the shelves. The door of this room was closed, and outside it he paused, some instinct telling him that behind it lay the intruder, if intruder there were. So strong was the feeling that when he at last jerked open the door and flashed the light round he was disappointed to find nothing. He went to the window and examined it. It had evidently not been opened for a very long time.

He turned round, then stood motionless. At the open door stood a dog, a thin creature whose every bone showed through its yellow hide, its tongue hanging out, and its lean head held stiffly to one side.

"It's you, you brute, is it?" Carstone said with a laugh. "A nice specimen you are to frighten a whole village. Get!"

But the animal did not move. In the surrounding darkness he could see the deep gleam of its eyes, as when one sees the eyes of a cat under a table.

He took a step forward and stamped his foot with a violence that raised a small cloud of dust. But the eyes still gleamed at him from the passage.

He was annoyed. It was a mangy brute, anyway, and useless. His revolver spat a bullet right between the eyes in the passage.

But they never moved or wavered.

And then the lean brute came into the room and slank along the farther wall! Carstone noticed that the hind legs dragged and that the head was held askew, as though the animal had been hurt at some time. And then for the first time he noticed something else, and that was that the creature made no noise. There was not a sound in the room save his own heavy breathing.

He could not understand it, and so he did what many men do when there is something they cannot grasp—he lost his temper.

"Confound you!" he said, and another bullet flashed out.

Something sniffed at his foot. Distinctly he felt something touch him, and the yellow dog still crouched by the wall, its head turned towards him in an attitude that was oddly pathetic, appealing.

And then Carstone was afraid. A thrill of acute fear ran through him, a dread of something, he knew not what. Some creature he could not see was still sniffing at his legs, and in a sudden panic he rushed from the room. He slammed the door as he went, but he knew that something followed him, and felt a shrinking apprehension lest it might snap at his ankles.

He did not pause to get his rugs, Lamp and revolver still in hand he almost fell down the stairs, dashed headlong through the hall door and down the weed-grown garden.

Then he felt bitterly ashamed. He had been as bad as, and worse than other fools before him. He hesitated, half resolved to go back.

"That you, Carstone?" a voice said, and the fact that he started violently spoke eloquently to the strain his nerves had undergone. "I couldn't rest, so we came over to see what you were doing."

"And I'm very glad to see you," Carstone answered hoarsely. "The fact is, Brendon, I don't believe I could stand another hour in that house if I tried."

"Hm!" Brendon grunted, "neither would I. I didn't tell you before, but I may say now that Vivian was believed to be a vivisector, as Gray found dozens of animal skeletons in the garden. My own idea is that the frightful amount of suffering undergone in the place has left its impression on it. Don't know what you think."

"The house has got something about it that I don't understand," the other said. "One of the dogs came and looked at me and I shot it, but I did not kill it."

He shivered. He was glad Brendon was with him. Even now he could see the gleam of eyes, feel the snap of invisible teeth at his ankles.

THE MISSING WORD

Austin Philips

It is surprising that Austin Philips (1875–1947) has become so forgotten. He was a prolific and popular writer in his day, particularly of short fiction and poetry, but also of stage plays and novels, and he was known for the originality of his fiction and his observations of social life. One of his stories, "The Fourth Man" (1914), which was made into a successful one-act play, considers prejudice and morals in society just before the First World War. Where Philips made his mark was on stories, particularly detective stories, set in the Post Office: The Man in the Night Mail Train *(1927),* The Unknown Goddess *(1929) and* The Real Thing *(1933) are distinctive crime novels.*

Philips was drawing upon his own experiences. He had followed in his father's footsteps as a postmaster, but also served in the Post Office's investigation branch which co-operated with the British Intelligence Services in checking suspect mail. He had also been part of a Postal Surveying Service and performed special duties in South Africa, so he had a fund of experience. In February 1907 Philips married Iris Bland, the daughter of Edith Nesbit. Philips had sold a few poems to magazines but now, with Nesbit's encouragement, he turned to short stories and began to sell regularly to The Strand Magazine, *which was arguably Nesbit's major market. One of his first sales was an article, "Crime in the Post Office". Many of his early stories involve investigations in the Royal Mail, including several supernatural stories, such as the following.*

A T THE GREAT HOUSE BEYOND THE TOWN THE PRIME
Minister lay at death's door; in the Murcester telegraph
gallery we sat, we dozen telegraphists, waiting for the news
that should bid us tell the world how a stormy soul had passed
where courts and kings and cabinets are not. And as, between
midnight and slow dawn, we waited, weary-eyed and idle, the
heavy tempest drops hammered hard upon the glass roof of the
gallery, frequent lightning forked, and clouds clashed together,
thunderously at war.

A blue flame sparkled in the periscope of a double-current
sounder; the needles of the instruments on the Sub-office Circuit
swung in sudden unison, so that they stood a-row like compasses
and pointed, each one of them, at the selfsame angle, no longer
northwards, but north-west by north. And then the electric current
sparkled on the sounders themselves, and the lights died swiftly out,
leaving us in darkness and dismay.

Old Shayler, grey-bearded and grey-moustached, the doyen of
us all, jumped away from the instruments and pulled his chair into
the open space in the middle of the gallery.

"Come away, boys!" he shouted—"come away from the sounders!
I'm not taking any risks!"

There came a rush and scrape of chairs across the wood-block
floor; the old man had done what we were too cowardly to do. In a
second or two we sat, ringed round him, huddling close and fearful.
The storm had raged since eight o'clock; for four hours we had terrified ourselves with tales of crime and horror.

"What a night!" gasped Wollen of the race-staff. "I've never known such a night before. Not in twenty years' service!"

Then once more the lightning forked across the hall, reflected in the glass roof above, footing, as it seemed, some *Danse Macabre* upon the gallery floor. The needles of the instruments on the Sub-office Circuit almost seemed to pirouette before they swung back again to their fixed position. Long after the flash had passed, the periscopes belatedly gleamed; the heavy sounders moved, as if driven by some strange force to babble in a code unknown to man of the mysterious power which set the elements at strife.

I drew my chair an inch closer to the man on my right; on my left hand I felt Beechcroft shudder and do the like. He was a poor creature at the best of times—to-night he was almost beside himself with fear.

"I knew just such another night," said old Shayler presently—"the night that Jacky Soames was killed at Bromyard and the office ransacked. But it wasn't lightning that killed him. Lightning seldom hurts people indoors, they say. It was a man that killed Jacky Soames!"

The chairs moved again, a full dozen of them, till we sat, huddled closer than ever, cold and fearful, for all the night's midsummer heat.

"Tell us about it, Shayler!" I cried. "Tell us what happened. Did they ever catch the murderer?"

And three or four voices echoed what I asked; for indeed it seemed better to hear of man's work than God's that night. One or two, indeed, cried "No!" but they were in the minority, and, sitting there in the middle of us, old Shayler began. And as the thunder, clamorous and insistent, growled above us, louder and more near, I felt Beechcroft shudder beside me, and his fingers, unconsciously, met on my wrist and stayed there. But I let the poor devil keep his grip, for I could hear his teeth chatter and his breath come and go in the darkness.

Then old Shayler cleared his throat and began.

"It was fifteen years ago, to this very night, and Jacky was sent in charge of the Bromyard office. It was a small enough place in those days, and a one-man show. But Jacky was nearly off his head with joy. He had just got a girl, and it seemed like promotion coming, and he went about the place singing and whistling till it wasn't big enough to hold him. I remember seeing him off from Murcester station after having a drink with him at the Old Dun Cow. It was the post-office house then, just as it is to-day!"

"Was that the last you saw of him?" interrupted little Teddy Saunders—he was only a boy, and couldn't let the old man tell the tale in his own way. "I mean, did he die?—was he murdered the same night?"

Old Shayler frowned and sat silent, and seemed to dry up.

"Go on!" said some one sharply—"go, on; and, Teddy, if you interrupt again, I'll put you in contact with the wires!"

The old man, somewhat appeased, cleared his throat again. "It was the last I saw of him," he said slowly. "But it wasn't the last I *heard* of him. I was on night duty, and at about half-past eleven we had a chat over the wires. He told me how lonely he was in that house all by himself, and how he couldn't sleep for the sense of responsibility, and I joked a bit to cheer him up, and told him to go to bed. But he said he couldn't sleep, and that he would sit up in the office all night. And then, as there was nothing doing here, I began to sleep."

Then old Shayler paused.

"Has anybody got a cigarette?" he asked. "Telling it makes it all come back again, and I shall talk easier if I smoke!"

Some one leaned across and fumbled for the old man's hand, and thrust a cigarette into his groping fingers. He lighted it, and at every puff I could see the white faces round me, and I felt that my own was whiter than them all. But no one spoke.

"About midnight," went on the old man, "I woke up with a start, in a cold shiver. Something was happening to Jacky. I didn't know what—I only knew that he was in danger; and it seemed as if I had been dreaming, and, though I couldn't remember my dream, I had waked up to find it was true.

"Then the Bromyard needle began to click, and, though the sending was jumpy and uneven, I knew it for Jacky Soames—I should have known his touch on the keys anywhere."

"What did it say?" cried Teddy Saunders, almost beside himself—"what did it say?"

And this time no one chided him for an interruption which seemed to come from us all, even though it was only Teddy that spoke. Even old Shayler showed no annoyance, for he knew that Teddy couldn't help but speak.

"It said," he answered slowly—"it said, 'I am being murdered by—'"

He stopped short, and puffed at his cigarette.

"Yes!—yes! What more did it say?" we clamoured.

Old Shayler puffed hugely, so that the glowing tobacco, before it sank into hidden greyness, shed a bright light on the faces round him.

"It said nothing more!" he answered, in slow tones, "But I rushed out to the police station (there were no telephones in those days), and when the storm was finished I got the sergeant to drive out to Bromyard; for I couldn't leave the office myself for any length of time. And when he got there he found poor Jacky's body on the floor by a parcel hamper, and his head hammered in with a poker, and the safe open and all the cash and registered letters gone."

"But was there no clue to the murderer?"

"None at all. There were all sorts of theories, though. And I had mine!"

"What was it?" asked Beechcroft, shuddering, at my side. It was the first time that he had spoken, and his fingers on my wrist were wringing wet.

"Yes; what was it?" I echoed.

"Have any of you young fellows another cigarette?" came the question, with aggravating lack of haste.

I thrust a packet into his hand. He took one, lit it, and then went on between great puffs.

"The police thought it was a skilled burglar, because the safe was opened with skeleton keys. But I think it was one of Jacky's own colleagues!"

"Good God!" cried some one. "You don't mean—!"

"I mean," went on old Shayler, "that it was some one who knew Jacky, and whom Jacky was glad to see. At first, when the fight began, he was able to hold the brute off with one hand while he sent the message with the other. And then the burglar must have hit him on the head and stunned him, which would have been easy, for Jacky was a small man, and no bigger than little Teddy here."

"But why did he have to kill Jacky, if he was stunned?"

"That's what makes methink it was some one that Jacky knew. And dead men tell no tales!"

The lightning lit up our faces again, the rain had grown to hail, and the thunder still rumbled across the glass roof. Beechcroft at my side looked almost moribund with fear. I tried to loose his fingers from my wrist, but it was useless. And before I could remonstrate Teddy broke in. "So Jacky Soames was killed before he could signal the murderer's name? But it was a pretty near thing!"

For the first time that night old Shayler answered a question swift and direct. "I believe he *did* signal the name!" he said.

"But how, if he was overpowered?—and if before, why didn't you hear it?"

"Because the wires were broken," said the old man triumphantly. "Because the lightning struck a tree on the high road, and a branch fell and broke the wires. That's why I never got the name!"

"Nor never will!" put in Beechcroft, in his high-pitched voice.

"I'm not so sure!" cried Shayler. "The word was sent, and the word is floating about yet, and some day or other it will find the wires again and tell the murderer's name!"

He fell silent.

"I've had enough of this!" said Teddy Saunders. "It's giving me the horrors. I can see the whole thing quite plain!"

"Strikes me we shall be here this time to-morrow," put in somebody gloomily. "The Prime Minister's a long time pegging out!"

As he spoke, an instrument in the far corner of the gallery began to vibrate. M.R., M.R., M.R. it clicked, in Morse code. M.R. was the call for Murcester.

"He's dead!" cried Teddy Saunders. "They're calling us from the Towers. And how are we going to manage without the light?"

I leaned forward and listened hard.

"It isn't from the Towers at all!" I shouted. "The Towers wire is on the other side. It sounds like Bromyard. But it can't be!"

Old Shayler leapt to his feet.

"It's Jacky Soames!" he cried. "I should know his touch among a million!"

None of us spoke; none of us dared to move. If we doubted, it was only because we dared not believe. And the nails of the fingers that held my wrist dug and twisted and tore into the flesh.

M.R., M.R., M.R. clicked the key, and then spelled out a word.

"By God!" cried Shayler, "Beechcroft!"

The fingers on my wrist relaxed; the man at my side fell to the floor in a heap; old Shayler had been right. The word that for fifteen years had floated in the void had found the wires again.

PHANTOM DEATH

Huan Mee

From 1894 for almost twenty years the by-line Huan Mee appeared in many of the popular fiction magazines, often with stories of the bizarre and unusual. There were also several books, including crime fiction, such as A Diplomatic Woman *(1900) and* The Jewel of Death *(1902). Those who read the theatrical press would soon have learned that Huan Mee was the pen name for two brothers, Charles and Walter Mansfield, as they declared their identities in a letter commenting upon the possible plagiarism of one of their librettos. Both brothers were journalists and though Charles (1864–1930) also wrote fiction under his own name, Walter (1870–1916) wrote only in collaboration as Huan Mee. Charles had turned to writing fiction when he became tired of his reportage on financial matters which is why so much of his material is escapist and larger-than-life. The Huan Mee by-line became so popular that Charles retained it for his fiction even after his brother's untimely death in 1916. They produced scores of stories, and here's one highly imaginative example.*

T HE PICTURE HAD WEIRDLY FASCINATED THE WHOLE OF
Europe.

In every capital where it had been on view thousands had flocked
to see it. Thousands had gone, often again and again, drawn by
some unaccountable attraction, impelled against their own desires.
Thousands had spoken the same words.

"I have seen it, yet I wish that I had stayed away—I would have
given anything not to have seen it—it haunts me. But, go!"

And I, in a wandering life about the Continent, had chanced
time after time to come upon the city where it was drawing its
morbid crowds, where it had become the sensation of the hour;
and I, time after time, had visited it, ever like the others, drawn
against my own will to stand before the canvas and drink deeply
of its horrors. Not the horrors that were depicted there, for the
vast picture was not revolting. It merely exercised a terrible and
all-absorbing control upon the mind of the onlooker, that set his
imagination at lightning speed to work, conjuring up—what? Who
can say? One left, wishing that fate had led one's steps elsewhere;
and yet tomorrow one returned.

Perhaps it was not wholly the picture that exercised this terrible
mastery over the senses, but its surroundings added something to
its magnetic influence.

An ingenuity of mind had conceived the strange idea that the
picture must be viewed in solitude and amid funereal environment.
Singly the visitors entered a room draped in crape, where the picture,
set well back in a frame of polished ebony and encircled by a black

silken rope, stood, with hidden lights directed full upon it, the room itself in darkness.

The master mind which had conceived the idea must also have planned the sullen surroundings.

With a crowd of merest idlers about it, who would have passed their little opinions upon the work, it might, perchance, have been as all others; but in the deadly life of that sombre room, in the terrible silence that seemed to cling to the very hangings, it became the weirdest masterpiece of the world.

The spectator entered alone, his nerves tingling with the suppressed excitement of wonder as to what the visit would bring forth, a little cynical, perhaps, because of the peculiar manner in which the picture had affected others—others are always so different from one's self; then left, silent and ghostly as the room from which he had departed, and become, as others were, weirdly fascinated, drawn back to it again and again, speaking of it with an awed shiver, refusing to describe it, but saying to others, "Go!"

Yet, with it all, what was it? "The Last Moments of Yevan Lestoki." Only the courtyard of a Russian prison, the snow driving before the wind, the shadowy sentries standing in the background, and Yevan Lestoki living the last few heart-throbs of his tortured life.

It was the brain that told, or seemed to tell, with ghastly vividness, what a hell his life had been since first he walked through that snow-bound courtyard.

It was one's senses that fathomed the unrecorded past and cried aloud the whole story of the picture. That Yevan had been racked, torn, and tortured at the callous bidding of him who stood there enveloped in his furs. Tortured in vain, for he had scoffed and taunted his persecutors, still holding back what they tried to gain by cruel force, until, at last, in this courtyard, he who had devised with devilish ingenuity all that the man had suffered, in a paroxysm of brutish rage, fell upon him and strangled him with the leather thong of his driving whip.

Yevan writhed before our eyes in the last agonies of death; it was the madness of the painter which gave to him an expression of mocking hate, to his murderer a haunted look of agonised horror, his mouth half open and his eyes dilated as though he were dying the death of his victim.

It was in London that I saw the picture last. Who knows but what I may have been the last one to gaze upon it? For it is well known to the art world that the masterpiece was utterly destroyed in the fire at the Mecklenburg Gallery on the night of the 12th of March, 1888, the very day of my visit.

I sat and looked upon the canvas, the whole mystery of the subject enthralling, as it ever did, my very soul; sat and looked until it seemed that it was not a picture I gazed upon, but reality itself. It was life, in which every figure seemed to live and move and have its being, and even the snow beat pitilessly upon the grey-coated sentinels in the background, gathering thicker and thicker before my eyes; and then—my heart for a second seemed to pause—my glance fell upon a man standing by the silken rope absorbed, like myself, in contemplation of the picture.

A man enveloped in a long fur coat, a man with the same twisted black moustache, the same cruel eyes and vicious mouth as the man in the picture, the governor of the Vyshne-gradski Fortress. *The same man.*

It was folly, an illusion, madness; yet there he stood and gazed upon his counterpart, while the atmosphere of that death-like chamber seemed to become heavier and more heart-chillingly oppressive.

Then as I looked towards him he turned and came closer to me.

"A marvellous work," he said with a slight bow. "I have seen it so often; and yet, like a magnet, it draws me to it whenever I am near."

"Marvellous," I acquiesced, for I could say no more.

He seated himself by my side, and a cold rush of common-sense came over me as I felt the sable cuff of his coat touch my hand, and realised that he was a man and not a phantom. Though how it was that he and I were there together, the traditions of the gallery broken, still perplexed me.

My eyes sought the picture again, and it seemed to grow more lifelike than ever before. I could see the throbbing breast of Yevan, the tightening of the thong about his neck. I could see the white flakes of snow whirling wildly in the cutting wind, and feel the chill air as it swept across the frozen courtyard.

"You were the model for Yevan Lestoki?" the stranger exclaimed, breaking the silence and turning suddenly towards me.

"I?"

"Yes, surely; it cannot be coincidence. If a man knows his own face, there in the features of the unhappy wretch dying beneath the torture, are your own, as truly as though a mirror were held before you."

He laid his hand upon my shoulder, and my skin seemed to prickle at the touch, and yet as my eyes followed his extended finger, as I gazed again at the dying man, I started in wild surprise, in terror that went icy to my heart, for truly, as he said, though to me it had never been clear before, it was as if I looked into a mirror.

"It is a wonderful likeness," he muttered.

"No more wonderful than the other figure," I forced myself to say, with a short, harsh laugh.

He raised his eyebrows in mild inquiry.

"The governor of the prison," I said; though I knew, despite my will, my voice was trembling. "Who is that but yourself?" and

I pointed my finger at his counterpart, as he had done at mine. "It is as though we both had lived in the past in those wilds of Russia, and now meet again in Bond Street."

"Ay, lived and died!" he answered, and, rising, walked once more towards the painting, and, resting both his hands upon the black silk rope, stood gazing long and steadfastly upon it.

"Lived and died," he said again, and then, with a careless shrug of the shoulders, as one who dismissed a matter from his mind, turned towards me and addressed me in the flippant, easy tones of a thorough man of the world.

"It is odd," he exclaimed, "curious; but let it pass as simply such. The fates have brought us together; so let it be." Then in a gayer tone he continued, "You will dine with me to-night, and let us celebrate the wealth of coincidence that one hour has brought into both our lives."

I wanted to say no, but I could not. All that this world had given me—my hopes, aims, most secret ambitions—everything, I would have gladly sacrificed for freedom, for the power to refuse, for the sake of being miles away from where I was, standing by his side before the picture; but my heart was as water, and I accepted.

And then, as we walked out into the spring sunlight, I could have laughed at my own folly, laughed as one laughs with relief when one awakens from an ugly dream, laughed at the distorted vagaries of a weak mind that could turn into supernatural fancies the well-knit frame and athletic proportions of my newly-found acquaintance, who strolled by my side talking of the latest comic opera.

In ten minutes we were merry at what before had filled me with undefined horror, joking at the tremor it had occasioned both of us; and when we separated it was with pleasant anticipation that I pledged myself to dine with him that night.

Yet a dozen times before the appointed hour arrived I had sworn to myself I would not go, a dozen times I had tried to fight down the fascination that seemed to draw me towards him. I determined at last that I would *not* go, and as I fixed the resolve he entered.

"I was passing in my brougham," he exclaimed, taking my hand in his; and I stepped back amazed, for I had given him no knowledge of where my chambers were situated.

"You will pardon the intrusion. You gave me your card, you will remember."

It was a lie. I had given him no card, for I had forgotten my case when I went out in the afternoon.

"Why look so astonished?" he queried, with a light laugh.

"I am sorry, but I cannot come."

"Tut—tut!" he deprecated, spreading out his hands.

"I am too unwell to-night; I should be but poor company. You must excuse me."

He placed his hand upon my shoulder, and that same chill feeling as before crept like a web across my face and spread itself around my temples.

"Now, dress at once, there's a good chap," he continued, with a sudden return to that second volatile self; "I'll give you ten minutes, and help myself to a whisky-and-soda."

And I obeyed him.

Why dilate upon the dinner? It was the best that the most fashionable hotel in London could serve.

I led the conversation to that which I would most have shunned, and spoke of "The Last Moments of Yevan Lestoki," of our meeting that afternoon, and the mysterious, unexplainable resemblance of ourselves to the chief characters.

For a moment he seemed inclined to pass the subject away, and talk of something else; and then there grew upon his face a look of terror, and he suddenly pushed back his chair and retreated, as though he feared I would attack him. As a spasm, it passed, and he was smiling upon me once again.

"Have you ever—" he commenced, paused, and lighted a cigarette.

"Ever what?"

"Oh, nothing," he answered, and we sat looking at one another until he spoke again, and then it was as a man forced to speak against his will, at the dictates of a power which controlled his lips, while he but gave voice to what he would have kept unsaid.

"Ever heard the story of Yevan Lestoki's death?"

"Never."

"No man on this earth could tell it save myself," he cried, "or the man who, prompted by Satan himself, set such a scene on canvas. The world whispers about a weird incarnation as they gaze upon those faces; the world cries, 'What insanity to reverse the expressions!' Only I and he who painted it, whosoever he be, know that things were as they are there depicted."

He sat back in his chair, as though the subject were dismissed, and placidly smoked his cigarette; and then, still as if urged to speak against his will, leant forward again, rested his arms upon the table, and looked keenly into my face.

"The old story," he continued, bitterly. "Yevan Lestoki and His Excellency Count Dalroukoff loved the same woman—"

"Then Count Dalroukoff—"

"Is the governor, yes."

"But it is a picture of barbarism, of bygone times," I said.

"Sometimes men's souls survive on earth from age to age, that Fate, or destiny, may work itself to finality," he answered. "Pass me another cigarette, and let us get away; this room seems as though it would stifle me."

He rose suddenly from his seat, and then, before I could move, as abruptly seated himself again.

"Of what were we talking?"

"Yevan Lestoki."

"Then away with him!" he shouted in a paroxysm of fury. "Curse Yevan Lestoki, and all such fiendish horrors. I'm tired of this room, and its suffocating atmosphere. I'm tired of life, of everything. Let us go."

He bent his gaze upon me, and repeated, "Let us go." Yet I could not stir. Somebody seemed to be clutching me, holding me back where I sat; and so we silently watched one another, and waited.

"Yevan Lestoki was a a cur," he muttered at last. "A—bah! Let us go, I say. Let us go!" And still he did not move; and I, who would gladly have departed, could not.

"She whom Yevan loved, Olga," he continued, speaking in the same ghastly tones, "married him. Count Dalroukoff swore that his rival was a traitor to Russia, and had him arrested and confined in the Vyshnegradski Fortress, of which he was the governor, and there he died. Come, that's the whole story. Now let us go."

It was as though a child repeated a lesson, and waited for release.

"Curse you, that's all," he cried again. "Let's go."

"Very well," I answered. "Let us go;" and with an effort of will I rose from my seat, and walked towards him.

"Stand back, Yevan Lestoki," he yelled, his hand reaching for a knife upon the table. "Stand back, or I will kill you."

"You're mad," I retorted, shaken with apprehension, and trying to bluster my nerves back to strength. "You're mad, you've lashed yourself into frenzy over an affair of a hundred years ago."

"It is a hundred years ago," he answered grimly. "It happened on the 12th of March 1788. To-day is the 12th of March again. Sit down, and you shall hear it all."

"Nonsense, let us go."

"Sit down," he repeated furiously; and I, scarcely knowing what I did, obeyed him.

He was leaning back in his chair, his hands clutching the carved arms until the bones of his knuckles seemed almost as if they would break through the skin, his head inclining slightly upon one side, his eyes half closed, and the tones of his voice like those of a man speaking in a trance.

"The horrors and tortures that the Count Dalroukoff inflicted upon his rival in that fortress would chill even your philosophical nineteenth century soul," he continued; "but Yevan Lestoki endured his tortures with contempt, his rackings and woundings with taunts. Dragged from his wretched dungeon, almost naked, into the icy courtyard of the prison in the early hours of the morning, he scoffed again, and reviled that fiend Dalroukoff, laughed beneath the lashes of the knout, and boasted that his murder would be all in vain, for Olga Lestoki was dead; she had visited him that morning; in an hour their souls would be united. 'Kill me,' he cried, in an ecstasy of passion. 'Kill me, you incarnate fiend, and send me to join the woman who is mine.'"

"And Dalroukoff murdered him even as he spoke. With the leather thong of his whip he choked the man. Twisted it around his neck and drew it taut, until his limbs quivered, and he fell back dead."

"He was dead, and yet no sooner had his spirit passed than a spasm convulsed his body, the glazed eyes cleared, the distorted lips resumed the natural form; and, with the thong still round his throat, he spoke:

"'You, Count Dalroukoff, and I, Yevan Lestoki, shall live and haunt this world, even if æons pass, until I have killed you, as you have murdered me.'

"Then the flickering soul died out, and the bruised and beaten body fell from the hands of his tormentor."

My host finished; slowly his eyes opened to their full extent, and he gazed stonily across the table.

"And how did Count Dalroukoff die?" I asked, with a shudder.

"He was killed in a duel five years later."

"Then, after all, you have simply related a weird legend that time has proved to be folly."

"Utter folly," he acquiesced, with a nod.

"Utter fol—" I stopped short, with a start of terror. A voice shrieked in my ear, "Kill him, Yevan, kill him; kill him, kill him!" My hands were grasping the edge of the table, my legs were twisted beneath my chair; my whole frame quivered with the longing to murder that man who sat opposite to me.

His head was upon one side, and he only looked at me with staring eyes, as if he, too, could hear that voice—"Kill him, Yevan; kill him!"

It was ghastly, horrible. With my clenched fist I smote upon my knee, striving to destroy the monotony of the dread silence, broken only by that awful voice shrieking in my ear.

Why didn't he speak or move? I hummed a refrain from an opera for a few bars; and then stopped, for the terror seemed to have left me. The voice was stilled.

"Come, let us go," I said, with an effort at gaiety I did not feel, and, rising to my feet, I took a step towards him; and then stopped, rooted to the ground. Behind him hung a curtain, looped back by a silken rope.

I needed no insidious voice to urge me now. I would kill him. If I could creep along and pass him, if I could reach that silken cord, then he should surely die.

I stood upon that spot for what seemed hours; and then silently I advanced one step, and waited—one again, and waited—and one again, and passed him, and took the rope in my hands.

I could hear his breathing as I stood and listened, and yet he did not move; and slowly and gently I disengaged the cord, and then crept down close behind him.

He shivered ever so slightly, his eyes lifted and looked into mine; and then, even as it seemed he was about to speak, I flung the cord around his neck and drew it tightly with a sudden twist.

He turned his face upwards for a second with agony upon his features, and, with twitching fingers, plucked at my two hands.

"It is well, Yevan Lestoki," he gasped; and then I drew the knot with all my brute strength until he sank back upon his chair dead.

I released him, stood looking upon him for an instant, and then the whole thing came upon me like a flash; I was back in myself, a murderer! In a paroxysm of homicidal mania I had slain the man of whose hospitality I had just partaken.

I dropped into a seat, and gazed with terrified eyes at my victim, lying huddled in his chair; at the cord, where I had flung it upon the carpet.

I was mad! For years it had lain dormant, and to-night it had burst forth. I crept to the door and listened—no sound without; and I locked it, and returned and stood beside him—thinking not of him, but how I should escape. And through it all, like a misty mirage, rose up that picture, "The Last Moments of Yevan Lestoki"—the central figures, the driving snow, the shadowy sentinels.

I touched his cheek; already it was cold as ice. At any moment I might be discovered, and yet I could only think in a brooding, feeble way how strange it was that I should have killed him.

But I must escape. His fur coat was lying on a lounge. I would put that on, and walk out of the hotel. And yet what need to do that? I had but to stroll out, and nobody would know.

I put on my own coat, and then, clutching him by the shoulders, forced him beneath the table, and drew the white cloth down to the ground.

I should be far away before he was discovered; and so, with a smile of cunning satisfaction, I slipped into the corridor, locked the door, and placed the key in my pocket.

A waiter was ascending the stairs. I paused until he reached me, and then something compelled me to speak. I could not resist.

"I've murdered a man in that room," I cried; "he's dead, I've hidden him beneath the table." And the tray he was carrying dropped with a clash upon the floor.

"What, sir? What?"

"I've murdered the man I was dining with—strangled him."

"No, sir; it's not true."

"Come and see," I answered, again impelled by a power beyond myself; and, unlocking the door, I entered, and he followed.

"That's the cord I did it with," I said calmly, pointing to the silken rope upon the carpet; "the body is hidden by the cloth. Look at it."

"I dare not," he cried, slinking towards the door.

"You coward, he can't hurt you now," I burst forth in violent rage. "Look," and I caught the long ends of the cloth, and threw them back upon the table. "Look! you fool; and then tell them all I killed him, and I'm waiting."

The man glanced beneath the table, and then sighed.

"Lor sakes! sir, how you did scare me! It ain't fair to play these practical jokes on a man." He mopped his white face, and helped himself to a glass of brandy; and I, following his gaze, looked beneath the table too, and saw—nothing.

I had flung the body there; I had not left the door of that room; my eyes turned mechanically to where my host's coat and hat had rested. The lounge was vacant.

"Look here, sir; it ain't fair, really it ain't," the waiter said again, liberally helping himself. "It ain't, really, you know; you're such an actor, I thought you'd done it, you know."

"I did do it, you doddering idiot," I cried, shivering as I dropped into a chair.

"Would you like a cab, sir?"

"No; fetch the manager."

The man left; and I went on my knees, and crept beneath the table. I stretched out my hands and felt the carpet, thinking there must be some horrible illusion, and the body was still there, though I could not see it; and then, in terrified bewilderment, I returned to my seat, and held my racking head between my trembling fingers.

Where was he? Who was he? Whom had I murdered?

The waiter returned, and the manager with him, both looking as though they feared they had a maniac to deal with. A commissionaire hovered around the doorway.

"The waiter has told me of your hallucination," the manager remarked. "I can assure you that you are wrong. I have known Count Dalroukoff for the last five years, and—"

"Heavens! Was that his name?" I gasped.

"Count Nicholas Dalroukoff. He was a constant visitor, almost a friend."

"I murdered him."

"Believe me, you are in error," he suavely murmured. "Not ten minutes ago he came to my office, paid his account for the time he has been staying here, and I myself saw him into a hansom."

"You swear that is the truth?"

"Absolutely, and I am much grieved at his departure. He was a man I greatly esteemed. I am sorry he has left us for ever."

"For ever?"

"Unfortunately, yes. His last words were, 'Good-night, and good-bye, for we shall never meet again.'"

THE WRAITH OF THE RAPIER

Firth Scott

George Firth Scott (1861–1935) was descended from an ancient Orkney family but was born in Sutherland, where his father was a land surveyor. He emigrated to Australia around 1883 where he became a journalist. He established a reputation as an exciting writer not only of mystery and adventure stories but also of stirring accounts of polar and Australian exploration. Scott himself undertook several expeditions into the outback. He was involved in various business ventures and though he and his wife returned to England around 1895, he occasionally returned to Australia until a scandal in his involvement in a tin mining concern in Western Australia caused him to leave Australia for good in 1906. His reputation as a writer, though, continued unsullied, for several decades. Today he is remembered, when remembered at all, for The Last Lemurian *(1898), in the style of H. Rider Haggard, where explorers discover the remnants of the lost continent of Lemuria buried beneath an extinct Australian volcano.*

Scott wrote several books set in the Australian outback, notably Track of Midnight *(1897) and* A Rider of Waroona *(1912), whilst of supernatural interest is* Possessed *(1912), an ingenious thriller of apparent spirit possession. Scott had a gift for ideas and the following has a phantom image that will remain with you long after finishing the story.*

I HAD BOUGHT SOME OF THE BEST WEAPONS IN MY COLLEC-tion from old Andrews, so that when I received a note from him telling me he had just secured a fine specimen of a fifteenth-century Toledo, with a history, I lost no time in proceeding to his shop.

Andrews, as I entered, was polishing the blade of a delicately fashioned rapier.

"Ain't she a beauty?" he said, holding the weapon by the point of the blade till it sprang to the weight of the hilt. "As fine a piece, of armoury-work as ever I see."

I reached to take the rapier from him, and he turned the hilt towards me. My fingers closed round it, and I was conscious of a curious pricking sensation which ran through my fingers to my wrist, and passed, in a quivering tremor, up my arm. With my other hand I took hold of the open basket-work forming the guard, and looked, first at the hand that tingled, then at the hilt I had held.

"You get it too?" the old man asked, with a chuckle. "Sort of pin-pricks running up your arm?"

"It is very curious," I said, examining the weapon closely.

The blade was grooved and thin; the guard more than usually long, made of a steel bar, twisted into a graceful spiral. Dark maroon-coloured leather, rough in the grain, yet smooth to the touch, covered the part where the fingers gripped. It was an interesting specimen of Toledo workmanship, but I could see nothing to explain the tingling I had experienced.

"What do you make of it?" I asked, looking at Andrews.

"I give it up," he said, with another of his chuckles. "The gent I got it from said it was witched; said it wouldn't hang on the wall nor stand on the ground, was always tumbling about and stinging whenever he picked it up. His wife, he said, got so scared of it he had to get it out of the house. I picked it up by the hilt, and I tell you I dropped it quicker than a hot poker. Bit queer, ain't it?"

I took hold of the hilt again. The pricking sensation ran through my fingers and numbed the muscles of my wrist. Overcoming the desire to let go, I held on firmly. My fingers stiffened and pressed against the leather with a grip like the convulsive spasm of writers' cramp, while the nerves of my arm throbbed and the muscles set taut and hard.

"What is under the leather?" I exclaimed.

"I ain't looked," Andrews replied. "The work was too good to tamper with if I wanted to sell her, so I just sent along word to you. She's genuine, for here's her pedigree. Have a look at it."

He produced a sheet of blue foolscap covered with small, close writing. The story I read was dated late in the eighteenth century, and was signed by the British Consul at Lima. It stated that the rapier had been in the possession of a Spanish-Peruvian family for over three hundred years, having originally been made for one of the family ancestors. This man, a noted duellist in his day, always had fought with this rapier, and the reputation he had acquired was shown in the name by which he was known among his compeers, a name untranslatable into English, which was just as well, the Consul added, seeing that it implied something utterly unspeakable.

How the man met his end was a mystery. The family legend asserted he had been carried off bodily by the Prince of Evil, but the Consul scoffed at this as a mere ignorant superstition, clinching his contention by asking how, if the man had been carried off, the sword had been left behind? Perhaps, he suggested, the devil had overlooked it, or had dropped it in his hurry, for it had certainly been discovered in the armoury years after the owner had disappeared. From generation to generation his descendants had guarded it with pathetic loyalty, until the last of the line had passed away, and the rapier, with the rest of his effects, had come into the market.

Following were several short paragraphs with various dates and signatures. The first, signed by the original purchaser, was brief and to the point. "This is a cursed thing," it said. The second stated the owner ran himself through with it. The third asserted the owner had had such hopeless ill-luck since he bought the weapon that he gave it away in disgust. The curator of the museum, to which the disgusted owner had given it, alleged the rapier fought with all the other weapons in the institution, and did so much damage that the authorities had no further use for it. A disbeliever in the supernatural bought it from them, but a few months' experience with it satisfied him. "I bought it in derision, I sell it in despair," he wrote.

When I had perused them all I looked again at Andrews.

"Faked," I said.

"The gent who brought her here said that's how it struck him when he first read it. That's how he came to buy her. He said someone else might like to have a taste now. He had had enough, and he reckoned she was a long way from being played out, to judge by her latest tricks. What do you say, sir?"

I glanced at the rapier where it lay on the table. A thin ray of the winter's sun stole through the dusty glass and struck across the hilt. Specks of light, some ruddy, some white, showed on the surface of the maroon leather. I picked it up and held it where the sunlit streamed over it. Thus illumined, I saw how minute points pierced the leather at irregular intervals.

I pointed them out to Andrews.

"Copper and zinc." I said. "Someone has put a miniature galvanic battery under the leather, and as soon as one's fingers close on the metal points a slight current passes through them. A very ingenious contrivance to give colour to that prettily told wonder-tale over there."

"Seems to me you're right," he said. "Still, it wasn't on the pedigree I fixed her price. It's cheap, as a fine made weapon, at what I'm asking for her. I'll take two quid."

"Story and all?"

"Pedigee, curses, *and* record," he answered.

I closed the bargain, and with the record in my pocket and the rapier under my arm I returned to my rooms. I was tempted to open the maroon leather covering of the hilt and examine in detail the contrivance I was convinced was secreted there, but on second thoughts I decided to postpone this until I had the advice and assistance of a friend of mine, one Charlie Manners, an enthusiast in all that appertains to electricity and psychic manifestation. Of the latter he was a profound and pronounced sceptic, more so even than myself. Trickery, aided occasionally by hypnotism and obscure electrical contrivances, were the trump cards he relied upon whenever a manifestation could not be otherwise explained. I wrote him a brief note saying I had secured a unique subject for investigation, and asking him to come round to my rooms at nine o'clock to help me solve the problem.

Selecting a spot for the rapier among several others on the wall, I hung it up. Then, having to be away for the rest of the afternoon, I left, carefully closing the outer door after me, for I had had trouble with my cleaner a few days before, and had summarily dismissed her. She had retorted with threats of summons and other dire proceedings. She was Irish, and she drank.

It was past seven when I returned. Switching on the electric light as I entered, I started hack in amazement.

The room was lit by four electric lights ranged round the walls. Plain, simple, and tidy were its ordinary characteristics, and so I had left it a few hours earlier. Now it appeared as if it had been the scene of a madman's exploits.

The tablecover was flung into a corner, and the table set up on end. The chairs were overturned. The bookcases were opened, and their contents strewed pell-mell on the floor. The hearthrug was stuffed half up the chimney. The Persian rug lay in a tumbled heap on the top of the writing-table. From the walls all the weapons had gone, and were heaped, in confusion, in the far corner.

As I viewed the scene of chaos, my late cleaner recurred to my mind. It was just such a silly piece of wanton mischief as one would look for from a drunken Irishwoman.

"What a silly creature!" I said to myself as I set the table on its legs and spread the cloth upon it. "But if she can get in once she can get in again, and will probably do more damage next time. I had better see the police at once if I am to avoid further trouble."

I righted the overturned chairs, set the Persian rug in the centre of the floor, and was about to replace the books, when the pile of weapons in the corner caught my eve. They had better be replaced first, I thought. Going over to them, I picked up the first to my hand. As my fingers closed on the hilt I flung it from me. It was my latest purchase, and the sting of it ran up my arm like the pain of a searing burn.

"You cursed thing!" I exclaimed as I saw it fall with a clatter on the other side of the room, for in the start it gave me I put more strength into the throw than I intended.

I picked up the next, one, a beautifully balanced Italian rapier of magnificent workmanship and a favourite of mine, for with it I had won my best prizes in the fencing-ring. As old Andrews had said, I was "a bit of a swordsman," and the instinct of the art came to me as I gripped the hilt of my favourite and paused for a moment to feel the spring of the thin, nerve-like blade. There are few swords of to-day to compare with those of the time when the highest skill was lavished on the production of a single blade.

With every part fashioned by hands skilled to the highest perfection, and guided by an artist's reverence for his craft, what wonder that such a weapon as I now balanced sprang to my touch like a thing of life? The thin blade quivered like the wings of a dragon-fly poised in the sun; as I turned my wrist it sprang almost to a loop and rang with a clear bell-note as it came again to the straight. With this I would not hesitate to meet——My eyes turned towards the corner where the Spanish rapier lay.

I have said I was sceptical on all things supernatural, sceptical to the verge of bigotry, but as my glance turned to the corner a shiver ran down my spine. In the clear space of the air I saw, for an instant of time, a gauzy, filmy thing, akin to the wisp of light thrown on floating dust by a weakly reflecting glass, only the wisp would have been formless, while this was a vague human form.

Even as I looked it vanished. The rational explanation that it was but refraction from the electric lights came to my mind and disposed of it. But nothing rational came when a moment later I saw the Spanish rapier rise from the corner where it lay—saw it move, in long, swinging steps, as though it were being carried in the hands of a man who was walking towards me.

Gripping my sword with a grasp made rigid by mingled astonishment and awe, I stepped away as it advanced, away until I was well across the room, and was standing with my back nearly touching my writing-table. Then I raised my sword-arm to bar its further advance.

A yard from me it stopped, and the long, grooved blade lay motionless in the air, levelled directly at my heart. With an upward fling I brought my blade across it.

Immediately, with graceful sweeps and flourishes, as though it were held by a master-hand, it went through all the stately motions of what was known as the Grand Salute three hundred years ago. As it floated on before me, paying me the homage which, as often as not, was done in cold-blooded treachery in the so-called good old days, I scarce knew what to believe. Was I going mad, or was I dreaming? Could I trust my senses, or were my eyes playing tricks with me? On the point of the Italian rapier I pressed my finger till the smart of pain convinced me I did not sleep. I felt the table behind me—it was solid to the touch. But still there was that weapon turning and curving in the air, as it might turn and curve were it in the grasp of a human hand, but with no visible hand to hold it nor visible form to support it.

The tales in the record were true! The spirit of the Spaniard still haunted the earth, still wielded his favourite weapon, still sought for blood-lust victims, still fought in duels to the death. Weariless, merciless, invulnerable, what mortal who faced him could hope to escape? And I, heedless of the power I was invoking, had in my blind ignorance and folly, challenged him!

I remembered my open door, and the thought flashed through me to fly. At the moment the clock in the church tower close by began to chime the hour. Nine o'clock, I told myself as the sound reached me. On the last stroke I would make a dash for the door, and, once outside, I would wait till Manners came. The final passages of the Grand Salute were being made, and I watched them as I counted the strokes of the chimes, counted with a grim sense of security, as though the vibrations had some subtle hold over the disembodied entity in front of me. Yet as the big bell boomed the hour a growing tension held me. The rapier was moving quicker as the first deep notes rang out. It had doubled its speed when the fifth stroke fell, it was quicker still at the sixth, it flashed when it turned as the seventh came, and whizzed through the air at the eighth. The salute was ending. I strained my ears to catch the last note of the hour—eight—eight—eight. Would the last note never come?

Slowly the reverberation died away. The last stroke had already come. It was eight o'clock, not nine. There was an hour before Manners was due—an hour in which I had to face, alone and single-handed, the impalpable thing that mocked me with its homage.

As the last tremor of sound ceased the salute was finished, and the rapier shot out straight for my breast, vibrating so that the light danced along its polished grooves.

Again I flung up the blade I held, crossing it over the other, ere I thrust straight at the eyes I saw. But the ghostly hand, or power, or whatever it was that wielded the haunted rapier, was masterly in fencing skill. With a wonderfully agile parry the point of my blade was turned aside, and the answering thrust was so swift and keen that it was inside my guard before I could turn my hand. I flung myself to one side as the thrust went home, went home through the space I had occupied and penetrated deep into the hard oak end of my roller-top writing-table.

I stared blankly at the rapier stuck in the writing-table. I saw it bend and spring. I saw the wood gripping the point against the force trying to wrest it free. I saw the hilt twist one way and the other, as though the hand that held it were striving recklessly to drag it from the wood, and in my stupor of fear a marvel came to me at the temper and strength of the steel which could stand so great a strain. To and fro the hilt swayed and twisted, bending the blade, jerking, tugging, wrenching to get it free from the grip of the close-grained wood. The lifeless steel was springing, writhing, twisting, and wriggling like a living serpent pinioned by the tail.

The ring of steel as the blade sprang free, and the gleam as it flashed through the air, brought me back to the danger I was in. The rapier was level in the air, pointing again at my breast. For the fraction of a second, behind the hilt I saw the shadowy outline of a man's head, and two eyes glaring into mine. It was the hate in the eyes that roused me. The side-swerve with which I had avoided the fury of that thrust was a trick a brilliant swordsman would have foiled. What if I were the better swordsman? What if I could drive back, by simple skill of arms, this weird presence? What if I could wrest the rapier from its grasp? There would be scant satisfaction in thrusting through the air where that outline showed visionary and vague, but—like an inspiration the thought came to me—I could hold it at bay till Manners came. Oh, the strengthening of my flagging nerves when I remembered that arch-sceptic and decrier of the supernatural! What ghost could stand before the cool-reasoned onslaught of his unbelieving mind? With my skill at fence, and his skill at argument, the disembodied entity of my scowling Spanish foe would soon tire of confronting us, would only be too glad to escape back to the darksome void whence he had come to injure and destroy.

Fired with the impulse, I sprang to the attack. The steel of the blades rang as they met. In thrust and parry they crossed and uncrossed, so quick, so keen, so vigorous that the silence of the room was broken by the steady sibilant sleethe, the sound that tells of smooth-faced, firm-held blades gliding, sliding, slipping, in a fierce endeavour to beat each other down. At the commencement thrust for thrust was given on fairly even terms; while I held my ground, my opponent, if I may so describe the invisible entity I was facing, held his. But the rapid movement of the rapiers, the skill with which my subtle tricks were met, and the quickness with which the thrusts were made in response, amply justified the reputation for swordsmanship my opponent, while in mortal life, had held. First one and then another artifice I tried, but every time my subtlety was anticipated and my effort foiled, until, with my arm growing weary and my wrist becoming stiff, I turned to a feint and rally I once had learned.

It was a trick not to be used in ordinary encounters; rather was it something to hold in reserve until one were in a tight corner fighting almost hopelessly for life. To one unacquainted with it, the feint would induce an attack by a thrust to the full length of the sword-arm, a thrust which would bring the maker of it beyond his limit, and give the opening to get within his guard, the opening which was the object of the feint. Once inside the guard, the rally was invincible. The keenest swordsman must fall back, a lesser master must be run through. As the thought of it flashed through my brain I acted.

The long, grooved blade sprang out. I knew the ghostly arm I could not see was stretched to the limit of its length. All my strength I flung into the rally. My upward parry would have hurled the sword from an ordinary fencer's grip. The Spanish blade barely moved aside. Had I not known before, I must have realised then the strength that held it. But nothing could turn aside the vigour of the thrust I made. Only by leaping back with lightning speed was escape possible.

Yet, as I thrust, the Spanish blade lay a foot beyond my reach. No earthly creature could have made so sudden and so great a leap, but in my haste to follow the advantage I had gained I scarce noticed it. I sprang forward, thrusting fiercely, madly into the vacant air before me, heeding only that the gleaming conqueror of so many a bygone fight was slowly but surely falling back. Inch by inch it gave way, step by step I advanced upon it. My blood was up, and with the fascination of the contest in my brain I forgot the conditions of the fight—forgot that while I was growing weary he whom I was fighting was tireless and incapable of fatigue. I even forgot how impalpable was the presence I was facing until there came that which brought home to me the weirdness of it all and nearly led to my own undoing.

With my eyes fixed on the vacant air where my opponent's ought to have shown, I was able to see everything in front of me: the wall at the other end of the room, the big armchairs by the fireplace, even the rugs upon the floor. Thus it was that, as the Spanish rapier retreated before me, and I advanced upon it, I saw the Persian rug spread out upon the floor slowly curl at the corner as though a trailing foot had caught it, a foot trailing so stubbornly that its owner would not deign to raise it from the ground.

The sight filled me with a numbing horror. What was behind that rapier? What was this thing, invisible to me, incapable of sound or speech, yet able to roll over the end of the rug when its trailing foot dragged against it? The sickening qualm which had swept over me when I saw the rapier wriggling free from the wood of the writing-table came upon me again. For I moment I faltered, my head grew dizzy, and the sound of my own voice, wailing, broke upon my ears. The curl of the rug fell over as the rapier sped toward me, and with panting lungs and trembling limbs I was fighting for my life.

Oh, the fiendish strength of that onslaught! Like a spiteful spitfire the rapier flashed as it made thrust after thrust with faultless aim until I was driven back almost to the wall. A rage of helpless auger swept over me. What chance had I against this formless foe? My body was vulnerable at a hundred points, but what harm could I do to the bodyless thing in front of me, even though I ran my rapier through the empty air a thousand times? A single thrust of his, and Manners might find a sorry welcome; no thrust that I could give would do more than exhaust my already failing powers. What was I to do to outwit him? What could I do to disarm him? In an access of folly, I sprang forward.

Once more I got within his guard; once more I beat him back, slowly, slowly, till I saw the rug curl up again as his dragging foot caught in it. This time the sight maddened me. Reckless, I sprang after it and pressed a furious attack. Still it went backwards. Directly behind it one of the armchairs stood. I saw the chair push back; I saw it come in contact with a pile of scattered books and tilt over till it fell. From behind the shelter of the fallen chair the Spanish rapier quivered in defiance.

I stood breathless, nerving myself for a final spring, when, through the air, there came the sound of the church clock chiming a quarter past the hour. I could not last much longer—I could not last! Like a stab, the thought went through me. There came a drumming in my ears, a mist spread before my eyes.

Dimly I saw the Spanish rapier leap towards me, as though the man who held it had bounded over the fallen chair. With numbing brain and failing strength I met the attack, but it was a struggle of despair. I could not stand against the fury of the thrusts; my hand could scarce retain its hold upon my rapier hilt. For a second I lowered my glance and saw how the crumpled rug lay on the floor between us. The advantage was taken on the instant. There was a fierce lunge, the point of the rapier pricked through to the flesh of my forearm; desperately I parried, and sprang back. Then the rug rolled over, and the rapier shot out in an aimless way, wide of all harm for me.

Ere the thought could take words, I knew my enemy had tripped. I lunged against the fall. More by accident than skill, the blade of my rapier went through the openwork of the hilt of the other weapon, through the curious open strands which sprang from the cross-guard to the head, until hilt clashed on hilt, and my sword went home, deep into the misty, visionary shape that loomed for a moment again before my eyes.

I saw the face grow clear in outline and in feature—I saw the spasm of anguish contract it—I saw the mouth gape in a gasp of agony—I saw the shadowy arms flung up—I saw the eyes' swift change from gleaming hate to a vacant, glazing stare—then my knees gave way beneath me, and I fell headlong into darkness.

So Manners found me when he came, lying face downwards across the disordered Persian rug, my sword-arm flung out in front of me, gripping the Italian rapier, the blade of which was locked in the curving spirals of the Spanish hilt. A speck of blood showed on the point of the Spanish blade; the Italian, which I always kept bright as new silver, was tarnished as dull as lead from the point to within fifteen inches of the hilt.

Manners scoffed at my story when I told it, jeered at my tumbled room, laughed at the scratch on my forearm, and pooh-poohed the tarnished blade. Nerves, nightmare, or bad whisky he suggested as the explanation, till we examined the maroon-leathered hilt. It was not copper and zinc which pierced the leather, but minute, needle-shaped crystals, which we afterwards learned were an obscure but deadly poison.

"There you are! There is the whole solution!" Manners exclaimed. "You were fooling with the thing; your hand was hot and moist; the poison affected you, and you went off your head. All the rest is raving delirium."

In vain I protested, and pointed to the sword-mark in my writing-table.

"What about the record, and the experiences of all the others who possessed the accursed thing?" I asked.

"Oh, rats!" he answered rudely. "Rats—rats—rats!"

It was useless debating the point. Manners was satisfied he had solved the mystery. Though I knew him to be wrong, I had nothing but my story to advance against him. I could not subpœna the Spaniard.

THE SOUL OF MADDALINA TONELLI

James Barr

James Barr (1862–1923) was the younger brother of the better known Robert Barr. Although James was just as prolific, it is Robert who is remembered, both as the founder and editor of The Idler *magazine in 1892 and for his clever crime stories featuring Eugene Valmont. It is long overdue for James to step out from the shadow of his brother and be recognised for his ingenious and atmospheric stories.*

Barr was born in Canada where his parents had emigrated from Scotland in 1854 but he followed his brother back to England in 1883 and became a journalist and story writer. Although he wrote many stories for the popular magazines he did not produce much in book form, unlike his brother, and even then the most popular, The Gods Give My Donkey Wings *(1895), a satirical tale of a mountain-top utopia, was under the alias Angus Evan Abbott, a name not designed for memorability.*

Many of James Barr's stories fall into the categories of weird fiction and early science fiction. The following dates from 1909.

A FTER ALL IS SAID AND DONE, HERMAN YORKE'S ELATION WAS excusable. To be chosen to play first violin in the Amateur Orchestral Society does not fall to the lot of every man who loves a fiddle; and Yorke was delighted in proportion to the rarity of the distinction. His hobby, made possible by ample means, was the picking up, in out-of-the-way corners, of fiddles; his religion the playing of them. During the twenty-six years of his life he had possessed himself of exactly fifty-two violins. Many of these he first sighted in the windows of pawnshops, a few in second-hand shops, three he bought at first hand, and five were presented to him by admirers, for he played surpassing well. Herman Yorke loved each fiddle, tenderly tended them all, kept each carefully wrapped in a white silk handkerchief, played on each in turn so that existence might not be wearisome to even the least gifted of them. He kept them all free from resin dust, clear of damp, and in each least particular out of harm's way.

Each one of them Herman Yorke loved with a full-hearted love. They were, to him, fair-faced, sweet, full-voiced children who respected his moods, inflected his moods, and reflected his moods, as the occasion called for.

Pity it is—but so it is—but even with his own children a man has likes and dislikes. One, owing to some subtle cause, physical, mental, emotional, spiritual, is preferred above the rest of equal blood, of equal wish to please, and equal, often more than equal, desire to be loved. Like many a parent, Herman Yorke endeavoured to school himself to an impartiality in his regard for his family of fiddles; yet, in spite of all he could do, one crept deeper into his heart and was more wistfully caressed than any of the others.

This fiddle he had picked up in a pawnshop Ratcliff Highway way, and, to be sure, in its depths a time-stained snip of paper bore the magic name Stradivari. Forty-eight of the others were similarly besnipped, the accredited makers being pretty evenly divided between Stradivari, Amati, Stainer, and Montagnana. Of course, no one but the halfwitted or wholly unversed pays the least little attention to these labels; indeed, it is to the credit of Herman Yorke that he proved so broad-minded as to refuse to be irritated by the impertinence. Herman Yorke bought the fiddle, and, as time passed, he fell into the habit of calling it his "Stradivari."

In tone and timbre it was a glorious instrument, yet it just failed to touch that ineffable grandeur, that haunting witchery of Stradivari at his greatest. Like Herman Yorke's own playing, it fell just short of the superlative. However, the Amateur Orchestral Society was happy in gaining two such recruits as Herman Yorke and his "Stradivari." For it was the "Strad" he chose to use at his first appearance in Queen's Hall.

The Amateurs give four concerts each year, on which occasions Queen's Hall is filled by the members and guests of the society. Herman Yorke made his début at the first concert after Christmas. A "smoker" it was, and, as it took place on the anniversary of the distinguished composer's birth, there was much more Mendelssohn than smoke in the hall that night, for ladies largely outnumbered the men in the audience. Yorke feared stage fright, but when he sat down in his chair at the very rim of the platform nearest to the stalls he experienced not a tremor.

Many a criminal, who has passed long hours in abject fear, walks unafraid to the scaffold; many a man sleeps soundly on his pillow when the disaster has befallen the very fear of which had kept him through long, long nights pitching and groaning on his bed. So Herman Yorke found when he took his seat and plucked his strings to the proper pitch. He found his nerves steady, his head cool, his eyes clear, and his fingers supple during those trying moments when the conductor's baton poised aloft bidding him prepare.

He played through the symphony as coolly correct as though he were in the music-room of his own house at Primrose Hill. And when the symphony had ended he sat back in his chair, and closed his eyes to float, in remembrance, again through that cloud of ethereal delirious joy which the enthusiast experiences who has taken his part in an exquisitely played symphony. In his delight he neglected to glance even one glance towards Esther Burnaby who, in all the austerity of Norman blood and twentieth-century riches, sat haughtily in the stalls. The girl noticed the neglect, but cared very little, as she was given to looking upon Herman Yorke as a poor thing, notwithstanding that she wore an engagement-ring placed on her finger by this same fiddler. Indeed, she rather enjoyed his neglect, if "enjoy" be not too burning a term to use in connection with one so dully frigid as Esther Burnaby.

It was shortly after the beginning of Mendelssohn's "Overture to Fingal's Cave" that a weird feeling crept over Herman Yorke. For the first time that evening he felt burning eyes upon him. Was stage fright to unnerve him now that he thought himself well out of danger of any such disaster? Surely not! He knew that he was playing as well as ever he had played, he knew that already he had won the conductor's confidence, yet, notwithstanding this, a sudden fear of himself fell upon him. As he played his temples began to burn as though two eyes—or two hundred—were focussed upon him, and that their concentrated gaze amounted to a flame. Fiercely he bit his lower lip, rapidly he blinked his eyes to clear his brain of fog.

Savagely he longed for a respite in playing that he might lift his eyes from the part.

That respite came at last.

Herman Yorke rested the nut of his fiddle on his left knee, and turned his face towards the audience. His gaze flickered across the upturned faces of the people, lightly as a butterfly zephyr dances over the heads of ripening corn, then, on a sudden, he stopped transfixed. For his eyes met those of a girl and the eyes of the girl seemed to look into Herman Yorke's very soul.

Before the thought came to him to turn away Herman Yorke had gazed into those other eyes more seconds than he cared to think about; and, when the part again called him to play, it was only at the expense of a mental effort that he wrenched his attention back to his fiddle. And all the time that he played he felt those eyes fixed upon him steadfast, unwavering, till their effect verged on physical pain.

What a girl, too! Hair black as an Eastern midnight; eyes luminously flashing as a phosphorescent sea; full, luxurious lips; round cheeks of the warmest sepia-red—a being alive with the passions and emotions of a clime where fierce sunshine burns and luscious grapes ripen, where each flower is an intemperance, and the wafting of a butterfly a carousal; where life is tempestuous and death an orgie.

What grotesque wind of fantasy had wafted this passionate creature, superb in her trappings, into dun London? And why, why did she perlustrate him so? In her gaze, too, he read a world of meaning; yet what meaning? He could not guess. Her look seemed to envelop him in fire, to burn longings she harboured into his brain. Herman Yorke could not fathom the mystery, so he resolutely kept his gaze from wandering in the direction of the fascinating creature, notwithstanding that his desire to solve the meaning of her look almost overpowered him.

Herman Yorke fiddled on, and at length came the interval. Then he raised his eyes. Yes; her eyes were still full upon him. He had never before been called upon to bear such a look, one so full of longing, of pleading, of imploring. Never spoke gaze more eagerly of a desperate desire to attract attention. Clear-voiced it called upon him to hearken. Again he found need for all his strength of will before he could turn away from her.

"What boldness in a girl," he began, but instantly checked himself. "No; it is not boldness. There is something deeper in that look than boldness. What that something is how can I guess? But she must not continue to gaze at me in this marked way, else undesirable attention will be attracted to her—and to me. I will go to the side of Esther Burnaby, and, if it be in my power, act in such a manner as to convince this strange Southern girl that I am not my own master quite."

From the flower-befringed platform Herman Yorke passed round to the stalls. Esther Burnaby received him with her accustomed hebetating superiority, yet Yorke was all gallantry and attention. And when he believed that he had made his relationship to the girl quite plain, the violinist turned his face to where he had last seen the Southern girl. The seat was empty. He glanced about him. Brilliantly dressed people were on every side of him, in knots, in couples, standing singly, but nowhere did he catch a glimpse of that raven head or those haunting, burning eyes.

The interval came to an end. Herman Yorke watched the raised baton, the seat in the fifth row of the stalls was empty. The first violinist plunged into Mendelssohn's "Spring Song," when, again, the pain struck into his forehead, causing him fiercely to contract his brows. Then the girl had not gone? Moreover, she sought to attract his attention! Very well, he would disappoint her. Without allowing his eyes to wander, he played through the "Spring Song" and the "Bees'

Wedding;" indeed, it was not until he stood up to play the National Anthem that he condescended to flash a glance. Tears stood in the girl's eyes; yes, he could see the glint and glisten of them. And the look upon her face was one of ineffable sadness. But, strangest thing of all was that when she caught his eye she held out her left hand, palm uppermost, fingers crooked, as though holding and fingering a fiddle; then she reached out with her right hand and apparently tightened the "E"-string peg of her imaginary instrument. Intently Herman Yorke listened until he was satisfied that his string was quite in tune. What in the world could the girl mean?

"She is certainly mad," he said to himself. "By what bad chance has she come to fasten her attentions upon me? I trust to Heaven that Esther Burnaby has not noticed. If she has—squalls!"

The young man put his "Stradivari" in its case, careful as ever then turned to watch the throng move towards the doors. He failed to distinguish the figure of the black-eyed girl. Doubtless she was there, jostling in the crowd, but he could not manage to pick her out.

Many times during the weeks that intervened between his first concert and his second Herman Yorke thought of the girl who had so annoyed and charmed and puzzled him. He wondered who she could be, whether she, too, played the violin; and, most of all, why her strange pantomimic signalling? At times he thought that she criticised his manner of holding the instrument; at times that her ear led her to believe him playing out of tune. By what right did she interfere? Who was she that she felt called upon to signal and to stare?

Always at the weekly rehearsals—those delightful blossoms that in the fullness of time lead up to the full-blown flower, the concert— many guests were present; and on each of these nights Herman Yorke kept a sharp look-out for the girl. She did not appear.

The night of the Spring Concert came. Herman Yorke was the first player to take his place on the platform; and he watched the people filter to their seats with much shaking of hands and merry chatter, for the audience was a gathering of friends and acquaintances. Listlessly the first violinist looked on at the kaleidoscopic intermingling of the atoms; and, in a lack-lustre way, he wondered if the strange girl would appear. To-night he was in no wise so anxious about her presence, for Esther Burnaby had decided to grace a whist drive rather than Queen's Hall. Like to like.

In the beginning the orchestra plunged into Glazounow's "Scenes de Ballet," and, within a very few seconds of drawing his bow, Herman Yorke realised that those eyes were again upon him. At the first opportunity he furtively glanced into the auditorium, and truly, as on the previous occasion, five rows back sat she of the raven hair. A little paler she looked, a little thinner, but her eyes were as large and her gaze as intent as on the first night of his seeing her. His was but a momentary glance, yet in that brief time the girl managed to finger an imaginary peg of an imaginary fiddle. There could be no mistaking her action. And each time he glanced she went through a similar performance.

When the piece was finished, and the applause had died, Herman Yorke rested the fiddle on his knee, and with the index finger of his right hand tapped the "E"-string peg, as he did so keenly watching the girl. A smile of exquisite radiance illuminated her face, she lifted her dark eyebrows in ecstasy, and nodded her head three times. Then she closed the index finger and thumb of her right hand as if grasping the top of the peg, and gave a quick jerk.

Herman Yorke turned his attention to that peg, but could see nothing out of the common about it. Critically he examined it. A plain peg, the mate of the other three! Was it really the peg she worried about? To make sure he inquiringly touched the tail-piece.

The girl energetically shook her head.

He wished that she would be less demonstrative, otherwise she was bound to attract attention. He was glad to see that no one appeared to have observed them as yet.

He touched the bridge.

The girl shook her head.

He touched the finger-board.

The girl shook her head.

He touched the "D"-string peg.

The girl frowned and shook her head.

He touched the "E"-string peg.

The girl smiled and vigorously nodded affirmatively.

"Whatever is up with her it has to do with this blessed peg, and, much as I would like to continue the pantomime, I fear notice. During the interval I shall go boldly to her and ask her to explain. Until the interval I shall refuse to look her way."

At the interval Herman Yorke shot a glance towards the girl, a glance which he believed would tell her that he wished to speak with her; then he quickly made his way behind the platform, and so round and out into the auditorium. The girl was nowhere to be seen.

"Confound it all, why has she run off? She must know that her signallings have aroused my curiosity, and that I cannot interpret them without word of mouth; yet she has flown. I shall pay no further heed to her pantomime show."

However, this resolve was soon broken. Yorke had noticed that his friend Tomson sat in the same row, and only four seats off from the girl; and he further knew that Tomson allowed few pretty girls to pass him unnoticed. No doubt he had observed she of the large dark eyes.

"I say, Tomson," said Yorke, off-handed—"I say, that's a remarkable-looking girl who sits four seats to your right. Is she an acquaintance of yours?"

"What right have you to be taking notice of pretty girls? You are here to play the fiddle," Tomson replied jocularly.

"Oh, I can do more than play the fiddle, at times. I take it that I am at liberty to look about me on occasions?"

"I noticed no striking girl in our row," admitted Tomson, now speaking seriously. "The fourth seat to my right? I thought that seat was empty."

"Empty!" laughed Yorke. "Empty! Not a bit of it. Far, far from it. You take a squint at it when we begin again, and see if it be empty."

"I must get glasses, Yorke. Hang me if I noticed a girl! I wish I had."

"There's a chance for you yet. When she comes in take a good look at her. I have reasons."

"Reasons or no reasons I shall certainly look, but, further than that, Yorke?"

"Oh, nonsense!" laughed Yorke, passing on to greet other acquaintances.

Once again Herman Yorke was playing, once again the girl's great eyes were upon him. Yorke glanced inquiringly at Tomson. Tomson looked blankly at Yorke. Delicately Yorke nodded towards the girl. Deliberately Tomson turned his head and stared; deliberately he turned a blank face to Yorke, and shook his head. An eerie feeling crept over Herman Yorke, and all the time the girl pulled at an imaginary peg. Herman Yorke fidgetted even as he fiddled.

The symphony ended, the next item happened to be a song. Unostentatiously the first violinist arose and signalled Tomson to the artists' entrance.

"Do you know her?" he asked eagerly of Tomson.

"Know her? Yes; as well as anyone can know her, for there is no 'her' or 'him' or 'it' in the seat you speak of. That's how much I know her."

"Please do not banter, old fellow, for she is disconcerting me, I fancy, too, deliberately. Do you know who she is?"

"Yorke, your nerves are off colour; you are seeing things; for, on my soul, there is no one in the fourth seat to my right! That's the seat you mean?"

"Of course it is."

"Well; it's empty."

"Tomson, you must be blind! A girl with jet-black hair, jet-black eyes—"

"Cut the description, or, when you're about it, be original, and give her red eyes and green hair. If there is a girl in that seat, then I swear she is made of invisible fabric, a sort of wireless-telegraphy girl! She does not interrupt vision."

Herman Yorke drew his hand across his forehead. Tomson sympathised.

"When this song ends, I'll return to my seat, and you to yours," he said. "Then, if you still see her, and if you have made no mistake as to the stall she occupies, nod to me, and I shall see her, even though I am obliged to borrow a microscope to catch sight of her. I take it that you are in earnest?"

"Never more in earnest in my life! The matter has gone so far that it must go much further; in fact, quite to a finish."

Yorke was quickly in his place; the girl still sat devouring him with her eyes. Tomson stood at the end of the row of stalls until he saw Yorke nod, then he deliberately walked to the seat indicated, and sat down. In a flash the girl reappeared in the stall Tomson had previously occupied. Tomson raised his eyebrows as who would say: "You see, old man, there is no pretty girl here, worse luck!"

A flurry of fear swept over Herman Yorke. The girl, then, was a vision seen only by himself. Transparently, Tomson, sharp-eyed, had not seen her; yet there she sat, yearning of look, impatient of look, imploring of look! And see with what fierce energy she withdrew the ghost peg from the phantom fiddle! And, as time passed, her looks became darker and darker, till they said to him, plain as words spoken: "Refuse, at your peril!"

"Did I convince you that there was no one in that seat?" asked Tomson, when the two met after the concert.

"You certainly did convince me," answered Yorke, with diplomatic ambiguity.

That night Herman Yorke sat in his music-room glowering at his "Stradivari." That he must do something—something if he was not to be haunted until his nerves cracked—he realised in the full. His soul revolted against laying rough hands on his "Stradivari", yet something must be done. That "E" peg! What about it? He removed it from his fiddle, substituting a peg from his second favourite violin. At the first draw of his bow, what a mighty change!

Clear as a bell rang the notes—exultant, triumphant, as if in jubilation at freedom from a thing that had benumbed it through many years. Seraphic notes poured forth, notes of haunting, ineffable timbre. At first, Herman Yorke almost feared to continue to play; later, he completely lost himself in the magic of its music—music incomparable, transcendent. More than an hour he continued to play, his features drawn as in pain at the splendour of it all; then he slowly collapsed in his chair, placed his arms on the table, and, gazing upon the fiddle, sobbed in the stress of reaction.

A Stradivari, a veritable Stradivari! Its own soul had now proclaimed the truth of its birth. And on the floor, whither his hysterically flung arms had tumbled it, lay the spurious peg which heretofore had vulgarised the tones. Herman Yorke heaped blessings upon the head of that strange black-eyed girl—or ghost! Which? He did not care a rap which. Enough that she had discovered for him the soul of the Stradivari.

The paroxysm of surprise and joy ended, Herman Yorke tucked his violin under his chin to play one last piece before putting it away for the night. Then it happened that disaster nearly overwhelmed the fiddle. Yorke's foot trod on the discarded peg; it skidded under him, he pitched forward, and it was only by allowing his head to come heavily against the wall that he saved his precious fiddle.

Flying in a temper, the young man crunched his heel upon the peg, which, as if in anger at its dethronement, had so nearly destroyed the Stradivari. When he lifted his heel, there he saw a few fragments of wood, and in the midst of these a core that had not gone to dust. Reaching down, Herman Yorke picked up a tiny metal cylinder.

Here, then, was the foreign matter that had made this superb fiddle sound second class. How got such a thing into a fiddle-peg? Assuredly Stradivari had never stultified his handiwork by inserting deadening metal plugs into pegs. This peg must have been substituted for the original by some blunderer in later days.

Between thumb and finger Herman Yorke held the cylinder the while he examined it critically. The first thing that struck him was the metal's inconsiderable weight. Next, on a sudden, he made out a cap or lid on one end. In an instant he had this off, and had shaken into his palm a tiny roll of thinnest parchment. Under a magnifying-glass he roughly construed from the Latin, this:

"For the peace of the soul of Maddalina Tonelli, read!

"That injustice may not be eternal, obey!

"This Stradivari was the property of Signor Umberto Canini, master player of Verona. Lying on his deathbed in Rome, to me, Maddalina Tonelli his pupil, he entrusted the violin to be delivered to his one child, Signorina Carina Canini. The temptation is too great. My passion for the fiddle is such that I shall not fulfil my promise until I feel death stealing upon me. But in case death comes upon me unexpectedly, each time that I lay aside the fiddle, I substitute a false peg, containing this message, in the sure knowledge that the dwarfed sound of the violin will discover to the discerning the presence of the spurious peg. Know you who finds this message that the soul of Maddalina Tonelli can find peace never until restitution is made. Search out Signorina Carina Canini of Verona, or if, unhappily, she be gone to her rest, then her nearest descendant, and restore to its rightful owner this precious Stradivari.

"That the soul of Maddalina Tonelli may have peace, obey!

"That injustice may not be eternal, obey!

"Blessings manifold be upon your head.

"MADDALINA TONELLI. 1707."

Herman Yorke sat back and closed his eyes.

"I have seen the soul of Maddalina Tonelli," he said, then sat a long time in silence.

The soul of Maddalina Tonelli, wandering, harassed, unquiescent, awaiting the time when injustice done should be undone, when restitution might bring to her peace! For twice an hundred years she had been a wanderer, following the fortunes of a fiddle. Had she been revealed to other possessors of the Stradivari? Perhaps not.

Perhaps the soul of not one of the former possessors had so burned with enthusiasm for the colour and life of sound as to be capable of seeing her soul. A Ratcliff Highway pawnshop suggested a succession of drunken sailor fiddlers, upon whose sight nothing less blunt than a belaying-pin could make an impression. To him the sight of the girl had been vouchsafed.

Herman Yorke leapt to his feet. What? Give up his Stradivari at the very initial moment of real possession? Never! Had he not come by it legitimately? Undoubtedly he had. Was it likely, then, that now he had tasted of its divine flavour he would put it away from him to expiate the sin of another, one of different blood, of different epoch? Never, never! The Stradivari was his by every right, that gave a man possession. His it should remain, despite imploring eyes and great round tears.

Another thing. Two hundred years had crawled past. Was it not absurd to dream of discovering the rightful heir of the long-ago Signorina Carina, daughter of the master fiddler? Utterly absurd! Descendants? There might be not one, there might be two thousand. Was it his business to search and sift among the population of Italy? Certainly not. Even in matters of conscience there must be a Statute of Limitation. Then and there Herman Yorke resolved three resolves. First, he would say no one word to any living being about his find of the scroll; second, he would pay no regard to the request of the long-dead Maddalina Tonelli; third—this to ease his conscience—he in his will would leave the Stradivari to the City of Verona. This last resolve surely should satisfy the soul of Maddalina Tonelli!

The night of the Christmas Concert arrived, and Herman Yorke waited behind the platform until the time came when he was obliged to take his place in the orchestra. Boldly he marched upon the platform, and, without a glance at the audience, he arranged himself, his fiddle, and the music. At the first sweep of the bow two things happened. First, he saw the conductor glance at him in pleasure amounting to amazement, for this was the first occasion on which the conductor had heard the real Stradivari; second, a sharp pain struck into Herman Yorke's forehead. Maddalina Tonelli, then, had her eyes upon him once again! He must be resolute. He must glance aside her glance, as armour glances an arrow. Not once during the evening must his eyes stray round to her face. It was sacrifice enough on his part; it should satisfy her, too, that in the end the Stradivari would pass into the keeping of Canini's native town, Verona. She must not trouble him more. He would show her that it lay beyond her power to disconcert him, haunt him as she might. He would keep his eyes from hers; and the very next minute his eyes were looking deep into her eyes.

The girl's eyebrows were arched high, her mouth was half open, her hands clutched one another nervously, she leaned forward eagerly, she nodded, once, her head. Plainly her whole being cried:

"You will; you will?"

Once for all he would crush her hope. Roughly he shook his head.

As a mother eagle, disturbed on her nest, ruffles and swells to double her real size, so the girl slowly began to develop and to expand until she seemed to fill the auditorium. Demon fire squinted and flamed from her eye, a hooked, horned beak thrust forth from her face, her ears lay flat back against her head, her black hair rose erect, stiff, and jagged as porcupine-quills; at a rustle and shrug of her body great coarse feathers thrust forth from her to stand angrily erect, her hands, one raised to either side of her head, grew scales, and each finger became a horrible talon, gigantic wings arched over her back, a curdling, hissing sound wheezed from her nostrils; then, with a scream and a skirl, this vampire shape launched itself hurtling straight for Herman Yorke's head.

Appalled orchestra and audience beheld the first violin leap to his feet in a spasm of fear; appalled, they heard his shriek:

"I will! I will! Mercy! Mercy!"

Appalled, they saw him fling his fiddle into the arms of the conductor; then, with a cry that was half scream, half groan, he fell flat upon his face on the floor. And next morning's newspapers chronicled the abandoning of a concert owing to the first violinist being seized with a fit.

Three months passed before Herman Yorke was strong enough to set out for Verona. Esther Burnaby showed a certain amount of consideration for the violinist. She waited till she heard that he had got upon his feet again, before sending him a note breaking off the engagement and returning his presents. He read the note, tore it into tiny pieces, and scattered these on the fire, then tossed the bundle of presents into a corner, notwithstanding the contents of that bundle were precious. He heaved no sigh at his release.

The volatile landlord of the little hotel which Yorke always made his headquarters when in Verona—he had visited Verona some half a dozen times in his life—welcomed him with great exuberance, and nothing would do but that the Englishman must drink a glass of wine with him. In the midst of a torrent of talk Yorke suddenly held up a silencing hand. The sounds of a fiddle danced and capered in from the street, to skip and play about the little parlour in which the guest and host sat. For a time the two men listened.

"That's good fiddling!" exclaimed Herman Yorke, at length. "Where does it come from?"

"The street, signor," replied the landlord.

"The street? Who plays?"

"Some ragged vagabond, doubtless," said the host, with a shrug of the shoulders.

"Lucky ragged beggar!" said Yorke, more to himself than to the Italian; then asked: "Can you induce him to come in here?"

"Doubtless. There is a glass of wine for him—"

"And twenty-five lire," supplemented Yorke.

"A glass and fortune? What more can man ask for in this world?" said the landlord, ambling off.

Five minutes later and the door of the parlour swung open. Herman Yorke sat thunderstruck. For there, framed in the doorway, stood the girl of the concerts. Poorly dressed, her face a little more drawn, yet the self-same girl! In her hand she carried a fiddle and bow, and she curtseyed to the Englishman with all the grace of a princess. Herman Yorke arose to his feet.

"I have the honour to speak to Signorina Maddalina Tonelli?" he asked.

"No, signor," she answered, looking surprised.

"Not Signorina Tonelli? Then, pray, your name?"

"My name is Carina Canini."

The truth flashed upon his brain. The ghost of Maddalina Tonelli had taken on the likeness of the living descendant of that Carina Canini of long ago, that he, Herman Yorke, might recognise the true owner of the Stradivari at a glance. He had no doubts, yet he chose to question the girl.

"Long ago lived a Canini famous for his playing?"

"He was my ancestor, signor. He left me his love for the violin, but, unfortunately, neither his skill nor his fiddle."

"He had a famous fiddle?"

"A Stradivari, signor, but it was stolen from him on his deathbed."

Carina Canini sat in a chair, her fingers toying with a glass of wine.

"Who could not be famous with a Stradivari to play on?" she added.

Herman Yorke gazed upon the girl much more frankly than he had gazed upon her spirit-counterfeit in far-away Queen's Hall. Nature had fashioned her to grace a palace; Fate had cast her in humble station. Hitherto Yorke had feared the bitterness of parting with the Stradivari, but now, as he sat feasting his eyes upon the glorious Southern girl, he realised that all the bitter had been turned to sweet. It seemed to him that he had known her through many, many months; in the circumstances, a not at all unreasonable seeming.

"I, too, have a fiddle," he said, breaking a long silence. "May I play to you a little while, just the while it takes you to sip your wine?"

"You are kind, signor," said the girl graciously.

Herman Yorke brought forth the Stradivari, and he played. He played with all his powers, he played with all his soul, he played as never he had played in his life, for the fear was upon him that this might be the last time he was destined to hold the divine violin close to his heart. As he played the girl's great eyes grew greater, her bosom heaved in ecstasy, and tears of pleasure glistened down her cheeks. And when the young man ceased to play she delayed not an instant but sprang to her feet, and, in a tumult of Southern enthusiasm and emotion, flung her arms round Herman Yorke's neck and kissed him passionately.

As, rather terrified at her own impulse, she started back from him, he held forth the fiddle.

"Signorina, once on a time this Stradivari belonged to one Signor Umberto Canini of Verona. Long years it has been a wanderer in the wilderness, but the gods watched over it, and, in the end, and at the right time, chose me to restore it to its rightful owner, Carina

Canini. Here, signorina, take back from bondage what is your own, and with it take this tiny roll of parchment."

Herman Yorke sojourned more than six months in Verona.

Again Queen's Hall, London, and again the Christmas Concert of the Amateur Orchestral Society. This concert will be remembered because historic, for at it Mrs. Herman Yorke, formerly Signorina Carina Canini of Verona, made her sensational debut on the concert platform, playing her famous ancestor's equally famous Stradivari. Herman Yorke occupied a seat on the platform, although he was not playing, and during the first part of the concert his gaze wandered over the faces of the people occupying stalls and dress-circle. There was one vacant seat in the fifth row, and this seat Herman Yorke watched closely. A symphony was played. The seat remained empty. A song was sung. Still the seat stood empty. But when his wife stepped upon the platform, and at the first sweep of her bow, the seat was occupied.

A girl, but not the girl of the previous concert! How could he expect that she should be the same girl, seeing that that girl now stood on the platform playing divinely? No; in the stall sat a different creature: altogether, a slight, frail, worn little creature a pale face pillowed in golden hair. Her eyes were full upon him, his full upon her. At length her lips parted in a smile of infinite sweetness, and, arising, she curtseyed low as though in fathomless gratitude to him. Then he beheld her begin to float into the air, up, and up, and up; and as she rose her eyes closed, and her head fell gently back in ineffable rest, and the whole great hall was filled with the splendour of her leave-taking.

Herman Yorke placed elbows on knees and buried his face in his hands. To himself he muttered:

"Now, indeed, has rest fallen like balm upon the tired soul of Maddalina Tonelli."

HAUNTED!

Jack Edwards

Despite extensive research I have been unable to find out anything about Jack Edwards. Like Elsie Norris he was a regular contributor to the Shurey weekly penny magazines Yes or No *and* The Weekly Tale-Teller *in the decade before the First World War. Many of his stories were supernatural or occult though he tended to write more for effect than substance. Once in a while, though, he controlled his exuberance and produced more memorable fiction, as in the following.*

WHEN ROYDON CAME DOWN THE STAIRS HE SAW IT WAITING for him, and as usual it vanished as he approached. He went into his bedroom, which, with the rest of the rooms of the flat, was on the floor below the studio. The chintz-covered chair complained in all its wicker frame at the heavy descent of his body. A large bluebottle from the lime-trees below the half-opened window buzzed in the silk of the casement blinds, and the hot sunlight lay in bars on the floor. The roar of the motor traffic on the north side of the square, modulated by the distance, bore with it the faint jangle of a piano organ like a treble melody half drowned by a tuneless bass, but he did not hear the noise of the street any more than he noted the golden noon or the buzzing of the fly or the creaking protest of the chair.

His hands were limp, and his legs stuck out stiffly before him. His chin was sunk on his breast, and his eyes goggled beneath his frowning brows. It was the face of a man who had begun to be afraid.

He sat thus, looking neither to the past nor to the future, but permitting only the horror of the present to absorb him.

To-day it had seemed more tangible. He had faintly discerned a face; the blurred outline of a form; a suggestion of limbs.

It was assuming personality; was progressing from a nebulous blur to definite shape; was entering upon a development a feature of which was that it no longer kept at a certain distance, but was apt to appear near at hand as though seeking to establish a ghastly intimacy.

Roydon fell to reviewing the incidents of the past weeks.

He had first seen it one late afternoon when coming down the short stairs from the studio.

At first he had thought it some strange effect of light in the darkness of the hall, but this idea was quickly dispelled.

Some unaccountable feeling had suspended his movement, and he paused with one foot on the step below the studio door and the other still on the threshold, while his eyes investigated the curious nebulous light that hung in a milky blur against the gloom below.

His arrested action was not due to fear. The moment he saw the apparition his mind cast about for a commonsense explanation, and, none being immediately forthcoming, he descended the steps slowly and noted the withdrawal of the blur of light towards the end of the hall.

He went towards it, and it faded and was gone. Before him were the panels of the closed door of his bedroom.

He dismissed the matter from his mind, telling himself that he had overstrained his eyes in the studio.

The second time he saw it in the studio itself. It loomed indistinctly at the far end, and as before, it dissolved on his approach.

He had been occupied on a largo panel intended for a mural decoration, and again he sought to explain the phenomenon by natural causes. The central figure in the panel was robed in scarlet, and Roydon had endeavoured to persuade himself that fatigue of the optic nerve, engendered by prolonged attention to the crimson figure, had produced a similar figure when he removed his eyes from the glowing canvas.

But there were two objections to this ingenious theory.

One was that the sympathetic colour to red is green, and therefore he might have expected a greenish-hued counterpart of the figure in the panel to confront him. What he actually saw was a shapeless white blur.

The other objection was that instead of being between him and the furniture of the room, as it would have been had it existed only on the retina of the eye, it came into view behind a chair which partially obscured the lower half. Moreover, it was stationary, whereas, had it existed only in his eye, it would have moved with the transferring of his vision and reappeared wherever his gaze rested.

Finally it had appeared to him on three other occasions, twice by day and once at night.

He had seen it establish itself at the door of a drawing-room in a friend's house as though it was waiting for him to finish his call.

The other daylight appearance was when he was crossing the square in which his flat was situated, and the night appearance was on his doorstep once on returning a little past midnight from conviviality in a neighbouring studio.

Roydon came back from his contemplation of the past weeks to a consideration of a triviality of the moment.

The buzzing of the fly on the pane had at last found an avenue to his attention, and aroused his annoyance.

He made as if to rise, and in the moment of action he became passive again. He had caught sight of his face and figure in the long mirror set in the door of the wardrobe.

The expression of his face startled him.

"Good God!" he exclaimed involuntarily, and again a moment later, "Good God! What would Mab say if she saw me with a phiz like that?"

He rose and shook the casement blind to expedite the escape of the blue-bottle, and then came back to the chintz-covered chair, which again protested at the impact of his body.

"I'll see Blair to-day," he murmured. "I'll 'phone."

The only son of well-to-do parents, Ernest Roydon had, during their lifetime, worked hard at the profession he had adopted and had succeeded in making, if not a name for himself, at least a small reputation and eventually a moderately good living.

On the death of his mother he had inherited enough money to render him independent of his profession, and when the demise of his father followed shortly after, he found himself, if not a rich man, at least one to whom the luxuries of existence were now more easily attainable than the necessities had been previously.

Instead of ceasing from the drudgery that had been his from the age of twenty-two, Roydon, now in his thirtieth year, worked harder than ever. Ambition took the place of need, and the sole difference his ampler means created in his life was that, whereas once he had seized every commission that came his way in order to provide himself with the necessities of life, he now only accepted such orders as he felt would advance him in his career, and gave himself over to the delight of creative work with indifference to the possibility of its ever having a market value.

The studio he had acquired in his student days still sufficed his needs. It was nothing more than a roomy attic with a large skylight in the sloping roof on the north side and two other windows. A flight of stairs led up to it from the four rooms which constituted his flat. It was, in reality, the upper part of a comfortable, old-fashioned house in a south-western square. The tenant of the lower part had moved recently, and Roydon, in view of his approaching marriage, had acquired the lease of the whole house.

At length Roydon rose from the wicker chair and set about changing his clothes, He looked almost anxiously from his bedroom door into the dimness of the hall before crossing to the bathroom.

The indistinct figure was not there.

"Why the blazes should it come and go like that!" he muttered as he filled the bath. "Why does the bally thing come at odd moments and then disappear for days! If I am haunted, why not a continual haunting? Why these haphazard appearances? Oh, it's a case of nerves! I'll 'phone to Blair."

He returned to his bedroom. "Let me see, what am I doing to-night? Oh, it's 'Traviata' at the opera. I'm taking Mab. Well, I'll see Blair this afternoon."

"Nothing whatever the matter with you," said his medical friend: "you're as fit as a fiddle. I wish I had your physique."

"You're sure?" asked Roydon anxiously. "You see, old chap, I'm to be married in September, and I want to know. I've been a bit 'off colour,' I fancy, lately."

"What are the symptoms?" asked his friend.

"Don't laugh," answered Roydon; "I've been having delusions—fancy I'm seeing things."

Blair was amused, and made an obvious joke.

"Don't be a fool!" said Roydon impatiently. "It isn't a case of that kind. You know I'm not much of a drinker." He related the occurrence. "I can't make it out," he wound up; "it's so bally casual in its comings and goings. I never know when I'll see it. Do you think it's really only a hallucination?"

"Of course," said the other importantly. "It's quite simple. It's a case of auto-suggestion really. You thought you saw something and it gave you a bit of a shock. That impressed it on your sub-conscious mind. Now, whenever you are a bit strung up, your sub-conscious mind projects the image on your brain—throws up a suggestion of what you are to see, and you promptly see it. You follow me?

You are unconsciously performing a simple little experiment of self-hypnotism."

"It's a 'simple little experiment' I'd give anything to lose the knack of," retorted Roydon. "What's the cure?"

"Rest and don't worry," said the other. "Here's Philpot's address. Go and see him to-morrow; I'll 'phone him up and talk about you in the meantime. It'll cost you a tenner."

That same evening Roydon sat with Mabel Wreford in the stalls at Covent Garden. They occupied the end seats of row H.

Roydon became conscious that someone or something stood in the gangway beside his seat. He turned with some impatience, expecting to confront a programme seller. Instead, however, he saw the same strange apparition to which he was now no stranger, but which none the less gave him an immense and sickening shock.

He saw the pale blur of light vaguely suggestive of a human form. It was nearer to him than it had ever been before, and as he gazed it retreated down the gangway and faded away at the point where a flight of steps provides the left-hand exit to the seats in the fore part of the auditorium.

In the darkness of the opera-house the luminous figure was plainly visible, and it seemed incredible to Roydon that others beside himself could not have seen it.

He looked quickly at the girl beside him. Her attention was riveted on the stage, where a great singer, famous alike for her acting and her vocalisation, was representing the pathetic end of the consumptive heroine. Miss Wreford was totally oblivious of all save the scene on the stage.

He looked round the house. Faces, palely indistinct in the gloom, were all turned stageward, and Roydon realised that to him, and him alone, had the apparition been visible.

"But why?" he asked himself in distress. "Why here? Why must it follow me?"

The sudden glare of the lights seemed to let loose the thunderous avalanche of applause from all parts of the opera house, and the greatest light soprano of the day came before the red curtains again and again to bow her acknowledgments.

"But why," Roydon's dizzy brain was asking, "why does it follow me?"

"It's horribly pathetic," his fiancée was saying. "I don't wonder you're upset, Ernest. It makes me cry inside, and that's much worse than crying with one's eyes. Don't say anything for five minutes. I want the motor and my handkerchief and some eau-de-Cologne and home."

"Why does it follow me?" Roydon continued to ask himself miserably as he went back to the studio after seeing his fiancée to her door. "What is the meaning of it? If it is only a thing of my brain, does it mean that I am going mad? And if it is something outside me, something occult and horrible, what is the meaning of it, and why does it come to me?"

He paused on the step with his latchkey in his hand, and then he came down the steps and walked several times round the square. "I can't go in," he murmured; "it may be waiting for me. I'm a coward. I'm afraid to go in."

He nerved himself to ascend the steps again, and finally inserted the latchkey and entered the darkened house.

It was on the steps leading to the studio. It did not vanish at his approach. He went past it and entered his bedroom, closing the door and shutting out the gleaming Thing in the dark hall. Then he flung himself on his bed in his clothes and lay there awake the whole night with the gas burning and his hands pressed over his eyes, afraid to look up lest the vision he dreaded should have entered the room and taken its stand beside him.

The next day he visited the specialist to whom Blair had recommended him. The verdict was the same, and a further physician whom he consulted endorsed the opinion that his health was perfect, and any delusion from which he suffered was the outcome of nervous tension. He was recommended to take a holiday.

Roydon found himself in the position of a man oppressed with a trouble and lacking a friend in whom he could confide, and, under the circumstances, he felt that a confidant was the one thing that could help him to bear the strain of the situation.

To mention the matter to Mabel Wreford was out of the question.

Although the tender relationship existing between them would have justified his consulting her on any other topic that might disturb his peace of mind, he felt that to approach her with the news of his hallucination was impossible for two reasons. She was of a highly-strung and sensitive temperament herself, and the shock of learning that her lover was the victim of such a haunting, whether self-created or not, would in all probability have a disastrous effect on her nerves.

Apart from the storm of alarm and fear that such a confession might arouse in her mind, Roydon felt that he could not burden her with so weighty and dreadful a confidence for the further reason that to broach the matter to the girl who was so soon to be his wife might have the effect of undermining his future.

A prospective bridegroom might well hesitate to impart a secret that would cause his future wife to regard him as an incipient lunatic.

At the same time, the growing need of someone to whom he could unburden his mind, and call upon for aid in such an extraordinary juncture, became almost as great as his dread that at almost any moment he might raise his eyes and see the object of his fear hovering in his vicinity.

Several times in the ensuing days he found the apparition at his elbow, and with the desperate feeling of a man at bay he began to make a note of everything in connection with the phenomenon in the hope of explaining its origin or mitigating its terror.

As a result of his observation, he noted that the phantom was seldom visible when he expected to see it. A hundred times during the day he would look round dreading to see his ghostly visitant, and each time his gaze would only encounter the familiar objects of his surroundings. It was only when absorbed in his work, or when his mind was similarly occupied with some matter inducing forgetfulness of his trouble, that he would look up and become aware of the presence of his unwelcome and strange visitor.

Now, too, he found that it remained visible for longer and longer periods. He was able to study its appearance, and, with a heart filled with terror and loathing, perceived that the blur of light obscured a dim shape within, as though the ghost of a person appeared enveloped in a semi-opaque haze like a dead body in a luminous shroud.

At length, one night in the studio, summoning up courage, he addressed the apparition.

The result was instantaneous and terrifying.

The apparition shook as with a ghostly ague. It developed an agitation as pronounced as that raised in the mind of the unfortunate young man who beheld it. Roydon's conjuration caused it an instant's palsy, as though it was an algæ-like organism quickened into active life by his words.

Roydon never knew how he got out of the room. He found himself, hatless in the square, having fled from the house, leaving behind that dreadful apparition quaking with a horrible spirit emotion either of mirth or fear.

It was late, and the upper windows of the adjoining houses were alight, while the downstair rooms were in darkness. People were retiring for the night.

Comfortable beds and the oblivion of sleep waited for these urban dwellers, but for him, sharing his lonely house with a spectre, comfort and sleep had become an impossibility.

He walked quickly round the square, pausing to look over his shoulder for fear that the quaking thing might be following. Panic gripped him. He felt that a gleam of white in his wake would cause him to take to his heels in terrified flight.

A church clock tolled midnight, and immediately on its staccato chime came the deep, reverberating boom of Big Ben, softened by the distance to a dozen mellow waves of sound.

A young man, hatless like himself, met Roydon at the end of the square. Their glances encountered in passing.

The stranger ascended the steps of a house, and Roydon heard a jingle of keys. He halted and looked back. An immense yearning for human companionship swept over the haunted man, filling him with a desire to buttonhole even this stranger and enlist his sympathy and aid.

The other was looking over his shoulder as he fitted his key in the door. Another moment and he would enter. Roydon's need drove him over the conventionalities at a bound.

"I say," he called, and then came to a pause in speech and movement. The man came down the steps.

"Yes?" he inquired tentatively.

In the light Roydon saw his face. It was young and fresh. He looked pleasantly human.

"You're—you're a neighbour of mine," stammered Roydon. "I've seen you often. I wonder if you would mind—" He broke off, his late agitation stirring him more than the astonishment on the stranger's face.

"Yes?" queried the other again, his surprised expression inviting Roydon's explanation.

"Would you mind talking to me a few minutes?" Roydon went on, with a rush. "I've just had a shock. I must speak to someone. If I don't I must shriek or run—I don't know which. I can hardly keep my teeth from chattering." His breath was uneven. He extended an uncertain hand. "I must touch someone and speak to them, or I feel I shall go mad."

His wide, startled eyes were fixed on the stranger's face, searching it with desperate eagerness for a sign of yielding or withdrawal.

"I'm not a lunatic nor am I drunk," went on Roydon. "I'm so badly frightened I'm not ashamed to show it and to ask for help."

"That's all right," said the other, and with his slow, genial utterance Roydon felt an immense relief.

"Tell me," went on the stranger, "what has upset you?"

"That's my house." Roydon indicated his dwelling. "I've lived there for years. I'm afraid to go in. There's a ghost there."

The other 's incredulous smile under the pale illumination of the street lamp suddenly brought to Roydon's mind the futility of his appeal.

"A ghost? Oh, impossible!" he heard the stranger begin, and with the conventionality of his attitude on the point Roydon was moved to impatient earnestness. He almost stuttered in his eagerness to convince the stranger of the truth of his words.

"Don't say that," he urged. "It sounds rot, I know; but I'm not a fool—I'm not a chicken-hearted craven, frightened by a shadow.

I'm"—the horrible truth welled up in his mind and flooded the moment with its horror—"I'm a haunted man," he concluded.

The other turned to the steps and Roydon clutched his arm.

"Don't go," he said quickly, in an extremity of appeal.

The stranger produced his key.

"Come in," he said gently. "You want a drink first of all."

He unlocked the door, and Roydon followed him into the dark hall.

There was the spurt of a match, and the stranger lighted a candle.

"Come up," he said quietly. "Don't make a noise, everybody's in bed. My rooms are at the top."

He led the way into a meagrely furnished room and indicated a chair, while he produced a bottle and two tumblers.

"Better bare it neat," he said laconically, pouring out a quantity of whisky and handing it to his visitor.

"My name is Gilbert Chalmers," he went on. "I know your name, and I have, now I come to think of it, heard that you were an artist. My landlady told me that you own No. 21. Now tell me about your spook."

Roydon plunged into his narration and Chalmers sat and meditated at the finish.

"An odd story," he commented. "You see the thing at odd times, you say, and in a lot of different places?"

On receiving Roydon's assent, he continued: "That points to the idea that it is a delusion of yours. You see, you carry it about wherever you go—into friends' houses, in the street, even in a theatre. Now, a ghost generally stays in one place. It haunts a locality, not an individual."

"It comes after me," said Roydon, making an effort to speak calmly: "and whereas once it kept its distance, now when it appears it is just at my elbow."

"I've never seen a ghost or any kind of disembodied spirit," answered Chalmers, "but I've studied the subject. It is said that there are spooks that try to take possession of a body. Those follow folk about. They are earth-bound spirits, so the jargon goes, and they only get a chance when a person is weak or ill, or goes into a trance or something. You are not given to trances?"

"I am awfully well," answered Roydon. "I've never had a day's illness, and a trance is simply a thing that couldn't happen. I've seen three doctors lately, a mental specialist among them, and they say that I am in splendid condition."

"H'm!" said Chalmers, and pondered. "Don't you think you had better go away somewhere and have a complete change? A sea journey for preference."

"I can't. I have some panels to finish—a commission, you know. I've got to finish by a certain date."

"Why not take 'em with you? Pack 'em up and go to the country."

Roydon brightened. "Yes, I might do that. But I'm going to be married soon. I did not want to go away just yet."

"I should think," returned the other, "it would be better to get rid—of this—this hallucination before you get married. Anyway, let's go over to your place and investigate."

He rose, but Roydon hung back.

"I can't go back yet," he said hoarsely. "I left it there, shaking like a jelly, a horrible, quivering white thing. I can't go back. Let me stay a little longer."

"Oh," returned the other, "stay all night if you like. There's a sofa. You can lie on that and have some rugs." He went into the next room, and after a few minutes returned with a pillow and an eiderdown quilt. He flung these on the sofa and turned to his visitor.

Roydon was sitting with his face in his hands.

"Buck up," said Chalmers not ungently, laying his hand on him.

Roydon raised his head and exhibited a haggard countenance, from which not merely the blood had ebbed, leaving it white and drawn, but from which hope, vitality, and even life seemed to be drained. It was a face of death in life that confronted Chalmers, who started back in alarm.

"Good heavens, man," he cried, "pull yourself together!"

Roydon's very tone was dead.

"It's here," he said—"it's on my left. Can you see it? It's followed me!"

Chalmers stared from Roydon to the spot indicated. "There's nothing there," he expostulated.

"It's shaking," pursued Roydon. "It's just here by me. It has come close. It almost touches me, and it is trembling. It is all misty, but I can see eyes, eager eyes." He suddenly clutched Chalmers. "My God!" he said in a tone of anguish, and leant heavily on him.

Chalmers, staring over his shoulder, saw nothing, and over his mind there flashed a conviction that his companion was insane. The next moment Roydon straightened himself.

"Ah, I'm behaving like a kid," he said. "Try not to blame me. It's an awful thing to be haunted." He went quickly to the door.

"Where are you going?" Chalmers asked.

"Anywhere," answered Roydon in a muffled tone. "All places are the same now."

His despairing voice echoed up the stairs as he descended.

Chalmers noticed that he had not once looked back.

"Wait. I'll light you down," he cried, and reached for the candle. But he heard Roydon at the foot of the stairs as he descended the first flight. Then came the sound of the closing of the door. He followed, and looked into the street. Roydon was nowhere in sight.

Chalmers concluded that he had gone towards his house, a few doors lower down.

A light, drizzling rain had begun to fall. The pavements glistened drearily, and a feeling of intense depression fell on the sympathetic watcher as he stared down the square, seeking the whereabouts of the man who had just left him.

Thus ended Chalmers' first adventure in connection with Roydon's hallucination. But in due course he was destined to learn of the progress of his strange obsession.

A few days later a silver-mounted walking-stick arrived for him. Neither card nor letter accompanied it to explain this anonymous gift, but Chalmers had no difficulty in ascribing it to Roydon's sense of gratitude over the episode of their recent meeting.

Four months went by in which he perceived no sign of life in Roydon's house, and early in December Chalmers noticed lights in the windows of No. 21, and concluded that Roydon had returned to town.

He wondered if he was cured of his strange obsession, and half expected that Roydon would call on him.

A fortnight later, coming down the steps, he saw him entering his house accompanied by a pretty, fair-haired girl.

Although several yards away Chalmers noticed the haggard look on the man's face, and perceived that his stalwart frame seemed to have lost something of its vigour and uprightness of carriage.

It was Christmas week, and on the eve of the great festival of the year he went to the pillar-box in the corner of the square with some letters. On returning past Roydon's house he saw the door open, and a woman, dishevelled and distraught, issued and looked wildly up and down the deserted square, wringing her hands.

She hailed Chalmers as he approached.

"Oh, do come—do come and help me!" she cried. "I don't know what to do." Her cheeks glistened with a ceaseless flow of tears. "It is my husband," she went on. "I am alone, and I don't know what is wrong."

"Is he ill?" Chalmers asked.

"I don't know," she returned. "His door is locked and he won't open it. He is ill or going mad—I don't know which."

In this brief colloquy Chalmers recognised the beginning of the sequel to his nocturnal adventure with Roydon some months before. He said nothing at the moment, but followed the girl into the house of tragedy.

He was not prepared for so rich a setting to the closing scene of the drama. Electric lights, tastefully shaded, illumined the hall and rooms. The house was decorated in a manner in which an artistic simplicity of effect was produced by the most costly means, and the originality and beauty of the interior was in striking contrast with the exterior of the house.

He followed Mrs. Roydon down the brilliantly lighted hall and up the richly carpeted staircase. As they went she spoke swiftly.

"He has been strange in his manner for some time. Both the servants left a week ago. They were nervous and wouldn't stay, and since then I haven't been able to get anyone else. One cannot get servants in Christmas week."

"Then you are all alone in this big house," Chalmers said in surprise.

"Since last Saturday," she returned. "He got worse then. I haven't seen him for two days."

They arrived at a closed door at the top of the third flight.

"This is the flat my husband had before he took the whole house," Roydon's wife continued. "The studio is up at the top. He—he has shut himself up here, and he won't let me in. I've heard him raving inside and crying. It has been awful. Now he is quiet. He may be dead, and there is this locked door and I can't get in. What am I to do?"

She leant against the wall and her tears flowed afresh.

The fair prettiness of her face vanished, and Chalmers saw in its place the grief-blurred features of a rather weak woman who was clearly on the verge of hysteria.

"Have you knocked at the door and called to him?" asked Chalmers.

"I have been knocking and calling all day," she answered. "I spent the night on these stairs listening to his ravings and asking him to let me in. He paid no attention at first, but twice afterwards he called out to me to go away. Oh, you don't know how awful his voice sounded."

She sobbed convulsively.

Chalmers listened at the door, but no sound came from within.

Mrs. Roydon had sunk down beside him on the stairs leading up to the closed door.

He rattled the knob, and rapped on the panel with his knuckles.

"Let me in," he called persuasively. "It is I—Chalmers. Don't you remember me?"

With his ear to the crack he fancied he heard a deep sigh.

"Won't you let me in, old man?" he called.

Suddenly a voice answered from inside, but it was not the unexpectedness of a reply that caused Chalmers to start back—it was something horrible in the sound of the voice, a ghastly quality of tone that suggested slime and viscosity.

"Chalmers, Chalmers," the slobbering voice cried thickly. "Go away—leave me alone. It has got me. I am possessed."

And at the conclusion of this speech the gelatinous utterance gave place to a string of cries and imprecations, so awful and agonised that Chalmers reeled from the door and stumbled downstairs in the wake of Mrs. Roydon's flying figure.

At the foot of the stairs she collapsed, and fell on the rich red Persian carpet of the hall.

"Oh, how awful, how awful!" she moaned. "Are there two in there?" She fainted, and Chalmers bore her insensible figure into the splendid dining-room, while outside in the square, to an accompaniment of musical instruments, the waits struck up a Christmas hymn.

Roydon is now in an asylum. In his studio was found a diary touching upon the hallucination which had finally unseated his reason. The entries were as follows:

"Sept. 22nd.—It has come back. My God! What am I to do? I am to be married next week, and now, after nearly eight weeks' peace, the cursed vision haunts me again.

"I finished the panels yesterday, and sent them up to town to-day. I went for a country walk this afternoon and felt well and happy. I saw a white figure on the stile at the end of the field I was crossing. I thought it was a country girl, and that I would have to ask her to move; and then I got near and saw that it was It.

"It melted away in its cloudy fashion, just as it used to do when it first came, but I saw a gleam of eyes from the midst of the cloudy blur. Those eyes have frozen my soul."

"Sept. 28th.—I saw it to-day, and it was quite close and stayed a long time. I have seen it every day since it reappeared. It is closer every time. I have tried to speak to it, but it trembles in such a ghastly way it makes me almost faint to see it. I shall go mad with sheer horror. Oh, if there were only someone to talk to!

"I must be brave, and never let Mab know.

"I am to be married to-morrow."

"Sept. 29th.—I was married today. It was there all the time. Poor Mab thinks I am awfully changed. My God! I am so well in body and so sick in mind."

There was a break in the diary, and then the entries began again in December:

"Dec. 10th.—We have been back in town some time. It is with me always. We have made the house beautiful, and all the time I feel that I am making it comfortable for a strange guest. Mab finds me moody and absorbed. Poor girl, she doesn't know.

"I have been to the doctors again. No help there. They all say I am quite well. I went to a City church, and after a service talked to a parson. I told him everything. He said it was sent as a punishment for sin. I told him I hadn't done any evil worth speaking about. He got huffy, and said he would pray for me. Up to the present his prayers haven't done any good."

"Dec. 15th.—It is with me all day. First on one side, then on the other. Quite close. It touched me yesterday. It was clammy and cold, like a huge slug."

"Dec. 17th.—It comes into bed at night. It is very cold. It touches my food at meals, and then I cannot eat anything. I don't know how Mab doesn't see it. It is there all the time. I cannot stand much more."

"Dec. 19th.—It is all around me. It is trying to take possession of me. Its eyes are close to mine."

"Dec. 22nd.—I have locked the door. It has never left me for several days now: This is the end."

There were no more entries in the diary.

Early in the New Year Chalmers went to the asylum and showed the doctor the diary, which he had fortunately been able to secure without Roydon's wife having seen it.

"It's a rum case," said the doctor, "He's absolutely insane. It must have been latent in him. He's quite happy and cheerful. Gives no trouble and has only one marked mania, He won't wear clothes. He'll wear a sheet or a blanket, and now we've given him a dozen yards of calico. He twists himself up in that. Come and have a peep at him."

Chalmers saw him. The madman was draped in a curious fashion. He looked as if he was wearing a shroud.

"Fairly normal in other ways," the doctor said. "Has a few un-nice ways—not very civilised, you know—and never says a word one can understand. Talks to himself in a strange, sloppy kind of lingo… Well, good-bye! Thanks. I'll let you know if there is any change."

That was the last Chalmers saw of Roydon. Sometimes he asks himself if Roydon was mad all the time, or if he really was the victim of a haunting by some strange and evil spirit that was visible to him and him only, and that, having marked him down as its prey, had eventually entered into him and possessed him.

But that is an uncomfortable idea. Chalmers prefers to think that there must have been lunacy in Roydon's blood.

OUR STRANGE TRAVELLER

By Percy James Brebner

*Percy James Brebner (1864–1922) is better remembered today for his crime
fiction, notably the two books featuring his eponymous forensic detective,*
Christopher Quarles, College Professor and Master Detective *(1914)
and* The Master Detective *(1916). Brebner's first book had appeared as
far back as 1889 and he wrote prolifically for the popular magazines. The
more bizarre adventures in his books appear in* The Fortress of Yadasara
(1899), with its lost world in the Caucasus, The Mystery of Ladyplace
(1900), with its mad scientist, and The Ivory Disc *(1920), with its mega-*
lomaniac mesmerist.

*Brebner's supernatural short fiction, though, has never been collected
in book form even though some of it was superior to his other work, such
as the following example from 1911.*

I WAS A MEDICAL STUDENT AT THE TIME, AND, ACCORDING TO MY father, had been an unconscionable time getting through my exams.

I explained to him that I had had the misfortune to deal with examiners who seemed to have a hobby for pitching on things which ordinary, decent fellows never worried about; and although I do not fancy I convinced him, it was proved that I was not fooling my time by the fact that after one of the exams—which I passed, by the way—I broke down, and our family doctor suggested a rest and complete change of environment.

That is how it came about that Frank Lascelles and I went on a walking tour in the North of France.

Lascelles you have probably heard about, since he is now a rather famous preacher at a fashionable West End church; and although you are not likely to have heard of me, I can assure you that Dr. Mark Glaisher has a very considerable practice in the neighbourhood of Wimbledon.

I just mention this in case you should underestimate us, and, as some others have done, accuse us of sticking to an imaginary story which, by a strange coincidence, turned out to be true.

We had been tramping for a week, having the time of our lives, and one evening were making for a village called Pedmont, where we intended to stay the night.

We were going along a road lying as straight as a road could lie across a flat bit of country, and were deep in some abstruse argument, when Frank suddenly exclaimed:

"Hallo! Where did that chap come from, I wonder?"

The man was about a hundred yards in front of us, going at the same pace as we were, and it was curious that we had not noticed him before.

He must have joined the road from some footpath across the fields; but even then we ought to have seen him, for there wasn't a bit of hedge or wood to hide him. He was a small man, round and stout, and carried a bag. He was neatly dressed, and was evidently not of the peasant class.

We dropped our argument, and, without agreeing together to do so, quickened our pace, partly out of curiosity to see what the man was like, partly with that natural desire which comes to so many people to overtake a person walking in front.

In a few moments we had doubled our rate of progress; but although the man in front never looked back, and seemed to be altogether unconscious of our presence, and although he did not apparently quicken his pace, we did not gain a yard upon him.

"Confound the fellow!" I said presently. "Let him get well ahead of us, Frank."

This, however, he seemed to have no intention of doing, for the moment we walked slowly he did so too.

The road dipped after a mile or two and ran between gorse hedges.

Now and again a bend in it would hide the fat little man from us, but directly there was a hundred yards of straight road we saw him again.

Coming to a bridge over a turbulent little brook we stopped, not to rest, but to let the man get away from us.

I am positive he never looked back, but the moment we stopped he sat down on a heap of stones by the roadside with his back towards us.

"He thinks it funny to play the fool in this way," said Frank quite angrily.

"After all, I suppose he has as much right to the road as we have," I remarked; "perhaps more, since he is in his own country."

"He doesn't look to me like a Frenchman," Frank answered. "And, anyway, he has no right to annoy other people."

I laughed a little at his annoyance. The stranger's behaviour had more effect on him than it had on me, and I have wondered since— But this is not the place to speak of my speculations.

Their worth will be better judged when the whole facts are known.

The instant we started again the man jumped up and went on. He appeared to hold himself in readiness to start at a moment's notice, as if his life depended on it, for he had not put his bag down, but held it in his hand all the time.

Pedmont was a fair-sized village and possessed a good inn. Travellers were frequent there on account of the ruins of a famous mediæval castle in the vicinity. We could see the broken walls and towers rising beyond the village street.

Our tormentor walked past the inn, and I was relieved, because I felt certain Frank would want to have a row with him.

We entered and washed the dust out of our throats with a bottle of wine.

In due course an excellent supper was set before us, and the old Boniface came and drank a glass with us, oozing the while good humour and local lore.

We were the only guests that night.

"Did you chance to overtake a small gentleman upon the road?" he asked when I mentioned the way we had come.

"Overtake him? No," Frank answered. "We did our level best to do so, but he would not let us. He went straight on through the village."

"Just now? Just before you came in, do you mean?"

"Yes."

"I did not see him, and I was looking out of the window."

"He was a small, round man, and carried a bag," I said.

"Yes, monsieur, that is right. It is very curious that he should go past. Yes, that was Herr Eckmann right enough. I cannot understand his going straight through the village."

Frank told him our experiences with the little German, and the landlord was more puzzled than ever. He declared that Herr Eckmann was such a sociable individual.

"Who is he?" I asked.

"He travels for a firm in Paris, and calls upon farmers with regard to seeds and roots. I think he does very good business, and every other month he is in this neighbourhood. It is always the same date he comes—regular, like clockwork—so I am always prepared for him. I know his taste and always have something special. This is his day, and for the last five years he has always remained the night here. We are very good friends. We were both through the Franco-Prussian war—on different sides, of course—but we have forgotten that. I do not like the Germans, no; but Herr Eckmann is the exception. He has lived in France a long time; that makes all the difference."

During the evening the landlord went to the door several times to look for his friend, and he inquired about him of every man who came in. They all knew the German well, but no one had seen him that day. An old road-mender said he had been working just at the end of the village all day and would certainly have seen him pass.

It seemed to me there was a general disposition to doubt our veracity, but Frank showed no annoyance at it, nor did I.

We spent an hour or two in the castle ruins next morning. We had arranged to make a short tramp of it that day, and decided to spend the night at St. Chade, where someone had told us there was a decent inn.

Our way lay through some pretty country, well wooded, and with distant peeps of quiet landscape which did not need the soul of an artist to appreciate. We had plenty of time and did not hurry. St. Chade lay at the end of a long valley, and we saw it from high ground when we must have been at least three miles away.

"Let us sit down and have a pipe," said Frank.

He had been rather silent all day. One would have commented on it in an ordinary fellow, but not in Frank. He was given to moods; his nature was artistic, and the artistic temperament is a thing apart. As a rule, I fancy it is a bit of a nuisance to its possessor, and I am very sure it is often a bore to the ordinary people who are brought in contact with it.

I understood Frank, however, and felt no surprise at his long silences.

"A smoke by all means," I said, and I climbed up beside him on to a bank of bracken at the edge of a wood raised a little above the roadway.

I didn't want to talk particularly—I am not quite sure that I didn't doze for a few moments; at any rate, we must have been there for the best part of an hour, and I was engaged in cleaning my pipe-stem with a stiff piece of grass, when Frank suddenly touched my arm.

"Look!"

"What is it?" I said, following the direction of his pointing finger.

At first I saw nothing to call for special notice—except for a bird or two, we appeared to have the world to ourselves—and then I uttered a low exclamation.'

About a hundred yards farther down the road, seated on the bank, just as we were, was Herr Eckmann.

"He wasn't there five minutes ago," Frank whispered.

"He must have been," I said.

"I am sure," was the answer. "I was looking at that queer-shaped tree five minutes since; he must be sitting on the roots of it. He wasn't there just now. I can swear to that."

"He was in the wood, I expect," said I, but I was conscious of feeling rather uncomfortable. Perhaps the fellow had accomplices, and—

"I don't like this, Mark," said Frank, as though a similar idea had passed through his mind; and then he got up, and shouted: "Eckmann! Hi! Herr Eckmann!"

The man must have heard him. Had he been half a mile away I think the shout would have reached him, but he took no notice.

He had his bag in his hand, his back was towards us, and he did not move until we slipped from the bank into the road, then he did the same, and walked on.

We made no attempt to overtake him, as Frank declared it was no use, nor did we talk much as we followed him. Perhaps it was his presence which made us think St. Chade rather a dreary place. This time he did not go farther.

He entered the inn—the Hôtel du Nord it was called—and I turned to Frank.

"We've got him this time," I said.

Frank did not answer, but quickened his pace and entered the inn before me.

Two or three men were seated at a table in the front room, but the German was not there. He had evidently gone straight through to the back part of the premises, or perhaps he had gone upstairs. I wondered if he had tramped on here last night.

One of the men, evidently the landlord, rose from the table as we entered. He looked as if he had consumed too much of his own liquor, and when we asked for a room his only answer was to call his wife.

"Have we a room, Jeanne?"

A woman came to a door at the end of the passage and looked at us.

"Of course," she said. "This way, messieurs."

"Don't say anything about Eckmann," Frank whispered to me as we followed her.

It was a pleasant room she showed us, and the meal which was presently served in an apartment at the back of the house was good.

Yet we were both silent and rather depressed, and I think the landlord must have continued to drink most of the evening, for he and his wife did nothing but quarrel.

Herr Eckmann did not put in an appearance.

"If this kind of thing goes on to-morrow, Mark, I shall get back home," Frank said as we went upstairs to bed.

"Oh, nonsense! Because a silly old German plays the fool you—"

"I mean it."

"But why, man? You must have some reason, something you are keeping to yourself."

"Yes, but—"

"Then out with it."

"I am not sure you would understand," he answered. "We'll talk about it to-morrow."

The two beds were side by side. At the end of the room, opposite the window, there was a small table and a deep and solid armchair standing on a square rug.

There was a key in the door, which I turned, and which Frank took out of the lock before he got into bed. Our window looked out at the back of the house, and just below it was the roof of an outhouse. There was a misty moon, and everything was as quiet as the grave.

St. Chade went to sleep early, and I never remember to have noticed the world so silent before.

I didn't mention it to Frank because he was a little depressed already, but before my head had been on the pillow ten minutes I began to long for day.

I hadn't the least desire to sleep; indeed, I almost suggested that we should get up and start off by moonlight. It would be more pleasant than this stuffy room. As a matter of fact, there was some exaggeration in this, for the room wasn't a bit stuffy; indeed, my bed being nearest to the window, I presently found the atmosphere rather fresh and cold, and drew the clothes more closely round my shoulders. The action possibly put me into a more comfortable position, and drowsiness came over me.

I suppose I had dropped off, for I suddenly started up into a sitting position, not knowing what had roused me.

"Mark!"

Frank was not sitting up. He was lying perfectly still, his back towards me. I thought at first he had called me in his sleep.

"What is it?" I said.

"Look there."

He did not say where, but since his face was towards the end of the room away from the window I looked across his bed in that direction.

The blind was up, a dim moonlight was in the room, and in the armchair I saw a man.

The chair was turned in such a manner that I could not see his face, but there was no mistaking his figure. He was leaning back, one hand resting on the arm, while the other grasped the handle of his bag.

It was Herr Eckmann.

"What are you doing there?"

I hardly recognised my own voice as I asked the question, not very loudly, but quite loud enough for him to hear.

It made no impression on Eckmann, but Frank was out of bed in a moment, and had struck a match and lighted the candle. I did not move until the flame had grown steady. I hoped the man would turn, and that I should see his face. He did not stir, and I slipped out of bed.

When I looked at the chair again it was empty.

"A phantom!" I muttered.

I hardly know whether I was relieved or not as this fact was suddenly forced upon me.

In an ordinary way I suppose I should have ridiculed the idea of such a thing, and should have sought for some simple explanation.

"Have you only just thought of that?" said Frank, in a low tone. "It has come for some purpose, Mark."

I did not answer. I think I wanted to argue the point, and certainly until now I had not supposed we were dealing with anything supernatural.

Evidently Frank had suspected the truth. He crossed the room quickly to the armchair, and I followed him.

"Move quietly," he whispered.

The chair was old-fashioned and heavy, and I watched Frank as he felt the stuffed seat and back.

His movements seemed to fascinate me; he gave the impression of knowing exactly what he was doing, what he was looking for and expected to discover. I made no attempt to help or interrupt him; I only moved the candle which he had placed on the table into a different position to give him a better light.

"Help me to move it," he said-presently. "Don't push—lift it. Carefully. We mustn't be heard on any account."

This done, he turned back the square rug and, taking the candle, examined the polished boards.

"Give me a knife," he whispered.

I got one from my coat hanging over a chair by the bed. Frank slipped the blade into a crack in the boards. That it differed from any of the other cracks might easily have passed unnoticed even after close scrutiny, but with some difficulty Frank prised open a portion of the flooring, some two feet square, which moved on a hinge.

The hiding-place revealed had not been made recently; the house was an old one, and in past times, no doubt, valuables had been concealed here. There was nothing of value in the hole now, only some clothes thrown in anyhow, a hat, a pair of boots, and a small bag. We both recognised them at once.

They belonged to Herr Eckmann.

Frank looked up at me, but for a moment neither of us spoke. I could not tell whether he was afraid, but I know I was.

The terror of the mysterious and unknown had gripped me.

"Let us dress," he whispered.

"Yes, and go—that way," and I pointed to the window.

I am certain I never got into my clothes so quickly before, and I do not believe either of us made a sound. The silence was intense. Not a breath of air stirred in the night, not a sound was in the house.

I was putting on my coat when the silence was suddenly broken.

Stealthily the handle of the door was turned.

It was a moment I shall remember all my life. I had a horrible fear that I had not locked the door, or that in taking the key out Frank had unfastened it again. Thank heaven, the turning handle did not open it or I should not be alive to set down this awful experience.

Again the handle was turned, not quite so gently, and there was a low exclamation of surprise.

I crossed the room quickly to listen.

"It's locked. I forgot to take away the key."

It was a woman who spoke, and the next moment there was an oath in a man's voice, followed by a violent attack upon the door.

"It won't hold many seconds," said Frank. "Run the chair against it and out with the light."

Pandemonium seemed to have broken loose suddenly, yet I was less afraid now than I had been a few moments ago.

This danger was something tangible, something I could understand; there was nothing mysterious to cope with.

I ran the chair across the room as Frank flung open the window, and as the man hurled his weight against the door I heard the woman run along the passage.

"Come, Mark," Frank called out, as he dropped on to the roof below.

As I scrambled through the window the door gave way. I think the man fell over the chair, fortunately for me. I dropped on to the outhouse, and not a moment too soon, for a bullet, fired from below, struck the window-frame even as I let go the sill.

"Quickly!" Frank shouted, and I slid from the roof to the ground, again only just in time, for the man fired from the window, chipping the tiles just behind me.

Then we ran.

We were without weapons to defend ourselves, and I do not think either of us thought we were running away from one man and his wife. The night seemed to be full of evil, the whole neighbourhood peopled with criminals who would strive to hunt us down.

As a matter of fact, I suppose our nerves were strained and under great tension. We were acting without thought, without consideration.

I was the first to stop.

"You weren't hit, were you?" asked Frank.

He did not seem to realise that I could hardly have ran the best part of two miles if I had been.

"No," I answered.

"Your escape was a miracle," he said. "They must have heard me open the window, for the moment I reached the ground the woman rushed out of the house. I stood still, so that she might not notice me; but she saw you at the window, probably thought you were the first to escape, and almost before I could move she had levelled a revolver at you. I knocked up her arm and then struck her with all my might."

"What are we to do now!" I asked. "I suppose we ought to go back and wake up the village, and—"

"No, no, that is not the best way," he answered. "They might not believe us. We'll go back to Pedmont, to the landlord there; he and Eckmann were friends."

I fell in with his suggestion. I really think it was the best thing we could do, but I had an unpleasant feeling that we were not being as courageous as we might be.

The landlord at Pedmont listened eagerly to our story, but I do not think he quite believed us.

As soon as possible we were on our way back to St. Chade, accompanied by two gendarmes, but we were very far from the end of our adventure.

We found the Hôtel du Nord closed. This impressed the gendarmes until the villagers explained that there was nothing curious in this. The landlord, whose name was Lemaistre, had sold the hotel some little while ago, with much of the furniture it contained. The new proprietor would not arrive until to-morrow, but everyone was aware that Lemaistre and his wife had arranged to leave to-day. There was nothing curious in the hotel being closed.

No one had heard any shots last night, but this might be accounted for by the fact that the nearest cottage was some little distance from the inn.

The keys, as arranged, had been left with the smith in the village, and we proceeded to examine the room we had occupied last night. The beds were made, the armchair was upon the square rug beside the table, everything was in perfect order. The hiding-place was there, but the gendarmes saw nothing remarkable about it, and it was empty now; clothes, hat, boots, and bag had gone.

It was rather an awkward position for us, for it was soon evident that our story was looked upon as a fabrication. Moreover, no one in St. Chade knew Herr Eckmann, and the neighbours were positive that he visited no farmers in that district.

Later, upon inquiry being made in Paris of the firm for which Eckmann travelled, nothing was known of his disappearance. Quite recently the firm had received orders through him. He was not often in Paris, and they imagined he was travelling the country as usual.

I need not recount all the annoyances we endured, all the formalities we had to go through, before we were allowed to return to England.

There was a general opinion that if Herr Eckmann were dead we were responsible for his death, and I believe the English Government had to undertake to produce us if subsequent discovery necessitated our trial for murder.

At home, as I have already intimated, our story was not credited. Of course we were not looked upon as criminals, but we were considered a pair of foolish young men who had allowed their imagination to run away with them and would not confess to it.

It was some months before the whole truth was known, and commend me to the French police for not letting go of a mystery.

The Paris firm heard nothing more from their traveller, so it became fairly certain that Eckmann was dead.

The first clue came from a farmer in St. Chade. He had been away from home for some time, was away when we were in the village. Herr Eckmann had called upon him a few days before his departure. He had not given him an order, but the German had mentioned that he was going to stay the night at the Hôtel du Nord.

Neither Lemaistre nor his wife was to be found, but eventually at Rouen a man was arrested for half murdering his wife, and in revenge she betrayed him.

He was Lemaistre, and she had gone in fear for her life for years, she said. She was afraid to disobey him. Her husband had killed Eckmann, and she had been obliged to help him to conceal the crime. He had intended to murder us, she declared. As they were leaving on the following day he said they might as well take whatever valuables we had about us, for as no one had discovered anything about the German it was not likely two cursed Englishmen would be missed.

I have no doubt the woman was just as guilty as the man, but while Lemaistre paid the penalty his wife received the benefit of the doubt and got off. I have my doubts, too, whether the main idea was to rob us. I agree with Frank in believing that they were both suddenly afraid we might discover that hiding-place under the rug.

I was inclined to speculate earlier in this narrative, but checked myself. I may do so now and leave others, who perhaps have experience to help them, to form an opinion.

I have wondered whether I should have seen the figure at all had I been alone. It may have been remarked that on each occasion it was Frank Lascelles who saw it first, that I saw nothing until my attention was called to it, and I am inclined to think that his more complex nature influenced me—that alone I should have been blind.

And there is one other point. That horrible woman explained that her husband had smashed the face of his victim so that he might not be identified. Had this anything to do with the fact that we were never once able to get a glimpse of the face of the strange traveller?

A REGENT OF LOVE RHYMES

Guy Thorne

One of the bestselling and most controversial books of the winter of 1903–4, was a thriller, much in the vein of The Da Vinci Code, *though a whole century earlier. It tells of an attempt to discredit Christianity by planting an antiquity which "proves" the Resurrection never happened, and then considers what impact that would have on civilisation. Yet it wasn't by any of the major writers you might anticipate—certainly not Hall Caine or R. H. Benson or M. P. Shiel. The book was* When It Was Dark *by Cyril Ranger Gull (1876–1923)—not a name that instantly springs to mind. It was published under his better known alias Guy Thorne, but again, unless you enjoy delving into the ancient worlds of science fiction and the supernatural, it's not a name we would all recognise. Yet Gull was one of the more prolific and respected writers of unusual stories of his day, noted for his sharp mind, his engaging conversation and his ever willingness to encourage fellow authors.*

A photo of Thorne in The London Magazine *in 1905 reveals a rather portly, medium-tall man who, with his waxed moustache and hair parted in the middle, might almost have been an inspiration for Hercule Poirot. Alas, neither Thorne nor Gull's reputation lasted for long, though there was enough for David Wilkinson to research his biography in* Guy Thorne: C. Ranger Gull: Edwardian Tabloid Novelist and His Unseemly Brotherhood *(2012), a resurrection of a life that was every bit as tragic as it was sensational.*

Several of Gull's novels—and he wrote over eighty in just twenty-five years—are available as e-books or print-on-demand titles, but his short fiction languishes. The following shows, though, that at times Gull could be hauntingly tender.

Whatsoever I have to doe before death, all leasure to end the same seemeth short unto me, yea were it but of one houre.

—MONTAIGNE

O THER MEN HAD BEEN DISCOVERED; TALENTED WOMEN WRIT-
ers had been found out; reputations had been invented; but
for many years. Glendinning still stood where he did.

He wrote stories which cultured people liked, and which cultured
newspapers spoke well of, but he made very little money. His work
vibrated in the ears of the general public with a dumb sound like
a drum beaten under a blanket. It was thought as well to know his
name, but to read his books was an indubitable bore.

He lived alone with his wife in an old granite cottage set among
trackless moors in the wild hinterland of Cornwall. For two years
they had dwelt thus, very happy in a simple life full of brave Atlantic
airs, majestic sunsets, the companionship of shy birds and beasts, and
the sound of God going by in midnight winds.

They had made their little home beautiful by simple means.
Gertrude had gone to small country sales at weather-worn farm-
houses and ancient cottages. Here was an old chair in which ancient
Celtic herdsmen had sat for generations, dreaming of things that
are forgotten. There a piece of Cornish cloam, so old and sturdy,
and yet so faintly beautiful, that it might have been a veritable find
from the Druid barrows under the mysterious cromlech hard by
upon Carn Galva.

Very poor though they were, their poverty was refined and irradi-
ated by the simple beauties ready to their hand. And on nights when

the wind was high and the Atlantic roared far below with a sound of kettle-drums, when the clots of spume were flying far inland over their steep-pitched roof, they sat by the fire and thought no couple more fortunate than they.

Each daybreak was a recurring joy, each morn a pious beginning of simple household business and high literary toil.

Then, quite suddenly and unexpectedly, the London people found Glendinning out. There were articles about his work in the papers that matter. People wrote to him kind letters of praise and thanks, and husband and wife saw that a real career was opening before them. Both said they never really wanted to leave their splendid solitude, that immense landscape which in itself was a rare bloom upon the fruits of peace and quiet. But both realised also that a duty, the duty of taking the sudden spring-tide at the flood, lay before them; and this was because before very long a child was to come to them both.

It happened later that Glendinning found himself pledged to produce a book for an eminent firm of publishers, for which they would pay him a large sum. Here was fortune indeed. They could put by a large portion of the money. A vista of splendid possibilities opened before them; both agreed that their former contentment with nothing was simply because, in the past, little more than nothing was to be had.

Three months later, and when the book was nearly done, their only local friend called upon them—their only local friend, that is, who could pretend to any culture or knowledge of affairs. He was the doctor of the neighbourhood, a justice of the peace for Portalone, the little fishing town five miles away.

They told him of their good fortune, of the new prospect that was opening out for them both; and the congratulations of the able, grizzled creature were hearty and sincere.

"Ah," he said, "I knew that it would come soon. Before long, in a year or two, I shall lose you both, and then there won't be a soul in the hinterland to talk to any more. But, my dear children, I can't tell you how glad I am! When baby makes his appearance, he will be born with a silver spoon in his mouth—or should I have said a gold-mounted fountain pen? Of course you will make a Charles Dickens of him!"

The good man stayed to lunch with the Glendinnings, and enjoyed an hour of wild speculative talk with the author. It was always a tonic to him to meet Glendinning, to discuss things that one can neither touch nor see, to argue about the reason of the Present and the possibilities of a Hereafter. The fact that both men held diametrically opposite views upon those questions that only the lords of life and death can really decide made their arguments most satisfying and stimulating events in the routine of a remote and quiet life.

"Death," said the doctor, as he went to fetch his mare from the little thatched stable behind the cottage, "death is simply cessation of correspondence with environment; and if you could only believe me, Glendinning, it is nothing more than that. We live again in nature, but that is all.

> "Out of his mouth a red, red rose!
> Out of his heart a white!

"We inform ourselves into all sensuous life. When we die our personality ceases."

Glendinning had argued the point until he was tired. He refused to believe that a man's soul was like the flame of a candle, blown out and then utterly non-existent, but he said no more. While the doctor was putting the bridle on the mare he let him run on.

But Gertrude, who had been listening to the talk without comment, contributed, no argument indeed, but simply a statement of personal opinion.

"For my part," she said, "I can't understand the doctor's point of view. I can't confute it, but, temperamentally, charm he never so wisely, I can't and won't believe in it!"

"Well," said the doctor, with one foot in the stirrup, "we shall all know some day, my dears."

With that he hoisted himself into the saddle, drew on his gloves of red dogskin, waved them a cheery farewell, and cantered over the heather towards Portalone.

They watched him till he became a black skeleton upon the horizon of the moor, then, linked arm in arm, they strolled along a footpath among the heath, towards a farm two miles away.

Glendinning began to talk business details with his wife.

"Of course I am not insured," he said; "we have never been able to afford the premium. But now I shall be able to put a hundred or two aside for you in case anything happens."

"Don't talk of such horrid things, dear," she answered, half laughing, but with brooding apprehensions in her gentle eyes.

They walked towards the farm. A mile away they met a plodding labourer, who greeted them and passed the time of day.

"Don't 'e go too near Trevarrick town-place, my dears," he said: "Mr. Trewella's bull 'e do begin to be getting a bit roguish, they do say."

They smiled at him, and, engrossed in their own affairs, wandered on towards the steading.

The doctor was back again, only four hours after he had left the cottage when it was happy. He was standing by the bed upon which Glendinning lay—his face was very white and set. He had been too good a friend to them for years not to tell them the truth now. He hadn't learned the suave and proper lies with which less rugged physicians oil the path of death. The sternness of the hard life upon the moors had entered into his blood; he believed that softness and half-truths were a cruel preparation for the grave. So he told them, quite simply, that in an hour or two Glendinning must pass away.

The furious creature, with its vast muscular neck, and head like a battering-ram, had done its work too well.

Glendinning felt no pain—he would never feel physical pain any more—but death was heavy upon him and life was going like a dying fire.

"Shall I stay, Glendinning?" the doctor said.

"I think not, old man," Glendinning answered; "I think Gertrude and I will be alone, please."

The doctor, who had seen many deathbeds, took up the hand of his friend, a hand that was still warm, full of blood, and unharmed. He lifted it to his lips, and then with a bowed head turned to go.

"I'll be back, child," he whispered to Gertrude, and left her alone with her husband.

Glendinning was unable to retain command of his brain for very long. He began to sob brokenly, and to moan that he had not finished *A Regent of Love Rhymes*. His last words were:

"You see, dear, if only I had finished the thing, then—then— you would have had something to go on with—only five thousand words—only five thou—" and with that he shivered a little and lay still, breathing heavily until his life was finished.

★

The midnight wind had wailed over the cottage so often, and Gertrude and her husband had read so many things into it—fantastic, romantic, and even holy—that it could now, even when Cyril was lying dead in the bedroom, have no extraordinary appeal to her.

The doctor had been there. The women from the farm, friendly sympathisers and kind-hearted Cornish folk, had sprung up on the moor and clustered round the house, and in it, like crows.

That was what Gertrude thought. She wanted to be left alone with her beloved dead.

Even now, down in the kitchen a farmer's wife was snoring on the settle. But Gertrude was alone—alone in Cyril's writing-room, with only the wooden partition between it and their own room, where he lay so waxen and so calm.

The time had not yet come for her to accept the gracious influences, the supreme consolations, the comfort that God pours into wounded hearts. She was stunned still, and as yet no echo from Paradise had come.

She had lit the lamp in the pleasant writing-room, and it shone on Cyril's pictures, on Cyril's books, on all the ordered litter of the great table where he wrote.

How secure, ordered, comfortable, and *right* it all seemed!

There was the typewriter, reflecting the light of the lamp from all its polished surfaces of black japan and steel, and by the side of the machine was the neat pile of manuscript, the final and uncompleted "copy" of *A Regent of Love Rhymes*.

The thing hypnotised her, and as she gazed at it the intense physical strain of the last hour had its result. She fell into a state, half-broken, half-stupor.

Through all her dream there ran these words—"*You see, dear, if only I had finished the thing, then—then—there would have been something*

to go on with—only five thousand words, only five thou—" She woke with
a start and sat up, rigid, in her chair, A clicking metallic noise filled
the quiet little room.

She plucked at her eyes with trembling fingers, for she had
thought that she saw an inexplicable thing upon the little green-
topped table where the typewriting machine was standing. She
thought that the keys were being depressed in the quick rattle of
an expert hand. The carriage seemed travelling rapidly towards the
imminent moment when she should hear the tinkle of the bell... The
bell sounded, the carriage was thrust back with its gritty, corn-crake
noise and the sudden clash of its impact upon the nickel buffer at
the end of the track. Then, once more, the enamelled keys began to
dance and glitter in the light.

No! This was not an illusion. *The thing was actually going on.*

Rigid as a corpse, she took two gliding steps towards the table.

As she stopped, the carriage was lifted up and the noise of the
keys stopped. It was exactly as though some invisible typist was
scrutinising the last sentence that had appeared upon the cylinder.
The carriage clashed confidently down. Once more the keys began
to race, the levers to hop up against the ribbon.

Then there was a screech of the cog-wheels. The filled sheet came
up into the air, as if a hand was holding it. It remained sustained for
a moment and then fluttered neatly down upon the thick pile of
manuscript, which was the almost completed story—*A Regent of
Love Rhymes*.

She staggered back to her chair. She knew.

She could not understand how or why, but she knew that some
superhuman force was at work. She realised that *A Regent of Love
Rhymes* was being completed—not for the sake of art—but for
her sake.

The clicking went on unceasingly. The mechanical movement which filled, completed, and removed the page did not stop.

She glided away from the machine, felt along the wall till she came to the door of the study, opened it, jumped across the intervening space at the stair-head and burst into the death chamber.

The candles round the bed burned still and cold. The shell which had been Cyril lay waxen and smiling.

Nothing had changed.

Again she hurried into the writing-room. The machine was going on towards its relentless completion of the tale.

Then, at last, she realised that, from some other world, her husband was writing the final lines of the tale for her—for *her*.

The lords of life and death had given him this little grace.

She drew nearer and nearer to the whirring, clicking thing, and, a yard away, watched the mystery, so stupendous in its operation, so commonplace in its material means, go on throughout the night.

The wind wailed and sobbed round the house; the dead body lay silent in the other room; and as she watched and listened, a sense of the august Powers which were at work for her came into her soul like balm.

She watched. She saw the very last lines of all, glowing, burning, wonderful lines were being stamped upon the linen paper which had been made in the United States. Then, as she held her breath in love, in gratitude, and in nameless fear, she saw the carriage lifted once more, and she saw that, in purple capitals, *FINIS* was written.

The loud clicking in the little room stopped suddenly. A heavy silence lay over the cottage, a silence which the terrific wind intensified, and could not break.

Gertrude rose up. She lifted her eyes, and called to Cyril's soul.

"Cyril," she cried, "Cyril," she called, "hear me before you go right away! Send me one more message—you have finished the book, dearest, tell me *where* you have done it—love—love of my heart—one word one word more—"

But the typewriter remained still and motionless. The love which was so strong that it had pierced through innumerable veils to help its object was not allowed to tell the lonely wife *why* it had done so, and from what near or distant place it had sent its last message.

We may get very near to the thick veil, we may think that the lords of life and death are kind and have revelations for us, but God knoweth His own time and place, and we are not allowed to understand.

We have not deserved it yet.

That is what Gertrude was taught.

She remained waiting very hopefully for the ultimate explanation, and the meeting with Cyril.

The book was a great success, but most of the critics, in their wisdom, agreed on one point. They said that, while the last two chapters of the story were well written, the author seemed to have attempted too exalted a note, and one which he was not quite able to sustain.

AMID THE TREES

Francis Xavier

I can find no information on Francis Xavier—or perhaps Frances Xavier as the name was spelled on one occasion. It was, of course, the name of a sixteenth-century Jesuit missionary, one of the founders of the Society of Jesus, and is thus a name adopted by some postulants when they enter the Church. It may well be the name taken by a sister of the church who was active as a teacher, but I can find no evidence either way. The name appeared on just a handful of atmospheric stories published in The Weekly Tale-Teller *between 1910 and 1912.*

E SSART WAS A LITTLE TIRED OF FESTA DO SAN PEDRO, AND TWO out of the five aggressively cheerful midsummer days that are given up to it were enough to render him stunned and deafened and altogether surfeited with the strident gaiety that is deemed necessary to make a Portuguese holiday really satisfactory.

He had been up and down, walking slowly with the great crowd, the lovely, tree-shaded Avenida da Liberdade a vast number of times, at first cheered and pleased with the splashy colour and gaiety of the people and their costumes; it was all so novel, so bright and absorbing to his unaccustomed English eyes. He had wandered about the sunlit streets of Lisbon, in and out of the dancing booths and the cinematograph shows, and been amused at the pandemonium set up by the clanging of tram-bells and the rattle of the headlong trams themselves, the hooting of the motor horns, and the terrible clangour of the electric bells hung outside the cinematograph booths to attract attention. In the nights he strolled through a warm, balmy air under the glow of a million swinging Chinese lanterns, watching the laughing crowd as it drifted by, dodging the showering confetti and provocative glances that laughing women with shining eyes flung at him, both of them for his excellent good looks, with reckless profusion. He had sat in cafés and watched the motor-cars parade, each picked out in firefly lights, the flower-entwined and Japanese-lanterned carriages, the eccentric and gorgeous state cars going by amid loud shouts of approval. It was a scene so full of soft, pervasive lights and velvety shadows, of subtle nuances of colouring and shade, that Essart, who was something of an artist as well as a shipping agent, found keen exhilaration for a time. Only for a time, however, for he soon grew tired of the noise and the heat, and the interminable bustle and passage of crowds irritated one so sensitive as he. At the end of the second day he found that he had had enough of the town, and decided that the country would be more charming and certainly more reposeful. Moreover, there was desire within him to see something of the country, for he had been busy during the two years that made up his stay in Lisbon, and had never found opportunity for holidays.

On the third morning of the festa, therefore he walked out of Lisbon when the day was so young that its freshness and stillness was dismaying, and he felt that his presence was alien and desecrating. He went out through this wonderful wine-like morning, choosing the road to Cintra that runs by Larmanjat at first, but quickly deserting it for a way, less obvious and hackneyed, of his own election, that branched off between hedges of aloe and cactus; along this road he wandered pleasantly, and at the pace caprice demanded.

He walked all day in this easy manner, making his own pace and passing and being interested in the many strange things he passed, the white, gleaming, Mooresque houses and the quintas and vineyards, and on occasion the straggled "great" patio house surrounded by its own fine plantations and gardens.

It pleased him greatly. The day was idyllic, hot with a level stream-ing sunlight; but his pace was too easy to entail heat or fatigue. There were many ravishing views and beautiful vistas in landscape, and, since the scenery had the constant piquancy of novelty, Essart saw many things he had previously but dreamed of, or at the best read about. Startling and craggy ravines, little streams that ran between rocks like fluid mother-o'-pearl, tremendously moulded slopes of rough, untended forest; now and then belts of immense cork trees were passed, and he saw, for the first time, orange trees set in rows like apple trees in the orchards at home, yet startlingly dissimilar in the knobbed glitter of their fruit in the sunlight; citrons he also saw, with their delicate, shining leaves, and the graceful, drooping pimenteiros; more than anything, he was held and fascinated by the trellised orderliness of the vines. He considered that the keynote of this glowing country lay in the vines.

Towards the middle of the day he arrived at a venda that pleased him, because overgrowing creepers that bore vivid scarlet blossoms shaded it from the sun's intensity; here he went in and ate an omelette and many oranges, and drank a yellow, thick, sweet wine from a wicker bottle. He might have had coffee, but he did not want coffee, for that had a flavour of city life that was abhorrent. He wished merely to drink sweet wine and smoke a cigarette and be immensely idle and look out over the incomparable view that opened before him. He wished simply and tranquilly to thoroughly enjoy the country and the day.

He spent an hour or two at the venda and left it with reluctance, for it was an agreeable place, and he went on walking (only an Englishman or a dog walks in the mid-day sun, runs the proverb) at his slow, enjoyable amble, until the evening crept down upon him in dusky, scented veilings of imperceptible delicacy.

The Southern darkness stole down upon him in soft, warm dusk and caressing gloom. There was a strange, moving fragrance in it, as though its secret was made up of exotic odours and the perfume of curious and lovely flowers. It kept one enthralled by this scent as one is enthralled by the essence of a scented woman. There was something veiled and mystical in it, something inscrutable, brooding. And it was quiet, too, very quiet, and in a manner that was palpable, like a texture, and there was suggestion that unnamable and unconjectural things were about, whispering in the tiny eddies of a nearly dead wind, in the secret, swimming rustling of the overhanging leaves.

As he walked through the deepening night Essart began to come under its spell. Its delicious luxuriance and tenderness engulfed him and his spirit in a gentle and lovely bondage. He moved daintily through it, his head aloft, as though eager to snuff in its essences, his veins gently throbbing with the subtle glamour and romance of the place and the moment; Fires awakened in his heart, and he began to glow and radiate with their spiritual suggestion. The wing of beauty and romance touched him, and he felt like a man walking through dreams. He saw these dreams peopling the night with a rich romance. He felt that it was a night for rich romance, for loveliness, beauty, for the soft laughter and silken voice of woman.

"It is a night ordained for the romantic," he thought. "And so is the place." He began to weave for himself bright patches of that moving colour of thoughts that is romance.

He began to look about, craving satisfaction of this desire. He said: "One should find a woman amid these trees. One should look up and see her looking down at once, a timid woman, a delicate, spirituelle, dryad sort of woman, outlined like gossamer against the darkling green-greys of these big trees. She should stand there very silently, something ineffable, something with gauze-like mystery about her, and she should have a thin, slim grace like the trees she stands among, and her eyes should be big, deep, unfathomable in a pale face, like the eyes and the face of a timid wood-thing" (he was unconsciously drawing upon his memory a picture by Arthur Hacker), "and she should stand among the trees very quietly, and we should talk."

He shivered with the thrill of real desire his imagery gave him. He was dreaming how wonderful it would all be, the woman standing vaguely outlined amid the trees in the soft and velvety dusk of this place, and in its hushed and breathless, almost airless, quietness, and this dream was so wonderful that he commenced to crave a fulfilment, a reality. He was young and ardent and ripe for love, and, like a nature that had been hitherto untouched with the divine passion, a desire for it came with a great power. Here he thought was the right place, the wondrous place, to meet love. It was a temple of love, the home of idylls, of arcadian glamour; here was a place fitted if ever there was one. Something within him broke loose and swelled out of him and carried him away with an intense fervour. What had been a dream had, for an instant, merged into acute need. He was trembling with a sudden gust of passion.

"A-ah!" he almost shouted, and he stood in the middle of the road. "Ah, a woman and love in this place! What would I not give for that—a woman and love!"

And he stood still and tossed his hands aloft.

"Oh," he said, "I wish I could invoke a woman. I wish, by some strange means, I could invoke a woman."

He had read many classical books, and enough of those dealing in psychic subjects to have a dim feeling that something might be gained by this attitude, that such invocation might put into motion things that he did not know or grasp, or that the intense projection of his will might attract someone, something—a woman. He sent his will streaming and feeling, wandering into the night seeking contact with some other will.

"Oh, a woman, a woman!" he cried. "I will a woman to appear!"

He laughed as he said this, but there was a real power of will under the laugh, and he waited with a certain frightened expectancy after he had spoken, for he had fancied he had heard something as he uttered the command, something that might have been a voice, a woman calling out. It was, he thought, rather shrill and painful, and ended on a choked and sobbing note. But though he waited it was not repeated, and in a second he shook his head to negative some inner question. "It was the wind," he muttered. "Probably it was blowing among the leaves, and—" He looked up to discover motion among the leaves, and, looking down at him, he saw the woman.

The place he had come to was guarded by steepish banks, for the road went by a cutting through the brow of a hill, and on top of these banks a thin fringe of cork trees soared up and met in a natural tracery above the roadway. The woman was upon the top of the right-hand embankment amid the trees, almost, it seemed, part of them; she was very silent and unmoving, and she was looking down upon him.

He was rather startled, but also he was attracted, and he could not take his eyes away from her. She stood there very quiet, in an attitude almost statuesque. The trees were not too thick, and he could see the outlines of her head and part of her body and something of the sweep of her gown. The head was delicate and small, he saw, but it was shadow amongst shadows, and he saw it only in certain delicate angles and phases—angles and phases that stirred him with a poignant sense of beauty. He could not distinguish her eyes, he could not distinguish features, but the pale, milky glow of her skin came down to him; he could see the glimmer, too, of a bare arm and a hand as she rested, supporting herself against the trunk of a tree. Of her figure, very little, though he felt that she was slim, for it seemed to grow up out of shadow and to be part of shadow wherever shadow touched. Indeed, she looked vague, impalpable, unreal herself, a figure of mist and delicate vapours, something fairy, elfin—a creature of the woods.

Essart stood still and looked up at her, and, though he was a little afraid, he was wrung with a moving passion as well. The glamour of the place was drenching him, and deep, trembling emotions stirred and beat through his body. He looked up to the woman and he whispered:

"Then you have come."

And he heard her voice answer him faintly, vaguely, like a breath among the trees.

"Yes, I have come."

"I called you," lie whispered. "Did you hear me call you?"

"Yes," she answered.

"I sent out my spirit, and it met your spirit and drew it."

"Yes," she said, "your spirit caught my spirit—that is why I am here."

"Oh!" he breathed, for it was very beautiful; and so they stood for a space looking at each other, and about them the trees and the air and the rustling leaves seemed to swoon with the heady glamour of the place.

Soon they began to talk, and of many things, not heavy, practical things, but of delightful, inconsequent things—the beauty of the night and the grace of the trees, the fragrances that welled out into this delicious place, of a myriad trivial, wonderful things—and they talked in little bursts and in the little silences that mean so much more than words, and always they found the world delightful, the moment celestial; happiness was in them, or so, at least, Essart felt, and flooding them and the quiet, quiet place with an equable, steady ardency.

The woman did not talk so much as Essart; but that was only seeming under the circumstance. And she never initiated remark; she answered only and never volubly, choosing mainly the monosyllabic "Yes" or "No." Only once did she break this habit and answer more lengthily and with greater passion than she usually employed.

They were talking very intimately of love, and suddenly she broke out:

"I have always needed love. I have prayed for it. I wanted it, craved it, and none came. Nobody understood—nobody—and I was so empty and lonely." He thought he saw her figure shake, and fancied he heard a sob. "Oh, I wanted it so; it is terrible to want and not to get!"

"Yes," he answered. "And that is why you answered me—came. Your spirit was heavy for love, and mine called to it. I was calling for love."

"That is the reason," she said, "I have sat in this place day following day for many years thinking a girl's thoughts of love, desiring love. I have peopled this place with thoughts of love; the spirit of my love must have drenched and filled this place, for here every day I have sat and poured my desires out." Essart remembered the feeling of indescribable passion that had seized upon him as he entered the cutting, and he felt he understood. She had filled the place with the fluid aura of her desire; the place was vibrant and charged with it, and he had responded because he was *sympatica*; the thought, he felt, was delicious. But the woman proceeded in her soft, mellow, and altogether bewitching voice. "Yes, I have sat here, lonely, very lonely, and thought my thoughts, and nobody has come to me, nobody looked into my heart. I ached for love, for I am a child of love, but none had love to offer. In the village they have a sore saying about me; when they do not revile me they jeer. I moon, they say; I am soft-witted, a little crazy, mad. But I am not soft-witted, and if I am mad it is that I am mad for love. I am lonely—lonely, cut off from the world, from the village, and I crave love."

"Ah," said the man, "and I felt your craving, and I came. Is it not beautiful? I wanted love also."

"O-oh!" breathed the girl, and he thought she drew back a little.

"I love you," he said. And now he was certain she shuddered, and when she breathed "Oh!" again it struck him that there was as much of pain as surprise or timidity in her voice.

"Yes," he said, and his voice was trembling with a genuine passion, "yes, I love you. You are very beautiful. You are the spirit of this beautiful place. I love you—oh, I do love you!"

She only sank deeper into the shade, and she put her hands to her face, and he saw that she was sobbing.

"Love comes now," he thought he heard her say. "I have asked for it so long and it comes *now*—now!" And she sobbed afresh.

Essart began to climb the steep bank; some burning and tremendous impatience was seething within him. He wanted to get up to this wondrous woman, to take her in his arms, to whisper to her, to touch her hair, to kiss her, to tell her that he loved her, loved her, loved her. He scrambled up the craggy road-bank to get at her, to tell her, and his clumsiness and inefficiency in climbing annoyed him. He stumbled so much; he made so much noise.

The woman amid the trees heard the noise. Her hands dropped away from her face, and she stared down at him as one terribly startled and awfully afraid. She put her hand out as though to stop him by a gesture, and she called out:

"No, no, no! You must not come up here. You must not come up here and see—it is terrible. You must not—"

"I love you!" cried Essart. "I must."

"No, no, no!" she cried.

"I love you!" said Essart. "I am coming."

He scrambled up the last few feet and stood a trifle blown at the top of the embankment—and the woman had gone.

He stood looking about him blankly. She had vanished; he could not see her at all or a vestige of her. He wondered if this was coquetry, but somehow he did not think so; something about the woman or the place forbade that thought. Yet she had vanished. He strained his ears to catch, perhaps, some hint of her movement through the wood, but all was quiet—deathly, heavily quiet.

He took a step forward instinctively, making for the exact spot upon which she had stood, and as he did so the silence was broken. An angry buzzing, whirring noise rose up, a whirl of tiny black objects swam by him—flies—and then he saw the woman. He knew at once that it was *the woman*—she was leaning in a sitting attitude against the trunk of a great cork tree, and she was dead. He saw the gleam of dark blood—blood that bad been congealing for half an hour—about the gash in her throat, and he saw the gleam of the knife that had done the self-murder in her little hand. He turned and rushed down the bank and down the road.

He remembered that half-strangled scream that he had heard before the coming of the woman, about half an hour ago, and he understood the significance of her wailing "NOW."

THE RIVER'S EDGE

Mary Schultze

Mary Schultze is another mystery name. She had a dozen or so stories in the cheap weekly magazines just before the First World War but none of those publications provided a clue to her identity. There were several by that name alive in Britain at the time, but none identified as a writer. She clearly had strong religious views as the following story, from 1912, reveals.

A LL THE MORNING IT HAD RAINED WITHOUT CEASING, AND Major Mercer had frankly been bored to death. He was spending a few days with an old friend, who had married and settled down some years ago; but the major had not been home on leave for a long time, and this was his first introduction to Lionel Deacon as a married man, and Lionel Deacon's wife and children.

After luncheon the rain mercifully stopped, and he announced his intention of going for a walk.

"Go to the river," Margaret Deacon had instructed him on his departure, "straight through the village. From the bridge you ought to have rather a fine sight—the river will be in full flood after all this rain."

So accordingly he turned his face in the direction of the little old village that straggled, in a long, uneven line of cottages, from the gates of The Manor. Once through the one main street, he thought he could hear the rush and roar of many waters dashing among rocks in their headlong flight.

A curve of the road, which hid the last red brick house of the village from his sight, brought him within full view of the river itself—a dark, seething, menacing mass of water rolling angrily between its banks. The bridge—an old grey stone one—spanned it at a considerable height. It lay about a hundred yards ahead of him, and he paused for a moment in the wet roadway to watch that roaring torrent. A little further up it spread itself regardlessly and recklessly over the meadowland on either side; but nearer to the bridge it entered a narrow, rocky channel, and seemed to gather itself into a great wall of roaring foam, as it hurled itself over the grey, ragged, slippery rocks from which the arch of the bridge reared itself defiantly.

For a moment he watched in admiration, tempered with awe, then suddenly gave a quick exclamation of horror at what he saw.

On the further bank of the river stood a small ivy-covered cottage, its little garden shut off from the spreading meadow in front of it by a green wooden paling. In the centre was a little wooden gate, and, as he looked, he saw it pushed wide open, whilst a child—a very tiny child to he running about alone, he thought—came trotting gaily out.

It made straight for the river's edge, just where the rocks rose steep and slippery with the hurling brown foam.

Major Mercer quickened his steps, anxiously watching the doorway of the little house to see if no one would rush out to take the child out of danger's, way. Apparently, whoever was in charge of it had not as yet missed it, and Major Mercer feared some awful calamity was imminent.

The bridge seemed further away from him in the last second, he thought, than before. And, though he quickened his pace, it took long—very long, so it appeared to him—to reach it. He drew hastily to the side, and glanced over the high grey stone parapet. The child was by then at the very edge of the raging torrent.

He commenced running as silently as possible—he knew he must not startle the child. To shout to it might be fatal. That one view he had when he had looked over the parapet revealed it to him, hanging fascinated over the leaping, rushing water, its little hands held out delightedly.

In the middle of the bridge he was impelled to look again. His heart leapt with thanksgiving—the child was at least still there. And, even as he looked, he saw that someone else was also there.

Just behind the child was the slight, graceful figure of a young woman in a pink frock. "She must have missed the child in time," he thought, "and followed it out of the little house." For the moment it puzzled him how she could have got so near to the child in so short a space of time, for she had been nowhere in sight when he had last glanced over the parapet, and he did not believe more than two seconds had passed since he had first looked to see if the child was still on the bank.

She bent over the little figure, and he thought it a little odd, comparing it with his own sensations of alarm and horror, that she should apparently take it all so calmly. She appeared neither afraid nor dismayed; just smiled placidly, happily, and, bending down, led the child swiftly back from danger towards the little house with the green gate.

The sun, which had for long been struggling to pierce the clouds, gleamed out from the stormy, cloud-flecked sky in one long, slanting ray of brilliance. It revealed her to him very clearly, and he remained standing at the side of the bridge looking over the parapet, seeing now no heed for haste. The woman's face was half-turned towards him, and he noted again, whilst he admired her utter coolness, that her expression was still absolutely devoid of any fear, and was just as placid and unconcerned as when she had first bent down and drawn the child to her.

"Nerves of iron," he commented, and agreed in his own mind that, on the whole, he had probably suffered more fright than she had.

"Women are jolly queer cattle," he reflected, astounded. "She's as cool as a cucumber—never turned a hair—while I'm perspiring with funk. Yet I don't mind betting she'd scream at a mouse!"

He resumed his walk, and, for a moment the parapet of the bridge shut out the woman and the child from his sight. He had a last outstanding glimpse of her erect, slight figure, the sun gleaming on her hair and on the child by her side, its yellow curls dancing in the light breeze that had arisen.

On the other side of the bridge the stone parapet sloped down gradually until it joined on either side of the roadway the low haw-thorn hedges that skirted the meadows. He glanced across quickly, then smiled. That show of unconcern had been partly feigned. Had she known she was being watched from the bridge all the time? He nodded wisely. It was obvious that the moment he was out of sight she had taken the last few yards to the cottage at a gallop, he thought, for the woman in pink was nowhere to be seen, not even the tail of her gown vanishing through the doorway. The child she had rescued was playing contentedly in the garden in front of the little house, busying itself with pulling off the heads of the nasturtiums that climbed riotously over the porch.

This time, though, the major did not fail to note the green gate was closed.

In discovering what was for him a new country, in getting lost, and finally finding himself again and arriving back at The Manor somewhat fatigued, and with very muddy boots and mud-bespattered clothes, Major Mercer, for the time being, forgot the incident at the bridge, and it was only later, when tea was over, and he sat with his hostess in the drawing-room that he recalled it.

It was in that pleasant, lazy hour before dressing for dinner Major Mercer, having enjoyed a hearty tea after his long walk, felt drowsy and contented as he sat in a big chair beside the fire. It was very comfortable and pleasant in the big old-fashioned drawing-room, and Margaret Deacon was rather a restful sort of person, he thought. She knew by instinct never to talk to a man unless the man showed unmistakable signs of wishing to he talked to. It may have been because she was holding the latest baby in her arms, and was looking across its curly head into the bright fire with a smile of placid content, that he suddenly remembered the other mother he had seen that day. The placid, gentle smile in Mrs. Deacon's eyes, or the curly-headed child in her arms, one or other—perhaps both—touched the chord of recollection, and awoke it with a swift start.

"I saw a narrow shave this afternoon," he said suddenly, and his hostess started at his voice, for it was some time since he had spoken.

"Where? What happened?" She looked to him with bright, inquiring eyes.

"It was at the bridge just beyond the village." He roused himself to tell her all that had occurred. "Rather a dangerous bit that, isn't it? The river is so unprotected. Don't you have accidents there at times?" He paused.

"No, I don't think so, except—oh, yes, there was last year." She shook her head sadly. "There was an—an accident there last year."

"Ah, I thought so!" The major was triumphant. "Well, there was jolly nearly another to-day. A child ran out of that little house which stands quite close to the river on the further side from the village—a very small child—but it went across the grass at the devil of a lick, straight for the river bank above the first fall at the bridge. I felt pretty sick with horror, I can tell you, and I was powerless at the moment, though I saw the whole thing from the road. I'd the bridge to cross before I could get at the kid. I put on a bit of a spurt, I can tell you, but I didn't dare to shout to it to go back. It was so small I might have startled it, and it would have been gone."

"What happened?" Mrs. Deacon asked anxiously. She was holding her own child very close, he noticed, as she spoke.

"Its mother appeared quite suddenly and carried it back from the edge."

"Its mother appeared?" she repeated quickly, and her eyes, looking to him across the baby's curls, were a little startled.

"Yes," he nodded. "For a minute it was out of my sight—the parapet of the bridge is fairly high. Halfway over I looked across, almost afraid I'd see no child there any longer. Instead, a woman in a pink frock—it must have been its mother—had appeared on the scene, pretty quickly too, for I was only out of sight a bare second or two. She was just bending forward as I looked. In another second it was safe. The whole thing was over so quickly I hardly realised it. But I saw her, of course, quite distinctly, and thought how calm and collected she seemed—not a bit flurried. When I got to the other side, and in view of the cottage, she had evidently gone inside, and the child was playing by itself in the garden, with the gate shut this time. It was a narrow squeak, though. Once in the water nothing could have saved it—neither I nor mortal man."

"Nor mortal woman," Mrs. Deacon repeated dreamily. And he marvelled at the strange look on her gentle face.

"Who lives in that little house?" he asked, feeling perplexed.

"Julian Leslie, an artist," she answered, briefly. Then, suddenly rising, she set the baby on the white, fluffy hearthrug, and, crossing the room, opened a drawer in the writing bureau. She took out a photograph and returned to the fireplace.

"Mr. Leslie lives there alone now," she said quietly, "with his child and an old servant. He is a widower. But tell me, do you recognise this face?"

He took the photograph from her in silence, and looked at it closely.

"Why, of course," he said readily. "That is the woman in the pink frock I saw to-day. The expression is different. Here she looks quite pleased with life and all that. But, somehow, I've never seen a look of such utter placid content on anyone's face as on hers to-day, in spite of the danger that had threatened the child. I suppose I was wrong, however," he ended lightly, "when I said I was sure she was the child's mother."

"No, you were quite right," she said in a low, strained voice. "That is a photograph of the little boy's mother."

"But you said this artist, Mr. Leslie, is a widower."

"Yes, he is a widower."

Major Mercer rose abruptly to his feet, the photograph in his hand. He looked at Mrs. Deacon, a perplexed line ruffling his forehead.

"But if I saw her to-day—" he began feebly.

"Poor Barbara Leslie was drowned during just such a flood as to-day a year ago—among the rocks above the bridge."

He was staring at her in speechless amazement.

"But yet you say I saw her to-day," he said at last slowly.

Margaret Deacon continued quietly:

"She was wearing a pink frock. She had run out of the little house to have a look at the flood. It is supposed she went too near, and slipped her foot on the rocks."

"But in that case," he persisted, "how could I have seen her to-day lead the child back from the river's edge? If I saw that woman"—he pointed to the photograph—"and I *did*, how can she be dead?" Still he did not understand; his mind groped wildly about trying to follow her.

She took the photograph from him gently, and a little smile of pity stole round her mouth at his look of bewilderment.

"Yes, you *did* see her save her child to-day, Major Mercer," she said softly. "Don't you believe, can't you believe, that such a thing is possible?"

And he was silent, knowing suddenly what she meant.

"I wonder!" he said at last. "It's extraordinary, because, you see, I am not a chap to imagine things. It never struck me that there was anything amiss—just a woman in a pink frock bending down over her child to lead it away from danger." Then he smiled a little nervously. "Of course, come to think of it, she looked almost unnaturally unconcerned about it. An ordinary woman would at least have looked in a blue funk. I thought she must have wonderful nerve, she looked so placid."

"That's just it!" Mrs. Deacon said softly. "She would, of course, look quite peaceful and unconcerned. Can't you realise a God great and merciful enough to allow those who have passed beyond our ken to return here at moments of intense peril to those they loved, still love? What more simple that they be permitted to stretch forth their hands to save. But no God of mercy would allow them to feel any fear of pain, or grief; they leave all that behind them. Sorrow may no longer touch them, the peace that passeth all understanding is theirs; that is why you were struck by the look of contentment on poor Barbara's face; she came back to save her little child gladly, happily, permitted by God Himself, but she felt no fear—she is done with fear."

Major Mercer sat down heavily in the chair out of which he had risen.

"If anyone else had told me about this I would have said it was rot. But I saw her myself, as clearly as I see you now."

"My dear man"—her eyes were very tender, she had lifted the baby on to her knee once more and was looking across its head to him very kindly—"don't try to worry over things, and don't try to understand. You yourself put the case quite clearly and simply at the start when you said 'Its mother appeared.' Those we love, and who don't try to understand. Those we love, and who are lost to us, watch over us—at times they come back to save us. They are always quite near us, in deadly peril they may stretch out their hands, and though we do not guess it, they may lead us into safer ways."

A FUTILE GHOST

Mary Reynolds

With Mary Reynolds we reach the author about whom I know the least, since I'm only aware of two stories by her, dating from 1897 and 1899. It is far too common a name to try and isolate an individual, and I do not know whether it was her maiden or married name. Whoever she was she produced this remarkable story which presents no ordinary ghost.

"FORGIVE ME, MARY, BUT HAVE YOU TWO NO PLANS FOR THE future beyond this hope of what old Mrs. Glyn may leave Hugh at her death?"

Miss Trevor's long, delicately-modelled hand trembled slightly as she pushed back the lace curtain beside her, and the involuntary movement belied the lightness of the voice which answered her sister's hesitating question.

"Plans, dear? Of course—yes. Have we not lived on our plans for the last five years? Hugh is almost willing to marry on them, but my more practical nature demands the addition of pounds, shillings, and pence. A truce to plans, Maggie—or, by the way, what are yours about this ghost business? Wells vows she will not stop her month out, and she is quite capable of spreading the tale among the housemaids."

"I wish you would be good enough to forget the whole story, Mary. Wells had nightmare, and fancied she saw something; if she had not overheard some stupid chaff of ours, she would never have magnified her fears into a black-veiled lady."

"Who was the first to see the said veiled lady, I wonder?" returned Miss Trevor. "If you remember, you were rather pleased than otherwise at possessing a family ghost, and felt able to snap your fingers at ill-bred people who talked of *parvenus*."

"I don't think anyone could have used that word to a Trevor, Mary, whomever she had *married*," retorted Mrs. Petersen, with asperity, "and if it required a family ghost to establish Charlie's claim to superiority, you must own that the game was hardly worth the candle. Besides, why should this apparition show herself by fits and starts to you and me, and end by frightening a staid lady's maid into fits?"

"Oh, you admit the incident of Wells!" Miss Trevor raised her pretty eyebrows in amusement; she enjoyed teasing her dignified sister, and she had pressing reasons for wishing to keep the conversation off more intimate subjects. But this time Mrs. Petersen was really annoyed; she paced the room in unusual agitation.

"Why do you harp on these things, Mary?" she said. "Surely we have had enough of the veiled lady already. Who is she? What does she want to tell us? I am sure she bodes us all no good."

"My dear Maggie, I had no idea of vexing you, and still less that your superstitions were so deeply rooted. Poor futile ghost, what harm can she do us? We have laid no sacrilegious hands on the goods of her order. We have done her no wrong, unless it be a wrong to amuse ourselves in the house where perhaps she ate her heart out. I'm sorry for her, Maggie, but she doesn't frighten me; you, who don't even believe in her, surely can't be afraid."

Mrs. Petersen stopped her walk, and met her sister's look with a rather tremulous smile.

"Frightened—I?" she said. "Hardly, Mary, but I think Wells has got on my nerves a little this afternoon. We must be going down now to give Charlie his tea—he has come in."

Half-an-hour later, Mrs. Petersen, left alone with her husband, took up the conversation at the point where she and her sister had dropped it, and told him shortly of Wells' vision and its painful, practical result.

"This horrid ghost tale will be revived again, and we shall be continually teased by hysterical servants. I'm unspeakably annoyed about Wells. She could not have chosen a more awkward time for her departure, and I'm sure no one feels the miseries of a new maid more than I do."

"I'm sure neither maid nor ghost is worth your tears, dear," said her husband, gently. His wife had slipped her hand into his as they stood together at his writing-table; now he stooped to kiss her with a tenderness which would have much surprised the outer world who looked upon the great ironmaster and his beautiful wife as the most frigid of devoted couples, while cynics even went so far as to doubt the devotion.

"What did Mary say about herself?" went on Petersen, anxious to divert the conversation, and, to do so, merely reversing his sister-in-law's tactics. Mrs. Petersen shrugged her shoulders.

"The usual thing happened; she so evidently wanted to avoid the subject, I dared not press it. All I could gather was that they have no hope of being able to marry unless Mrs. Glyn really does leave Hugh her money. I always think it doubtful myself, but the end must be near now—she is very ill."

"And failing Mrs. Glyn's money—"

"Further than that I could not get, Charlie. Mary only chaffed, and would tell me no more."

"I wish to Heaven," burst out Petersen, impatiently, "that Cardwell were not such an impossible person, or that Mary were not so blindly devoted to him; I hardly know which. She is the best girl in the world but one, and you know, Maggie, how many times I've tried to do a brother's part by her. Why, if you haven't sisters of your own, and you look on your wife's as very much yours, you should not be allowed to make things easier for her with your money, I own I never shall see. Mary herself would have no scruples about taking a settlement from you and me, you know. She can see what real happiness it would give us to make her happy; but in comes

Cardwell with his confounded pride, and swears his wife shall be no dependent on my charity. I believe he feels my money a sort of offence. Hang it all! I'm no cad, I hope. Better men than Cardwell are glad to call me friend, while he, from his lofty height, looks down on me as a mere business man. You needn't say 'Hush!' Maggie; it's painful to have such sentiments towards one's future brother-in-law, but he seldom pays us a visit during which I don't long to kick him downstairs."

"It's not Hugh's fault, dear," said his wife, gently, "that he's not able to keep a wife. He's a good landlord, and manages his estate really well, I believe. He simply has overwhelming odds against him. You have owned yourself that no one could bring that estate round without money, not to speak of the charges that are left on it."

"Then why doesn't he let me make a handsome settlement on Mary, I want to know?"

"He isn't made that way, that's all, dear. He has been very loyal, too. They have waited for each other five years already, and, remember, when he and Mary were first engaged, no one dreamed she and I were soon to be turned out into the world as beggars."

"Well, hasn't Mary been loyal, too? Confound it all! I should think *she* has something to boast of in that way. You aren't blind Maggie, and you must have seen that there is not one man only who would give a big slice of his life for the chance of winning her. There's Middleham; I don't speak of position only, but he's a good fellow who will make a name for himself in the world, and he loves Mary with all his heart. I assure you I could kick Cardwell more cheerfully than ever when I compare him with Middleham; a cold, prig of a man, against one who has a head and heart, too."

"What a perverse world it is," said Mrs. Petersen, thoughtfully, and then her face relaxed into a smile as she met her husband's look.

"I don't think it has gone very perversely with us, dear," he returned, as he sat down to his writing table.

"You forget the ghost, Charlie. Please don't laugh, but I have the most horrid presentiment about her re-appearance. I feel sure that something dreadful is going to happen. You remember when she came before."

"My dear girl," Petersen turned sharply round and spoke in his most emphatic tone; "when will you learn to bring your reason to bear even on ghost-seeing? If this unhappy woman wanted to warn you against something, would she begin by frightening your maid? Supposing she had a warning to give, how would she do it? Would prowling about passages convey to your mind that you were to look out for an attack of neuralgia within the next fortnight? A truce to the ghost, Maggie; believe that if she has a message to anyone, it is to a sadder person than you or me."

Mrs. Petersen took her usual place in a low chair by the table.

"You and Mary are very scornful, to-day," she said. "Mary calls her futile, and you say she prowls. I don't think I really mind her either when you are here, but I can't invent epithets for her. I'm tired and stupid; here is a third volume—stupid, too. I'm going to sleep over it while you write."

II

Yet Mrs. Petersen did not sleep. Her eyes wandered out to the sunny garden, and her thoughts wandered, too, to another garden, as sunny and bright with May flowers as this, which she had said good-bye to four years before.

Petersen's eyes also strayed from his writing and rested on the beautiful woman whose grace and tenderness were always new revelations to him, though she had been for four years his wife. No one thought of calling Petersen handsome, although some women professed to admire his strong, rather heavy personality, but about his wife's good looks there had never been been two opinions. Her graceful figure, fair face, with its delicate, well-cut features, and general air of high breeding, had long ago established her claims to beauty.

Her marriage, four years before, had been a nine days' wonder. That one of the Trevor twins, left unexpectedly penniless at their father's death, should exchange "her thousand years old name" for that of Petersen, the ironmaster, who had barely reached the skirts of the exclusive county set which called the Trevors of it, was surprising enough to the ordinary mind; only a cynic could suggest money as a factor in the matter. But that Margaret Trevor, who passed for an extraordinarily reserved and proud woman, should depart from her usual reserve so far as to assure her friends that she married Mr. Petersen with the deepest love and gratitude, since nothing but his great love stood between her and beggary—that both she and her sister should tacitly assume that on its social side her marriage needed no apology—these things passed the philosophy of Blankshire society. They also entirely passed the philosophy of Mary's betrothed, Hugh Cardwell, who could never shake off his aversion from "a tradesman brother-in-law," as he was pleased to call the millionaire ironmaster.

But time works many changes. In four years, Petersen had become a power in a bigger world than that of Blankshire. Perhaps his wife had helped him somewhat, for no one could ignore the beautiful Trevor sisters, especially since Margaret had all the external aids which wealth can give. Perhaps she had merely compelled people to recognise the force of character which had won her. The fact remains that Charles Petersen had become a personage in four years, and in the same space of time Cardwell had grown soured and almost middle-aged in trying to solve the impossible problem of bringing an impoverished and heavily-charged estate into order without the help of ready money.

In her way Mary Trevor had suffered, too. She was too sweet-natured a woman to envy her sister's happiness, but the shadow of long disappointment began to fall on her, the freshness of youth to pass away, and, beneath her light manner these last few days, her sister had guessed at the depression which would not be shaken off.

For Mrs. Glyn, who lay dying, represented Hugh Cardwell's last hope. If that eccentric lady chose to leave him her moderate wealth, his course would once more be clear. The many sisters and the fretful mother might take up their abode at the comfortable dower house. Farms might be drained, houses repaired, new buildings put up, and last, but not least, Cardwell Court itself might be set in order for its new mistress.

"If." Mrs. Petersen's thoughts dwelt so sadly on that fateful word that she was forced to turn them from it.

In her present mood, even the ghost was a welcome change, and her memory strayed back to that melancholy wanderer.

The luxurious library at Chilcote Priory hardly suggested age and ghostliness. It was so airy, so modern, so light; but beyond the cheery library wing stretched a very old house indeed, with galleried staircase, winding, shadowy passages, and latticed windows, with heavy, stone mullions darkening the rooms within. A fit setting for a ghost story.

But as, ten years ago, ghostly visitations carried little or no cachet with them—since ghost seers were looked on, rather as people a trifle wanting in mental balance, than as highly-strung natures to whom special revelations of an unseen world were vouchsafed—only vague rumours of the Priory ghost had reached the outside world.

Its inhabitants, however, knew that since, some years before, Petersen's father had fallen in love with the beautiful old stone house fast falling into ruins and degraded to the uses of a farm; had bought and restored it; laid out a lovely garden with infinite artistic taste; and, inside, furnished it with equal understanding of its possibilities; a mysterious veiled figure had, from time to time, haunted the house.

The *raison d'être* of the apparition had never been known. If wrong or violence had been done to the dispossessed nuns, centuries before, no memory of it remained. Any tragedy enacted within the Priory walls, earlier or later still, had been totally forgotten. Yet, sometimes by day, sometimes by night, one or other of the family, from time to time, met, in dim passage or darkened room, a black-veiled woman who vanished before one had time to grasp her shadowy garments.

The apparition was too rare and too erratic to give the house the name of being haunted. Sometimes, for several years, nothing was seen of her; oftener still, the appearance happened at a time or place which lent itself to delusion; still, the fact remained that, during the four years of their married life, not only the Petersens, but Mary Trevor, also, had severally encountered the ghost where there could be no possibility of mistake; and Mrs. Petersen, by no means a nervous woman, had conceived a positive dread of the veiled lady.

III

If there is one time in the day at which it is possible to contemplate the existence of ghosts with great philosophy, it is surely that when one comes comes down to breakfast in a pleasant room, to find the May sun streaming in on a well-ordered table.

Mrs. Petersen felt extremely cheerful on this particular morning—helped, one cannot doubt, by a most reassuring talk she had just had with Wells.

Wells, on the understanding that the whole family would depart to town for the season in less than a week, had agreed to reconsider her decision. Like her mistress, the morning light gave her courage, and she was even disposed to allow that the waving of tapestry and the flickering of a lamp might have played their parts in the apparition of a few nights before.

Hence Mrs. Petersen came down to breakfast in so cheerful and active a mood that she paid no particular attention to the sorting out of the letters, and was quite unprepared for a stifled cry which burst from her sister, as she laid one of her letters down on the table.

"I'm so sorry," said Mary, gently, in response to the startled looks of her sister and brother-in-law, "I—I ought not to have been so surprised, Maggie. It's a letter from Hugh." Her voice shook ominously, and she waited a minute before going on, then began to read in a quivering voice:—"'Aunt Glyn died yesterday. She was never conscious at all after I came. Gifford tells me that everything is left absolutely to him and his wife, with the exception of a few legacies to old servants.'" There was an awkward pause, in which neither of the Petersens found anything to say more comforting or original than "My dear," "My dear girl," with varying emphasis.

Mary made a forlorn attempt at a smile. "I think you've forgotten sugar in my tea, Maggie. Don't look so tragic over Aunt Glyn, please. It's my fault, I believe; I had the ill-luck to tread on her pug the first time we met, and she never quite forgave me, I'm afraid. Charlie, have you nothing interesting to tell us? You've been absorbed in your paper for quite half an hour."

By ill-luck, Petersen's eyes had just strayed to a short paragraph which announced, "We regret to record the death, after a long illness, of Letitia, widow of the late Charles Glyn, of Marylands, and daughter of the late George Cardwell, of Cardwell Court. The deceased lady was well known in the philanthropic world, and numerous charitable societies will lose in her an active patroness."

"Er—nothing, I'm afraid," he murmured at random, "except that the Government were defeated last night again."

"No? What on?" questioned Mary, who was a keen politician, and the unhappy Petersen had to own that he had made a mere slip of the tongue, and meant that they had secured a better majority. His wife was more fortunate, for her letters included one from her dressmaker with that enclosure of patterns so dear to the feminine heart. It was only when Mary was safely occupied with these that Petersen ventured to glance at her. She was a brave woman, he said to himself, as well as a handsome one, for only her unusual pallor betrayed the shock she had suffered that morning when the hopes of years were suddenly shattered.

The two sisters were strikingly alike in figure, in the shape of their graceful heads, and the curves of their delicate, oval faces. There, likeness ended. Miss Trevor's hair was darker than her sister's, her features less regular, her complexion less brilliant. People who didn't love Mrs. Petersen, spoke of Miss Trevor's expression as more animated, but her warmest admirers could find no other point in which she surpassed her sister.

Yet Petersen, as he looked at the pale, firm face, cursed the fate which had given this woman's strong love to Hugh Cardwell and denied it to a man like Middleham who would have given the world to win her, and who was held back by every tie of loyalty and friendship.

Mary herself was determined to be no subject for her family's pity that day. Hugh might have lost, but he was Hugh still; they were at least no worse off than they had been before. With these and kindred sayings she cheered her sister, when Mrs. Petersen, unwontedly demonstrative, took her in her arms and cried over her a little. One thing Mary did agree to: she promised to write and summon her lover at once to the Priory, and to use her best influence to make him allow her to accept the settlement which Petersen had so long wanted to make on her.

"I should do it if you were marrying a millionaire, you know, Mary," said the kindly ironmaster: "why can't I make it on Cardwell's wife? You know I have neither kith nor kin in the world but you. If anything happens to Maggie and me, you'll be a very rich woman indeed, my dear. Mayn't we have the pleasure of seeing and enjoying your happiness while we live?" Mary promised her influence with a rather sinking heart. She had not been engaged to Cardwell for five years without learning something of his character, but to cheer Maggie's evident distress she professed a faith she did not feel, and even went the length of discussing future plans with her sister.

These whiled away the morning, and various calls on neighbours consumed the afternoon. The two had only just returned, and were giving Petersen tea in the cheerful library, when the footman announced:

"Mrs. Neville, in the drawing-room, to see Miss Trevor, m'm. Most perticler business, she said, ma'am."

The sisters looked at each other in some surprise; Mrs. Neville's name suggested nothing to them.

"The lady said she was from a distance, ma'am, and she kep' the carriage, a hired one from the 'George' at Blankhampton, to wait for her, she said, m'm."

"Take tea in for Miss Trevor and Mrs. Neville, John. Mary, ask her if she will have the horses put up for a little while."

But the stranger whom Mary Trevor found in possession of the big, oak-panelled drawing-room, promptly declined these hospitable attentions.

She was a short, stout woman, handsomely dressed in silk that rustled and beads that rattled, and, at the moment Mary went in, she was in a state of heat aud flurry painful to behold, and made worse by contrast with the younger woman's graceful coolness.

"You must excuse me waiting five minutes while I get cool, Miss Trevor. My fan, thank you. The heat tries me terribly, and I really dare not begin to talk business until I have recovered myself a little."

Mary opened a window, and offered cooling drinks, which were declined with *empressement*. She was quite certain now of her unknown visitor's errand. Mrs. Neville had no doubt heard of Wells, and, being warned of Mrs. Petersen's wrath, had applied to her sister for their maid's character. She evidently belonged to that unfortunate class who play their part in life, from its tragedies down to the engaging of a new maid, in a state of perpetual flurry. Mary contrasted Mrs. Neville, stout and heated, with her elegant slim sister, and thought Wells hardly to be congratulated on her change of mistress. She had just reached this conclusion when Mrs. Neville suddenly ceased her fanning, assumed an upright position, and began with evident hesitation.

"You will be surprised at this visit of a comparative stranger, Miss Trevor, I—"

"Not at all," returned Mary, easily; "but would you not rather see my sister, Mrs. Petersen?"

Mrs. Neville made a gesture of decided refusal.

"I have to see *you*," she answered. "I—I—wish with all my heart this did not fall to my share, but—"

Again she stopped, and Mary, utterly unprepared for this tragic way of asking for a maid's character, made another attempt to help her out.

"It is about Wells, is it not, Mrs. Neville?"

"Wells?" came the unhesitating answer. "Good heavens, no! It is about you I came. You do not recognise me, Miss Trevor, yet I have met you, years ago, at Cardwell Court. I am a neighbour of the Cardwells."

Mary's colour changed.

"There is nothing wrong there?" she asked, with a little shake in her voice.

"Nothing that I know of just now. Mr. Cardwell is away, I believe. I have a most difficult task to perform; will you forgive me if I speak very plainly?"

Mary bowed her head; something in her guest's manner frightened her vaguely. She was not flurried now; agitated she might be, but it was wonderful how much dignity this undignified person managed to put into her last words.

"I must speak of myself first," she went on. "The Cardwells are old friends of mine. When I met you there, we were living some miles away, but a year ago, partly in order to be near Mrs. Cardwell, my daughter and I rented the Chase which joins the Court estate. I have a daughter—I—perhaps we were not careful enough, perhaps we took too much for granted, Mrs. Cardwell and I—my daughter is very impressionable—can you not help me, Miss Trevor?"

Mary had risen, and stood facing the older woman with an undefined terror in her eyes. She rested one hand on her chair, and, before she spoke, her nervous fingers tightened their grasp on it.

"You want to tell me," and there was a vibration of anger in her voice, "that Hugh—"

"No, no," broke in the other, quickly, "not that—not Mr. Cardwell. It is Cicely, my daughter; she is very young, and impressionable, as I said before, and—how can I tell you, she has grown to love him, and her love is stronger than she is; she is very delicate, and she is my only child, all I have in the world, and it is killing her."

"I don't understand," Mary struck in, in a voice so hard it sounded strange to her. "What can I do, Mrs. Neville? Do you want me to tell her myself that Hugh and I have belonged to each other since we were children together—that for five years I have waited, waited, waited to be his wife? How would that help your daughter?"

"I do not ask you to do that. I am telling you the simple truth. My daughter loves Mr. Cardwell, and she is dying. She desires to have the right to leave him all she has in the world, and she is very rich. She wants to marry him. She knows of his love for you; she knows that a man cannot love two women alike. I have told her all that, but it makes no difference. She is willing to accept friendship in return for her great love, if he will only marry her."

"But what can I do?"

"How can I tell you, Miss Trevor? I have told you all there is to tell: the decision rests with you. I might remind you that now Mr. Cardwell is a very harassed man, that his—difficulties have long stood in the way of your marriage. What difference Mrs. Glyn's death makes to him I do not know. I might tell you that my daughter asks nothing better than to leave him rich and free all his days, if he will only make the few months she has yet to live happy by making her his wife."

Mary had pulled herself together, and stood tall and cold before the unhappy mother.

"In other words, Mrs. Neville, you ask my consent, nay more, you even ask me to suggest to Hugh Cardwell this horrible mockery of marriage. You ask me, who love him better than my life, whom he loves with his whole heart, to give him up, to help you to coerce him into marrying a dying woman, on the understanding that hereafter he and I shall live easily on her money. Have you no understanding of the infamous bargain you propose to us?"

The other rose too, her flurry had quite vanished, and the amount of dignity she brought to bear on her very undignified errand was wonderful.

"It is you who do not understand. I have tried to put it before you plainly; perhaps I have failed. Cicely is very ill, the doctors give her six months at the most, she has the greatest desire to be Hugh Cardwell's wife, and, as his wife, to help him in a way she cannot do as a friend, for she is under guardianship until she marries, and she cannot now use her money as she wants. And I have come to you because you are a woman and know what it is to love some one—you have said so—better than your life. Let that love plead for me. I love Cicely in that way, too! I would give anything in the world to save her, but she is past that, and I am here to ask you if, for Mr. Cardwell's sake as well as hers, you will help to give her dying wish. You could not have humiliated yourself as I have done, I see it in your face. But you do not know what a mother's love is, Miss Trevor."

"No, nor ever shall," moaned Mary under her breath.

Mrs. Neville went on,

"I must plead for forgiveness again, and go, for mine is a long journey and I must return, to-night. Have you any hope to give me? Can you at least forgive me?"

"I must think, I must think, let me have time, please. Oh, forgive *me*, forgive *me*, Mrs. Neville. I will write to you in a day or two, I cannot say yes, to-night."

Something in her white face touched Mrs. Neville to the quick; her dignity vanished at once, and tears came into her round, kindly eyes.

"My dear," she said, taking the girl's unresponsive hands, "you cut me to the heart, yet some day I think you will know that my errand here wasn't all cruel or selfish. Try and keep some gentle thoughts of Cicely and me, when all is over with her, and I am left a desolate old woman."

Mary went out to the carriage with her visitor and saw her off with a dazed feeling. She felt numbed, and incapable of any more emotion just then, and not caring to face Margaret or Petersen, she wandered out into the bright garden, trying to collect her thoughts there. She was still dazed, and unable to think connectedly when, after a long time, she came back again, walking past the library window on her way to the garden door.

Petersen sat at his writing table, and Margaret in her usual low chair near him; he had stopped his work for a minute, and turned to speak to his wife, and the sight of their happy faces sent a sudden pang of loneliness into Mary's heart. Something like this had she imagined the cosy room at Cardwell Court that Hugh called his. She, too, had looked forward to a day when Hugh should bring his daily worries and his business to her, and find the unfailing sympathy she was so ready to give him.

She went in quickly, hardly knowing what she did, intending to go to her room for a quiet hour before dinner. The hall was very dark after the sunny garden, and Mary had fairly to grope her way up the dim staircase. A landing with a group of palms and flowering plants was at the top of the main stairs, whence shorter flights branched off to the right and left hand galleries. The heavy scent of flowers was in the air as she passed, turning to the right to her own room. Her eyes were getting accustomed to the gloom now, and she could distinctly see a dark figure gliding down the opposite gallery, in the direction of the staircase. Her dulled sensibilities were quickened by the sight, for she recognised the outlines of the veiled lady's figure.

She came down the panelled gallery with a gliding step, the blackness of her habit faintly defined against the dark oak wall behind her. A sudden impulse seized Mary to turn back and meet her face to face. She ran down the stairs again, passed the landing with its flowers, and was half way up the opposite steps before the apparition had reached them. She came on quietly, her face bent down, but clearly to be seen, white, against the dead black of her habit. Mary's eyes travelled upwards from its sombre folds to the face framed in hard lines of white and black. She was too absorbed to feel any fear.

The nun came nearer, she raised her face, it seemed, as she approached, and Miss Trevor's fascinated gaze rested on it.

It *was her own face*—changed, as pain and sorrow might change it, but her own distorted reflection looked back at her from beneath the nun's veil.

The ghostly figure came nearer; perhaps it held out a hand, who shall say? for, at that instant, Mary's fascinated gaze relaxed, and a look of terror came into her face. Her grasp on the balustrade loosened at the same moment, and, with a shriek and a crash, she fell backwards on to the landing below.

IV

After many days, recollection came back to Mary Trevor, and she found herself lying in a darkened room, and Margaret, with dark rings of trouble and weariness round her eyes, watching her.

Her first words were hardly calculated to reassure her anxious sister.

"I don't think the ghost will ever trouble us again, Maggie. I must have fainted, I'm better again now, and I'll get up in a minute or two."

The sound of her sister's voice seemed to be too much for Mrs. Petersen's overstrained nerves. A woman in nurse's dress got up and put her hastily into a chair. Petersen himself appeared from somewhere and took her away, while the nurse busied herself in forcing the invalid to take food.

"What is the matter? Am I ill? Where has Margaret gone?" Such were a few of the many questions the nurse had to answer with the usual formula, "You mustn't talk, please, try and go to sleep again."

Later on, Margaret came back, her usual, collected, quiet self, bending down to kiss her sister with a pitying tenderness, which helped Mary more than anything else to understand the terrible news she was trying to break to her. She was a cripple for life.

It came out bit by bit, partly wrung from, partly told by her sister and the nurse. The fall had hurt her spine hopelessly; she had had, at the time, concussion of the brain; there had, indeed, been days when Mrs. Petersen had prayed her beloved sister might die. That was over now; Mary would live, and live long, but she would never walk, probably never leave her sofa again.

She took everything with a quietness which astonished them all. When Cardwell arrived on a terrible errand of farewell, Mary was much the calmest of the family. The Petersens hung about the house in nervous misery, while Cardwell himself came down from a few minutes with Mary alone, so utterly broken and disconsolate, that Petersen's heart warmed to him, and he was able, for the first time, to feel for his brother-in-law, who was not to be, something like affection.

It was not, however, until some months afterwards that the approaching marriage of "Hugh Cardwell, Esq., of Cardwell Court, with Cicely, only child of the late Edward Neville and of Mrs. Neville, of the Chase, Dashshire," was announced on the best authority.

How much Mary Trevor had told her sister of Mrs. Neville's errand did not transpire, but the Petersen's intimates found, to their surprise, that that distinguished pair did not express the faintest disapprobation of it, any more than they shewed astonishment when, some few months later, the death of "Cicely, the wife of Hugh Cardwell, aged 22," was likewise duly announced.

Mary Trevor also—looking on at a world in which she had ceased to play her part—expressed neither sorrow nor surprise.

She has lain ten years, waiting, watching.

Petersen is a Cabinet Minister now, and his wife an acknowledged leader of society. Middleham has a great career before him in the great Colony he has gone out to govern. Cardwell is an authority on agriculture, and the second Mrs. Cardwell is the keenest sportswoman in the county.

All these pass before Mary Trevor, who learned to see the world with other eyes when, one summer evening, long ago, she met that ghost of the future face to face, and learned her own destiny there.

GHOSTS

Lumley Deakin

Lumley Deakin is another great mystery. He—I presume it's a man from the nature of the stories—appeared out of nowhere and caused quite a stir amongst readers of the fiction magazines published by the firm of Cassell during the First World War—Cassell's Magazine, The Story-teller and, in particular, The New Magazine, which ran his series of "Behind the Door" stories featuring the mysterious Cyrus Sabinette. The editor revealed that the stories had generated much correspondence from readers but at no time were any details about the author provided. He disappeared as rapidly as he appeared after just two years and seventeen stories, plus one long delayed story published in 1923 which I suspect had been held over in the inventory. All of his stories were of an unusual nature but not all were overtly supernatural. The following is one of the more straightforward!

I T IS A PLATITUDE THAT ONE-HALF THE WORLD DOESN'T KNOW how the other half lives. It is certain that the half which knew Grimshaw by night was not in the slightest interested in the other half that knew him by day. Dual personality is a fascinating subject, and yet it is much more common than the lay mind believes. Grimshaw played two rôles, and each was perfectly natural to him. Society regarded him as the most eligible bachelor in its ranks. If he were not handsome, his features were strong enough to make him highly attractive. Moreover, he was the most generous giver that Society had known for a decade. There was no charitable institution in the West End that didn't look to him as to a fairy god-parent. His contributions were large and frequent, and, most delightful of all, he was exceedingly modest in his generosity. As a rule his cheques were received along with a request that the donation should be announced as "anonymous." In a way such modesty was the surest way of gaining recognition, for it is the silent money that talks, and whispers concerning his benevolence were ever on the lips of those who flitted from one reception to another throughout the season. Many inquiries were made about the source of Grimshaw's wealth, but Society never learned the truth, for the cunning which made the wealth possible also framed the mask by which unthinking Society was blinded.

Cyrus Sabinette made the acquaintance of Grimshaw at the house of Lady Recker. The two were introduced to each other as being "the two most interesting men in London at the moment." Grimshaw, strong and somewhat rugged, gave the tall, slim figure of Sabinette a careful scrutiny before holding out his hand, and Sabinette's big dark eyes returned the stare, only slightly less insolently. No one in the company overheard the preliminaries, but, to the amazement of those who knew Grimshaw for a retiring, almost unsociable man, the two were apparently confirmed friends within an hour of meeting each other for the first time. Sabinette had a pretty wit, and he found the way to Grimshaw's confidence with ridiculous ease. Indeed, Grimshaw confessed, as he was taking leave of the hostess, that he had never met a more delightful personality, and begged her, if she had any regard for him, to bring them into even closer relationship.

Grimshaw lived on the south side of the river. His house was an imposing structure, standing in well-wooded grounds. If his tastes were simple, at least they were artistic, and while he kept only a few servants, there was everything in the house for which the heart of any self-indulgent bachelor could yearn. That night he went home with pleasant recollections of Sabinette's wit. Frequently, while in the cab, he burst into peals of laughter as he recalled some jest or other which the tall, dark, cynical man had evolved. He sent the sleepy-eyed butler to bed, and allowed himself a final cigar in the study.

Half-an-hour after he entered the house there was a rattle of gravel on the window. He went quickly to the door, taking a pistol from a cabinet in the study as he went.

Cyrus Sabinette was on the doorstep, and before Grimshaw could recover from his surprise the newly-made friend explained his sudden appearance.

"I am staying with friends in this district," he said, "and Lady Recker was good enough to tell me about your kind remarks before you left. This is the hour when most men are dull, and it occurred to me—"

"The very thing!" said Grimshaw. "Come in. I was thinking about that story you told us in the smoke-room, at Lady Recker's. I should love half an hour before turning in."

Sabinette followed him into the study, and gratefully selected a cigar from the proffered box.

"Now," he said, settling himself in a chair, "I'm an opportunist. I wonder if you'll give me credit for having brought a pleasant hour into your life to-night?"

"I've never laughed so much before," said Grimshaw.

Sabinette smiled an appreciation.

"I should say," he said, slowly, "that your life is not too full of brightness."

Immediately, Grimshaw's face took to itself a frown.

"I don't know that I've ever complained." he said cautiously.

Sabinette made an expressive gesture. "If you'll allow me to say so," he remarked, "bachelordom, at your time of life, is almost positive proof of—shall we say disappointment?"

"You're not nearly so witty as you were an hour ago," said Grimshaw.

"I hasten to apologise. I came here to press home a great desire upon you. It would be more than folly in me to court your displeasure."

"A great desire?"

"To beg from you a letter of introduction."

"To whom?"

"To a man whom, I am informed, is the most astute business genius in all London—Abraham Heischmann."

Grimshaw's frown deepened.

"You puzzle me," he said.

"Strange," Sabinette murmured. "I was sure that you were a personal friend of his."

"What is he, and who is he?"

"Mr. Heischmann is a large employer of labour in the clothing industry."

"I know so little about business men," said Grimshaw, sleepily.

"He is reputed to be making thousands by the careful selection of his work-people."

"Indeed?"

"He is so skilful in the handling of those who court his society that he obtains preferences in the way of Government contracts for the supply of official clothing."

"You left the door open. Do you mind closing it?"

"Certainly," said Sabinette, rising from his chair.

"From the outside," Grimshaw added, whereupon Sabinette resumed his seat.

"My dear friend," he said, wagging his cigar between his fingers, "you're not nearly so clever an actor as Society would have me believe."

Grimshaw had risen to his feet, and there was a threat in his attitude.

"Of course, I knew that Henry Grimshaw and Abraham Heischmann were one and the same person." Sabinette calmly blew out a wreath of smoke. "And, not being in clover myself—"

"You thought you'd come and blackmail me?"

"Sir!" And Sabinette lowered his eyes. "I never blackmail anyone. In truth, your dual role interested me. When I learned that the kind-hearted philanthropist, Henry Grimshaw, the man who was practically worshipped by every designing mother in Society, Henry Grimshaw, the man who is reputed to have spent as much as ten thousand on a ball in this very house where we are sitting—when I learned that Henry Grimshaw was the money-hungry Heischmann of the daylight, I said to myself, 'Here is something to keep you from dying of ennui.' You talk of blackmail. Pooh! I am not so greatly in need of money as that. I came to admire you—also, to inquire if there was any chance of your buying my services."

"I thought so," said Grimshaw, with a sneer.

"The services will be worth the money you may pay for them. Let me come in with you, as secretary, manager, or anything."

Grimshaw's face had lost the frown and assumed an expression of fear.

"Why should I?" he asked, timidly.

"Because you and I, working together, might achieve so much… You think you're on a good thing if that German contract is secured?"

"Who's been talking?"

"Never mind that. You've put in a price that leaves you only a small margin, but, provided you can get the labour cheaply enough, you'll make anything up to twenty thousand out of it—that is, if your tender is accepted."

"It will be," said Grimshaw, conceitedly.

"Meaning that no one dare tender a lower price? The others are not able to buy their labour so cheaply."

"What if I said yes?"

"You shouldn't be so cock-sure," said Sabinette. "As a fact, yours isn't the lowest tender. I happen to know. I'm in a position to give you inside information. I can give you names, if you want them."

"Where do you get your information?"

"It comes to me," said Sabinette. "I never go in search of it." He scribbled some figures on the back of an envelope and handed it across to Grimshaw. "That's the price you tendered," he said with a smile. "Don't work yourself into a rage and commence to accuse all your clerks."

Grimshaw's amazement was great. He knew that he couldn't accuse any one of his clerks of treachery, for he, himself, had worked out the estimate, and the tender was, so he believed, secret to himself.

"I admire you," said Sabinette, as he watched the shadows on the other man's face. "You're not altogether bad. You're not a hypocrite, although you do spend thousands in the West for which you make the East pay. In a sense, you're a curiosity. You'd interest even the meanest psychologist. I'm not certain that you're aware of the two phases of your nature. I was watching you at Lady Recker's to-night, and it was very difficult for me to believe that you were, in reality, Abraham Heischmann. You were so polished in your manner; you exercised so much fascination over the ladies; you were so—so English in your bearing. But I heard you muttering to yourself as you sat alone in the conservatory. You were speaking in Polish. The language is familiar to me."

Grimshaw's face was very white. Physically, he was twice as strong as the other man, but Sabinette's thrusts had weakened him. He had lost his nerve. At last he managed to stammer:

"Supposing I say that you're right—what then? What do you want me to do?"

Sabinette dropped his cigar-end on a tray and gave his man a steady look before replying.

"Want you to do? I don't know that I want you to do anything for me, save taking me into your confidence a little more fully. I'm a comparatively friendless man, and you interest me immensely. The dull dogs whom we met to-night leave me very disgusted with human nature. Your other life—down in the East End—has taken hold of me by reason of its striking contrast to that which you live in the West. I don't work for the sake of money alone. I think I told you a minute ago that I was not particularly in need of any money, but I'm always on the look-out for something new in kinks. Still, if you have the avarice fever, I might do a great deal for you. I have very influential friends in those quarters from which you derive your—shall we say patronage? When shall I come to see you at your factory?"

Grimshaw caught at his fleeting courage.

"It serves me right," he said, "for allowing sentiment to attract me to you. Lady Recker gave me to understand that you were quite an artist, in a way. I find that you are nothing more than a vulgar blackmailer. There's the door. Get out."

Sabinette went out without another word. Grimshaw didn't accompany him to the door, and he didn't hear the door close, but he knew that the man was gone.

The next morning, he arrived at his factory an hour earlier than usual. He had slept but little during the night, for Sabinette's seeming prescience had worried him not a little. He sent for his foreman, a vicious-looking, low browed Pole, and asked for the report of the previous day's working. He glanced over it, curled his lips in scorn, and wrote something in Polish on a slip of paper.

The waiting foreman cried out as in pain when he saw what was written there. Grimshaw seemed to enjoy the man's mental agony.

"I have every reason to believe, Kravinski," he said, "that for some time past you have been selling my secrets, betraying me to competitors, and that after all I have done for you. Very well. The English police will be interested to learn that they can put their hands on a 'wanted' anarchist within an hour."

Kravinski whined as though he had been whipped, and he fell on his knees and begged Grimshaw for another chance, swearing that never by so much as the movement of an eyelid had he betrayed his trust. Grimshaw began to open the correspondence in front of him. He came on a letter from a German military department. Almost before he had drawn it from the envelope he knew that the contract which he had felt was so safe had been given to another.

"Read that!" he said to Kravinski. "And then tell me that you have never betrayed me. We've lost that contract. It has been given to a wretched Pole in your own country, because he tendered slightly lower. Someone must have told him. If it wasn't you it must have been that sister of yours, whom I took the trouble to rescue from the Warsaw police. I have never trusted you wholly, Kravinski, but I had a reason for giving you a position of trust."

The wretched man had ceased to whine. His eyes were fixed on the steel paper-knife lying near Grimshaw's left elbow. As though he knew what was passing in the Pole's mind, Grimshaw placed the weapon at a safe distance. With the same movement he pressed a bell-button. A man in private clothes, who had been waiting in readiness as the result of Grimshaw's telephone message before he left his house, stepped out from behind a screen.

"There's your man," said Grimshaw, calmly. "Karl Kravinski, wanted by the police of three countries. I'll give you details of his career after you've put him safely under lock and key."

There was a sharp struggle, but Kravinski was too weak to make much resistance. As his shrieks came back along the corridor to the office, Grimshaw calmly resumed his opening of the morning's mail.

"Some day," he said to himself, with a smile, "these vermin will understand me."

Then he sent for Kravinski's sister, Yoli, the Pole. She was a wonderfully pretty woman, with a prettiness which her shabby dress only accentuated. Her face was very small and white. There was pronounced intelligence in her big eyes, and some pain. In years she could not have been more than twenty-two; in experience of the world and its ways she was nearly fifty. This girl, whom Grimshaw had said he saved from the Warsaw police, had appealed strongly to the man's baser emotions when first he set eyes on her. She was one of a thousand women engaged in the factory, but she stood out prominently from all the rest.

"You sent for me, Mr. Heischmann?" She spoke without a trace of accent, and her eyes were watching his face closely, as though trying to read his mind.

"Sit down, Yoli," he said, pleasantly, but she shook her head and remained standing.

"You become more obstinate every day, Yoli. Why?"

She did not speak.

"And I've done so much for you! I can't understand it."

With the Slav's love of the dramatic, she drew from beneath her shawl five pounds in gold, and placed the coins on the table in front of him.

"There's my bondage money, Mr. Heischmann," she said, and struck an attitude. "That's what you paid for me. Take it, and I shall then be able to answer freely any questions which you like to put to me. You provided the five pounds which the immigration department demanded. For five pounds you bought me, body and soul, just as you bought all the rest of the poor wretches who are in your factory."

"We'll forget all that for a minute, Yoli," he said, persuasively. "I have something of importance to say to you."

"I'm listening to you, Mr. Heischmann."

"Then come a little nearer."

"I'll listen from here."

He sat back in his chair and gave her a careful look.

"Tell me, Yoli," he said, "if you ever met a man named Sabinette—Cyrus Sabinette?"

She shook her head.

"Are you quite certain?"

"Why should I tell you whom I meet? I am only your slave in this factory—not outside."

"We'll try another tack. When did your brother tell you about the German contract for which this firm was tendering?"

"I have not seen my brother since yesterday."

"Well, he must have told you before then if he told you at all. But your answer is almost good enough. You may take it from me that you won't see your brother again for a long while. I've handed him over to the police."

She felt for the edge of the desk, and her eyes opened and shut as though she could hardly believe her senses.

"They have a very short way in England with anarchists," said Grimshaw. "They give them a rough trial, but they generally swing. Now, Yoli, tell me the truth about that German contract."

She fell on her knees and clasped her hands, swearing that she knew nothing about any contract, and pleading in behalf of her brother. Karl had been a father to her. He was the only relative that she possessed in the world.

Grimshaw listened to her pleading, then tapped on the desk to compel attention.

"If you will tell me all you know about this man, Sabinette," he said, "I will do my best to get your brother another chance."

She protested that she didn't know Sabinette, whereupon he struck her on the cheek with a folded newspaper, and angrily ordered her back to the workroom.

All that day, Grimshaw made the lives of his sweated employees a misery to them. In his eyes they were cattle, purchased with coin, and kept for the sole purpose of making profits for him. Every one of them was carefully selected; each had a past; a threatening sword was dangling over every one's head. All were refugees, fugitives from justice, men and women who had fled to this country for sanctuary, and whose names had been sent on in advance by Grimshaw's many agents on the Continent. It was a perfect system of slavery, which his brain had devised, and the price of each slave was five pounds, handed to them before they landed, in order that they might pass the immigration authorities, and subsequently deducted from their meagre wages. The majority hadn't been able to pay back the money. He took care of that. While they were debtors, they were abject slaves, and even after they had liquidated their debt, there was always the fear of the law.

At the end of the day, Grimshaw returned to his house on the south of the river, shed the skin of the wolf, and prepared himself for the Society in the west which had come to pay homage to his eligibility.

In two days' time he was to hold a garden-party, with dances in the moonlight, and all the rest of it. The letters of acceptance were piled on the table in the hall, and he and his butler went through them before dinner. A passion for detail was one of the characteristics of the man, and before leaving the house for the club that night, he reviewed all the arrangements that had been made for the garden-party. Everything was in perfect order, and he drove to the West End with the air of a man who feels that a good work had been well completed, and that everything must come out right.

And about the time that Henry Grimshaw was lolling in an arm-chair at the club, and discussing a political problem with an effete colonel, Yoli Kravinski was kneeling on a bare floor with her hands clasped and her black hair floating over her shoulders. It was a squalid tenement in which she and her brother had lived for twelve months. The two rooms which they rented were almost devoid of furniture.

The windows, looking out on a slum courtyard, were coated with grime; the wailing of a hungry, neglected child blended with her petition on behalf of her brother. She was still kneeling, when a white hand rested on her shoulder, and the most tender voice that she had ever heard inquired:

"You are the sister of Karl Kravinski?"

She screamed out in fear, and stumbled to her feet.

"How did you get in?" she asked, in a terrified whisper.

"How, my dear child? Through the doorway. My name is Sabinette—Cyrus Sabinette. Have you heard of me before?"

"No," she stammered; then—"Yes."

"Mr. Heischmann spoke to you about me?"

She nodded.

"Ah! yes," said Sabinette. "It was through him that I came to learn of you and your brother. He has been arrested—hasn't he? Heischmann told me that he was almost certain to be extradited."

The girl caught at his arm.

"Save him for me!" she pleaded. "Can you? Can you do anything? He is the only being in the world that I love. We are alone in the world, he and I."

"I came to talk about Mr. Heischmann," said Sabinette, apparently ignoring her agonised face. "Heischmann told me that you were very much attached to him."

"To my brother? Yes."

"No, to Heischmann himself."

She shivered, as though a cold wind had swept through the room.

"I hate him!" she said, and repeated the word "hate" three or four times. "They will send my brother to the mines if he is extradited, and he will never come back... Ah! you will help me? Your eyes are so kind, your voice so gentle. You understand."

"I *know* that he will be sent to the mines," said Sabinette. "See—" and he drew a blue document from his pocket. "That is a copy of the information sworn by Mr. Heischmann to the police. It gives the record of Karl Kravinski. No doubt a great deal of it is the result of his imagination, but they will believe Mr. Heischmann before your brother."

"Save him!" she pleaded again.

He took hold of her wrists, and in the gloom of the room his big eyes glowed.

"Why should I do this for your brother?" he asked.

She crept closer to him.

"If not for my brother's sake—for mine."

He smiled, well pleased, and releasing one hand, stroked her black hair in a tender way.

"You're a very beautiful girl, Yoli," he whispered. "Supposing I said that I would save him, what would you do for me?"

"Anything!"—and her eyes flashed.

"Anything?" he echoed. "That's much too comprehensive. Now, Yoli, supposing I were too late to help your brother—and I fear that I am—what then?"

She stepped back from him, and was silent for a moment.

"I should kill Heischmann," she said, "and then I shouldn't care what happened to myself." She turned her back upon him, and he could see by the movements of her shoulders that she was dwelling on the possibility of losing her beloved brother. He went up behind her, and placed his hand affectionately on her arm.

"Child," he said softly, "I am intensely sorry for you, because—something has happened already."

She turned quickly and faced him.

"Tell me!"

"Are you strong enough to bear it?"

She nodded, and her cheeks went a shade paler.

"Read that," he said, and held out a newspaper towards her.

Karl Kravinski, arrested earlier in the day, had destroyed himself in his cell.

She read the paragraph slowly. Instead of the tears which he might have expected, she laughed a little hysterically. Then, "All right—all right," she said, and the paper dropped on the bare floor at her feet. He regarded her pityingly.

"I'll help you to another and a better position," he said, but she threw up her head in disdain. "Come," he sighed, "you're much too beautiful to be sweating out your life in his den of a factory. I, too, am a Pole (he dropped into the language) and I want to help you."

The music that incites was in that tender voice, and she fiercely gripped his arm.

"Yes, help me," she whispered, and then laughed unnaturally. "Help me to repay Heischmann for what he has done, and—"

"And, then—"

"Anything," she breathed.

Sabinette's arms enfolded her.

"I will help you," he said, and the light in his eyes was brighter.

II

Grimshaw or Heischmann watched, from the window of his office, the passing out of the building of the horde of slaves. The day's work was done, the machines in the low-roofed shed were quiet, a film of dust was gradually settling on the piles of garments stacked on the huge counter in the middle of the room. An under-foreman came to the office door and meekly presented the keys of the outer gate. Heischmann, without looking up from his letters, said:

"Yoli, the Pole, hasn't been here today."

The under-foreman shrugged his shoulders. What was one woman, more or less, to him.

"See to it," said Heischmann, "see to it, to-morrow; she must be brought to her senses."

An hour later. He was almost through with his letters. The masked ball in the grounds of his house was to commence at midnight. He lay back in his chair and half-closed his eyes. It was very quiet in the office; the single jet of light seemed to deepen the shadows in the corners… Something detached itself from the shadows immediately behind his chair. He watched it in the tiny circular mirror propped up on his desk. A thin hand was raised. In the light of the gas-jet, the poised weapon appeared like a dagger. Heischmann possessed a strong nerve. He didn't move aside until the weapon was moving downward, and then he moved so swiftly that he was gripping the slender wrist before the cry of fear had died from Yoli's lips. He wrenched. She screamed in agony. The long scissors clattered on the floor. She twisted her lithe body, and slipped from his grasp. He darted to the right of her, just as her fingers closed again on the scissors. She was on her knees. He sprang towards her, stumbled over a fallen stool, and fell with his whole weight upon her. There was a faint moan—no greater sound. He scrambled to his feet, and groped a way to the wall, where he leaned for support, his breath coming jerkily. The woman on the floor lay quite still. The dull light of the gas-jet rested on her bosom, and picked out the ring of steel which he knew to be the crook of the scissors. He went back to her and bent down…

"Through the heart!" he muttered. Then, in a frightened whisper: "Yoli! It was an accident… your own fault."

He straightened himself, and made a frantic rush to the door. Then he covered his eyes and shrieked like a frenzied woman.

The door was standing open. Cyrus Sabinette was lolling against the jamb.

"I rang several times," said Sabinette, quietly, and pretending not to notice the agitation of Heischmann; "and, at last, I took the liberty of walking in." Then, his eyes rested on the form on the floor. He gave Heischmann an inquiring glance. "Fainted?" he asked.

Heischmann was rumpling the points of his lounge coat.

"No," he gasped, "she came here to complain—about work—and—I had dismissed her—one of my seamstresses."

"Ah!" Sabinette stooped beside the woman. "Suicide, I suppose. These poor creatures love the dramatic. I think I recognise her face."

Heischmann was swaying to and fro. Everything was unreal to him. Sabinette looked over his shoulder and smiled at the pitiable object near the door.

"Sit down, man," he said, almost soothingly. "This will be easily explained to the police."

Heischmann dropped on a chair; there was no strength in him now; all his muscles had become weak and flabby.

"Wait here one moment," said Sabinette, "and I will procure some brandy; you look positively dreadful."

"Don't go—not yet," pleaded Heischmann. "There's brandy in the cupboard above your head."

Sabinette turned, reached up to the cupboard and lifted down the bottle. He poured out a glassful, and came behind Heischmann's chair. "Now," he whispered, and forced the edge of the glass between the quivering lips. Heischmann drank deeply, and rested his head against the back of the chair.

"You'll be all right in a few minutes," said Sabinette; "just close your eyes, and try to forget this—this thing."

Heischmann was conscious of a blissful peace. In a little while, his senses seemed to fall into slumber; the vision of Sabinette became blended with the form on the floor...

When Heischmann opened his eyes again, he was lying on the bed in his own house. His man was in the room, noiselessly selecting dress-clothes and laying them in readiness for his master. Heischmann watched him curiously for a moment. Then,

"How long have I been lying here, Merrit?" he asked.

The man came to the bedside at once.

"Since early afternoon, sir," he answered. "You came back in the company of a gentleman whom I don't remember to have seen before. He told me that you had swooned in the club—he fancied that it was due to the heat."

"Since—early—afternoon!" Heischmann mouthed the words doubtfully. "Are you certain of that, Merrit?"

"Quite certain, sir. I have been in the room all the time."

The sound of music came up from the grounds below. Heischmann sat up on the bed. Merrit drew aside the blind and looked down.

"Everything is ready, sir," he said, softly; "the guests will be here shortly." He indicated the dress-clothes, and Heischmann slid from the bed and gave himself up to the dressing.

In the grounds, a myriad glow lamps had been strung from tree to tree, Chinese lanterns peeped wonderingly from the hearts of the bushes, and above the droning of the assembled guests the music of the concealed orchestra floated. The costumes of the dancers were of every shade and style; there was originality in every one, from the little gnome with wings of fire to the wonderful representation of a living opal. Heischmann of course had effected only evening dress, and he wore no mask. The midnight supper was laid in the grounds, the guests passing to their places through an avenue of swinging lanterns. Lady Recker was there, and familiarly she forced her way to the side of the host. She lifted her mask as she leaned towards him.

"You, darling," she said laughingly. "We didn't dream that it would be half so beautiful, although you have a knack of going one better every time."

He pressed her hand, lightly.

"You were always generous, Lady Recker," he murmured. "My only hope is that nothing may be wanting. An old bachelor is hardly expected to—"

She closed his lips with her fan.

"Hush!" she chided. She moved a little nearer. "I want to introduce the sweetest child you ever met." She turned, and motioned with her fan to a slim girl in the dress of a wandering minstrel, a girl whose eyes peered through a mask of flame colour and seemed to look straight down into his heart.

"Ma'mselle," whispered Lady Recker—"our dear delightful host."

Heischmann took a deep breath, and grasped the white hand that was held towards him.

"How cold it is," he said, and raised it to his lips.

"How gallant," the girl murmured, and seated herself by his side.

Those two led off the dancing. Heischmann's heart was beating rapidly; his blood was racing; the music quickened, the girl's feet glided over the lawn as though they did not actually touch the grass; she seemed to carry him with her; the smile on the rose lips arched so invitingly beneath the mask, thrilled him and set his brain dancing.

"Beautiful!" he whispered ecstatically, as she threaded a way between the dancers and brought him to the edge of the lawn. "You dance like an angel!"

"An angel!" she echoed, and flicked his hot face with her fan.

The music ceased, but she carried him on—across the path that fringed the lawn and into the shrubbery.

"We must go back," he sighed; "we—must—and yet I—I could go on like this for ever."

"For ever—and ever," she laughed. "You are tired?... No!... You must not do that!" He had raised a hand to her mask... "In a little while, we'll rest."

"Rest," he murmured. And the lights on the lawn had passed away. The voices of the guests could be no longer heard.

"Rest here," and with a quick movement she freed herself, and lay down on the grass at his feet. He lay beside her. The surrounding shrubs pressed against each other as though they would hide, the pair from curious eyes.

"I must go back," he said dreamily without moving.

She slipped a white arm under his neck as he lay there, and leaned over as though she would press her lips against his.

"Close your eyes," she whispered, and his heart thrilled in anticipation of the promised kiss.

He opened his eyes a second after he had closed them. Horror came into them. The mask had been torn away from the girl's face. It was Yoli, the Pole, that looked down upon him! He tried to cry out, but his lips were sealed; he tried to move his arms, tried to rise, but all strength was gone. He saw the flash of the weapon as she raised it above her head, and he saw behind her the tall sinister figure of Cyrus Sabinette.

And they called it Suicide! If they had known the truth!

Elizabeth Jordan

After several little known (well, unknown) writers to one who was much better known in her day although again, like so many, her reputation has faded. She's also, so far as I know, our only American contributor although the story, again so far as I know, appeared in a British publication, the extremely rare Premier Magazine, *three years before its American appearance. Elizabeth Jordan (1865–1947) was born in Milwaukee, Wisconsin where she became a local reporter by the age of twenty before moving to New York to work on the* New York World. *By 1901 she was editor of the prestigious* Harper's Bazaar, *whilst also writing stories for several of the leading magazines. She published over thirty books including many mysteries and society novels.*

Jordan was fascinated by the supernatural and even stayed a night in a haunted house—she devotes a whole atmospheric chapter to it in her wonderful autobiography Three Rousing Cheers *(1938) and it inspired the opening chapter of her novel* May Iverson's Career *(1914). I confess I am not fully au fait with the entirety of Elizabeth Jordan's output, though there are ghostly allusions in several of her novels and I know of two ghost stories in her collection* Tales of the Cloister *(1901). I expect there are more to discover, such as the following.*

T HE CLOCK ON THE MANTELPIECE STRUCK TWO, AND LIEUTENANT Belden, believing for an instant that it had awakened him, turned in his bed with a distinct sense of being ill-used. He had ridden sixty miles across the plains during the day, and it was hard luck if he could not have the night of uninterrupted sleep he needed after such a journey. He would throw out that clock in the morning, he reflected drowsily; it had awakened him before. Then, suddenly, he heard another sound which held him rigid, with every nerve strained to its utmost tension.

In the far corner of the room something had moved, and even as he turned his half-closed eyes towards it, it moved again. By the gleam of the starlight entering his windows, he could see that it was a large something, bulky, black, and awkward. It might be a big dog—but a dog could not possibly get into his quarters. Or it might be a man crawling on all-fours. Whatever it was, one thing was certain; it was out of place in his room at two o'clock in the morning. Very slowly, and with the utmost caution, the lieutenant's hand slipped under his pillow and closed on the revolver which lay there, ready for the emergencies attending life in a frontier army post, and as his fingers tightened on the butt, the young man sat up with a jerk.

"Who's there?" he demanded, in the crisp tones of the parade-ground.

There was no answer but the black object in the corner rose to a man's height for a moment, wavered uncertainly, then dropped again and crawled towards him. Belden leaned forward and stared at it, conscious as he did so of an unpleasant tingling at the roots of his scalp.

What the deuce was the thing, anyway?

"Stop!" he commanded sharply. "Stop, or I'll fire!"

The thing on the floor continued to move. As it came nearer he saw that it was a man, and that it held something in its right hand, something bright and metallic. He fired, and simultaneously with the explosion, leaped out of bed towards the intruder. He thought he heard a groan, but his blood was singing in his ear-drums and he could not be sure. A second later, however, he had touched the electric button, which was some distance from his bed, and in the centre of the now brightly lighted room was bending over a motion-less, silent figure.

It was a man, in the uniform of a trooper, and it lay face down-wards, with arms and legs sprawling, in an attitude of grotesque helplessness. Near the relaxed right hand was a silver pocket-flask—his own flask Belden now realised—from which the cover had been taken off and the liquor it held had trickled. From under the left arm, awkwardly crooked as if in a quick instinct of self-defence as the man went down, another small stream crept indolently along the polished floor—a stream whose nature Belden did not recognise until he took the figure by the shoulders, and with considerable difficulty turned it over. As he did so, the eyes of the dead man, wide open and full of horror of a violent passing, stared up at him, while the mouth, twisted by some muscular contraction at the end, bared its teeth in a sardonic grin. Belden, who had been trying to prop the dead body against his knee in the hope that life still lingered in it, dropped it after his first glance at the face, and rose to his feet, shuddering, while his brown cheeks whitened.

"Kearney?" he gasped aloud. "My God! *Kearney!*"

Kearney grinned on, and to Belden, who stood above him, stunned by the shock of the discovery he had made, the expression of this man, his servant for the past four years, seemed subtly to soften and take on a special meaning. It was as if Kearney grinned at him across the dark gulf that lay between them to give him comfort. He knew what Kearney would say if he could speak. He could almost hear the words:

"Well, sir, we've done it this time, sir. But it ain't your fault. You've warned me often enough. It's up to me, sir."

Belden knelt down and took the dead man's hand—the hand, he thought, of the best and most devoted "batman" an officer had ever had, a servant whose only fault had led to this incredible tragedy. Belden knew now just how it had all come about. Again he seemed to hear Kearney telling him:

"You see, sir, it was this way. When you left me behind, sir, it was bound to happen. It always did happen, sir, when you left me alone. By the time you got back I wasn't fit for duty, sir, so I kept out of sight, knowing you'd understand. I'd been drinking your whisky all day, sir; and by night it was all gone, and I was on the verge of—well, of you know what, sir. I had to have more whisky, so I crept in here and got the flask out of your pocket, thinkin' you'd sleep too sound after your ride to hear me. I've done it before, sir, and you never heard. But this time—well—this time, sir, it didn't work."

Belden passed his fingers across his eyes, and found that they were wet. Then, resolutely, he tried to pull himself together, and-from the whirling chaos of his thoughts to shape some plan of action. He had killed Kearney—his man, who for four years had given him the unquestioning devotion of a faithful dog. Kearney would have died for him at any time, he knew. Well, he himself would probably have died for Kearney, if it came to a show-down; certainly he would have risked his life to save Kearney's, and Kearney must have known he would. So now this Kearney who lay before him—this

strange, incredibly remote Kearney with the frozen smile—understood and forgave him. He was sure of that. Kearney's soul, still
hovering near them, must know what emotions were racking the
soul of the officer who had been his unwitting slayer. He, Belden,
would carry the memory of the tragedy and the regret of it to his
grave—that, too, was certain. But now there were things to do, and
he must prepare himself for the strains of the coming hours. He
was not afraid of the result of the investigation that was inevitable.
The case was perfectly clear, and half the men of his company,
who knew Kearney's habits, must have seen him turbulently drunk
during the two days of the lieutenant's absence. He must say his
say to Kearney, however, in these, the last moments in which they
two would be alone together on this earth. He pressed the hand of
Kearney, which was already growing stiff. As he did so, a spasm of
feeling shook him.

"You understand, Kearney," he said huskily, "and you forgive me.
I know you would tell me so if you could."

For a moment longer his eyes rested on Kearney's face, with its
fixed grin. Even in this short time the first horror was certainly leaving it, he reflected, and with the smoothing of the features under
the fingers of Death, the lips were taking on more and more the
familiar curves of Kearney's frequent and happy-go-lucky smile. The
thought greatly comforted Belden. He rose to his feet, covered with
a sheet the stark figure on the floor, and, dressing hurriedly, went to
his superior officer to make his report.

Five weeks later, following his acquittal after an almost perfunc-
tory trial, Belden dined with two of his fellow-officers, and then
went sombrely to his own quarters, exhausted by the strain of the
experience. He insisted on returning alone, shaking off with a word
of thanks his friends who were convinced that on that particular

night, at least, he needed their companionship and the diversion of "a stiff game" of cards. He had not yet chosen another man to take Kearney's place, and in the interval his quarters had been kept in order by the wife of Sergeant O'Toole, whose sympathy for him had been expressed in an almost passionate dusting of his effects.

As he entered the front door of the small house he occupied alone he was momentarily repelled by the darkness and silence that greeted him. He had intended to go directly to his bedroom, but with his foot on the lowest step of the short flight of stairs leading to the floor above he paused. For some reason, he did not care to go to bed just yet, so he turned and went into his study, where he switched on the lights, lit a cigar, poured out a modest drink, and opened a book, intending to read for half an hour. But he found it impossible to centre his attention on the printed pages. His thoughts were full of Kearney, and he seemed to hear again and again the mournful bugle call of taps ringing out over the soldier's grave. Well, it was taps. The whole thing was over now—ended; he must keep his thoughts off it, and resume his usual routine. He would go to bed at once and get a good night's sleep, as the best preparation for a fresh start in the morning.

He closed his book, crushed out the fire of his almost unsmoked cigar, turned off the lights, and started upstairs. As he did so he became conscious of an unwillingness to proceed, but he ignored this and ascended steadily. Then he thought he heard steps behind him, and stopped to look back, with the reflection that he had forgotten to lock the door, and someone must have entered. In the darkness he could see nothing, nor was there any sound, so he went on again, only to hear at once the steady fall of other feet behind his own on the uncarpeted, hardwood stairway. The sound was so unmistakable that he turned, listened, walked back down the stairs, switched on the light in the hall, and finally tried the front door. It was locked. He walked slowly through the three rooms on the first floor, flooding each with light as he entered it, and then examining its every nook and corner with the utmost care. Every room was empty. Belden experienced again the boyish sense of injury that visited him when he considered himself ill-used. If the fellows were playing a practical joke on him, they had chosen a mighty bad time for it; the thing was in abominable taste. He turned out all the lights and started up the stairs once more, and again the footsteps followed him. They were oddly familiar footsteps—resolute and quick. They were light, too; they were—why, yes—of course—Belden's mind worked very slowly at this point, circling round the idea without at first taking it in—they were like the footsteps of Kearney!

Belden knew now what was the matter with him. He was nervous, frightfully nervous, and no wonder. The shock he had had was enough to unsettle any fellow's nerves. He reached his bedroom, turned on the lights, and dropped into the nearest chair. His heart was beating a little faster than usual—a mere trifle. He held up his hand and looked at it critically. It was perfectly steady, and he smiled. Then, whistling under his breath, he made his preparations for bed as usual, if rather more deliberately, turned out the lights, and got in between the sheets.

Almost immediately there were sounds; in the room, as of someone moving about. Belden set his teeth and listened to them. Of course, it was a case of nerves, and it probably meant that he was going to break down, to collapse. How suddenly it had come, and what a strange form it had taken! He wasn't seeing anything—he was just hearing things; and he always supposed that if—if—anything— anyone—came back, it was more apt to be seen than heard. Now it was over in the corner—in Kearney's corner. Naturally—that's where it would be. If he looked there, he might see something, but he did not care to look.

With a leap Belden was on the floor. He switched on the lights and examined the room carefully, even bending down, with a grim smile at his own fears, to look under the bed. He had not locked the door of his room when he entered, but he locked it now; then, with one of the strongest efforts of will he had ever made, he turned out the lights again and got back into bed.

The instant the darkness folded around him the sounds he had previously heard were repeated, in that far corner of the room. For an hour, the longest hour of his life till then, Belden lay and listened to them. Then, with a groan, he rose and turned on the lights. For a time, he had no idea how long, he sat on the side of the bed and waited for what would happen. In the morning, he decided, he would go to the medical officer and get a nerve tonic, without explaining why he needed it. In the meantime he would see what effect the light had on his morbid imaginings.

That it had some effect was clear at once. The sounds ceased, and in their place a deepened silence hung over the room—the silence of something passive, watching and waiting. Belden became convinced that he was not alone, that something he could not see, and mercifully, for the moment, could not hear, was with him. He experienced a sudden trembling, as if he were in a nervous chill, and he slipped back into bed, where he lay with open eyes staring straight before him. After a time his trembling stopped, and he drew a breath of relief as his pulses steadied. His nerves were not up to bearing the dark, that was all; so he would keep the light on, and in the morning he would get a tonic and would soon, be all right. He was very conscious that he must not *think* about that room or about anything which had happened recently. He centred his mind on events long passed—on student days, on girls he knew in the past, on big game he had shot—but no, when he shot that game Kearney had been with him, and he must not think of Kearney. He drove his memory back to his boyhood home, to the old swimming-pond, to the quiet fields and orchards where he had played. He slept.

When he awoke the sunshine was flooding his room, and in its gorgeous radiance the electric bulbs shone wanly, pale reminders of the unsubstantial horrors of the night. With a great throb of thankfulness he sprang out of bed, and stretched his athletic young body, as if shaking from his shoulders the horrors that had ridden him in the dark.

As he bathed and dressed he whistled cheerfully, and he ate his breakfast with the best appetite he had known for a week. There was much to be done that day, for he had been lying back a bit, and now he attacked his work with vigour, rejoicing in the distraction it brought him.

Once, as he crossed the parade-ground, and observed the quarters of the Army surgeon in the distance, a sudden memory of a suggested nerve tonic shot into his mind, but he ignored it with a smile. An experience such as he had had might happen to anyone— indeed, could hardly fail to happen, he supposed, given the same conditions. But it was over, and, by Jove, he was frankly glad it was. He wouldn't have wanted it indefinitely prolonged. At the thought a sudden shiver struck him, warmed though he was by the grateful sunshine.

That night he worked until almost seven o'clock, and when he started for his room to dress for a "family dinner" at the colonel's quarters, his mind was still filled with the details of a project on which he and one of his superior officers were working together. If he had not wholly forgotten his experience of the night before, it was certainly overlaid by more important reflections. And it was, therefore, with a shock of genuine surprise that he again heard behind him, as he walked upstairs, the sound of quick, soldierly footsteps.

Even as he heard them, his first conscious emotion was not fear but annoyance. Was he going through that business again? If he was, it was carrying things a bit too far. He did not deserve it. And then his annoyance turned upon himself.

Why the devil hadn't he gone to Clark, that morning, and got the tonic he needed? He had had his warning, which would probably have been enough for anyone else. He entered his room almost sulkily, and, as he passed through the door, had an odd sensation of something squeezing in with him—something that brushed his shoulder as it went. It was so definite that he was glad to reach the electric-switch and turn on the lights. And as he did this he glanced around expectantly, but there was nothing to be seen, though the sense of a presence in the room, intangible but pervasive, deepened momentarily.

In his heart Belden was very thankful that he was dining with the Blakes. A good dinner and cheerful companionship would brace him up, and he would come back, no doubt, in a different condition of mind and nerves.

He crossed the room to a cupboard to get the garments he meant to wear, and, as he did so, felt again that odd sense of something accompanying him, pressing close to him. It was as if a willing, eager presence tried to get ahead of him, to anticipate his wants. And now Belden recalled, with a quickening of his heartbeats, Kearney's occasional tendency to "get under his feet," as he had expressed it, when he had been drinking. He sat down in a chair to pull off his shoes, and felt suddenly that unseen hands were pulling at them as well. The perspiration started out on his face, and he took his handkerchief from his pocket and wiped it off with a hand which now, he observed with disapproval, was shaking visibly.

"Jove!" he muttered under his breath. "It's getting worse. I'll get that tonic tomorrow—won't I, *just!*"

By the time he was dressed he was trembling all over. Each article he had picked up had seemed to be handed to him, and he had been unable to lose for an instant that sense of a crowding presence, so near that it occasionally touched him. He believed he would hear as well as feel it if he turned his lights out, but he did not dare make the experiment. Instead, he left them burning, for he knew he would not have the courage to enter that dark house at midnight.

On his way to the colonel's quarters he stopped at the surgeon's, and, finding that gentleman already at dinner, casually dragged him from the table to his consulting-room, to demand a sedative and a nerve tonic.

"I'm not sleeping well," he explained.

The doctor nodded, and turning to the shelves behind him, began to handle bottles, and make up a prescription.

"I think," hazarded Belden, "I'd like something now—something quieting."

Dr. Clark looked rather surprised, but he mixed a dose of bromide and gave it to the young man without comment.

"I'll give you a little sulphonal, too," he remarked. "The dose is ten grains at bedtime. And take the tonic three times a day," he added, wrapping up the bottles. "You'll be all right in a week or two."

Belden dropped the small package into the pocket of his overcoat, and agreed politely that he would. There was an immense comfort in Clark's matter-of-fact attitude, and he did not remind himself that the doctor knew nothing of his condition beyond the fact that he was not sleeping well.

He enjoyed his dinner at the Blakes', and was so braced up by it that he even smiled to himself as he opened the door leading into his brightly lighted hall. Strange that he should have got into such a blue funk. He had actually been afraid to enter his own quarters! He turned off the hall light with a grin, and cheerfully started upstairs.

Just behind him, and very, very near, sounded the quick tap, tap of feet that followed him. They stopped as he entered his lighted room, but again something entered with him and pressed against him as he walked.

Belden staggered over to his bed, sat down on the side of it, took his head in his hands, and groaned. Then he found himself moving, as if to make room. Something, he thought, was sitting beside him, very close to him.

The night that followed was the most terrible he had ever known. Again he kept the lights burning, but he did not fall asleep until dawn, after he had taken two doses of sulphonal. To-night the thing was not in the distant corner—its corner—but hovering close to him. Several times he fancied that it was sitting on the side of the bed; twice he had the feeling that the blankets were being drawn over him; and, for one black moment, which brought out a cold sweat all over his body, he was certain that something was trying to creep in beside him. At that he cried out and sprang up.

"Kearney!" he cried. "Kearney! For Heaven's sake go back where you belong!"

The sound of his own voice, hoarse and strained, brought him to his senses. He sat down again, weak and trembling, on the side of the bed.

"Heavens!" he muttered. "So this is nerves! This is the kind of thing they do to a man. I've got to keep tight hold of that. It's only nerves."

He dared not get into his bed again, so he put on a heavy bath-robe, and spent the remainder of the night in a big chair, where by turns he dozed and awoke. He was in Dr. Clark's office before breakfast, and this time, without going into details, he gave that gentleman an idea of the nature of his sufferings. The doctor nodded with portentous wisdom.

"I rather expected something of the sort," he murmured, and added a few technical remarks on the subject of shocks and high-strung nervous systems, which meant very little to the pallid young man before him.

But Belden had made his own diagnosis, and was glad to have it confirmed. He departed with an additional supply of tonics and sedatives, and the fight of his life was on.

Under normal conditions Belden was a man of steady nerves, and early in life he had acquired the habit of thought. This helped him now, for he resolutely proceeded to consider his case as if it were the case of another, and to apply to it the cool judgment he would offer that other if such a victim came to him. These, then, were the facts. He was in a nervous condition caused by shock, and which time would undoubtedly correct. For the present his disease took the form of hallucinations—extremely unpleasant ones, to be sure, but to be regarded sternly as the baseless things they were. Darkness aided them, so he would shun darkness. They did not trouble him when he was with others, so he would be alone as rarely as he could. Towards this end he would, first of all, secure another servant, and keep him around his quarters.

The fitting candidate for the place was one Regan, a trooper in his company, who had been the close chum of Kearney and had taken the latter's place as substitute during Kearney's lapses from sobriety. Belden knew that Regan expected the job, and that he had been both surprised and chagrined by the officer's failure to take him on. But for excellent reasons Regan was the last man Belden desired to have near him now. In appearance, manner, carriage, and briskness of movement, he was much like his dead chum, and Belden, who knew the strength of the friendship that had bound the two men, realised that thus far Kearney was rarely out of Regan's thoughts. He had not blamed Belden for the disaster; no one had done that, for, as Belden had realised from the first, and as the "hearing" subsequently proved, all the conditions were too thoroughly understood by the officers and men of his regiment to permit any criticism of him.

But he did not want Regan's face before him, with its oddly subdued expression; and it was characteristic of "Teddy" Belden that he did what probably no other officer in his regiment would have taken the trouble to do—he sent for the trooper and told him why he could not use his services.

"You see, Regan," he said, at the end of his few words, "you and I have both been hit hard by this thing, and we'd keep it fresh in each other's minds even if we never spoke of it. We've got to forget it—if we can."

He ended with a sigh, and Regan, standing before him very stiff and straight, saluted respectfully.

"I understand, sir," he said, "and I guess you're right. Thank you, sir."

He saluted again and started to leave, but something in the attitude of the officer checked his steps. Belden was sitting hunched up in his chair, with his chin in his hands, staring at a spot on the floor. It was clear he had forgotten that he was not alone.

"I'm—I'm sorry, sir," faltered Regan, and, receiving no reply, got himself out of the room.

Belden's new "batman," a trooper named Murray, entered upon his duties the following day, and performed them efficiently enough, but with an effect wholly unforeseen by his superior. From the first hour of his service Belden was conscious of an extraordinary increase in the activities of the thing of his hallucination. It was, he told himself grimly, as if Kearney resented the presence of the newcomer. "And I didn't expect *that*," Belden reflected, "so how the deuce could I have subconsciously brought it about?" The sense of the Thing's nearness—he had begun to call it the Thing in his thoughts, though he was conscious of the unwisdom of thus giving it a name—was incessantly with him. He felt it touching him, brushing against him, and, most harrowing manifestation of all, leaping in, as it were, between himself and Murray as if to intercept the latter's efforts. If Murray mixed a drink for him, an unseen hand seemed to push it toward him. If Murray held his coat, he was invariably conscious of the little pull with which, in the past, Kearney had drawn it down. Murray always kept at a respectful distance from his superior— a distance just great enough, Belden reflected bitterly, to permit Kearney to step in between them. More frequently than he realised, he himself stepped back on to one side to avoid the proximity of the Thing, and after this had happened once or twice, Murray began to look at him curiously.

"Nervous as a cat the loot'n't is," he told his chums. "Jumps at shadows, he does. And he ain't sleepin', neither."

It was true that Belden was not sleeping. The nights were full of horrors whose varied and malignant forms he would never have dared to reveal to anyone. He rode until he was half dead with fatigue, and then lay awake until dawn, staring with wide eyes into his lighted room, and hearing now the incessant stir and movement around him that testified to the nocturnal activities of the Thing, even when the lights were on. More often Belden sat in his big chair and waited for the dawn, which brought him the release of an hour's sleep. At first he had fallen upon Clark's drugs as an exhausted swimmer clutches at a rescuer, and had turned from double doses of sulphonal to repeated doses of chloral. But these things, he had discovered, merely made matters worse by destroying his reasoning power. "As long as I can think it out," he told himself, "and remember that it's really nothing but nerves, I can stand it." So he had thrown away the growing collection of bottles Clark had pressed upon him, and was making his fight on exercise, fresh air and will-power, which were efficient aids as far as they went.

In a few weeks he had to let Murray go. The fellow, he realised, was noticing things, and wondering about them. For example, it had become a habit of Belden's to rise suddenly from a chair in which he had been about to sit down, because he had realised that the Thing was occupying it; and to turn from his bed because the Thing was between the sheets; and to step aside to let the Thing pass him—all of which surprised and startled Murray.

These conditions, also, made it impossible for Belden to spend much time with his friends. They, too, began to notice things he did, and to exchange worried glances.

It was May, three months after Kearney's death, before Belden made the first acknowledgment that he was losing his fight; and he made it to Kearney himself toward two o'clock one morning. He rose suddenly from the big chair in which he had been sitting, and threw out his arms in a gesture of utter despair.

"Kearney!" he cried: "My heavens, Kearney, if it's really you, let me alone! Haven't you punished me enough?"

He waited, as if he had uttered, an invocation and expected a response; but none came, though the rustling, moving presence in the room remained there. Belden listened to it for an instant, and spoke again.

"What do you want me to do?" he demanded. "Is it this?"

He crossed to his desk, and, opening a drawer, took from it the pistol with which he had killed Kearney, and which he had not used since that night. It was loaded, and he picked it up, and, holding it in the palm of his hand, stood staring down at it.

"Is it this?" he repeated. "Well, I guess it's the best way. A life for a life. Is that what you want, Kearney?"

The room was very still. For the moment he heard no steps, felt no movement. That was it, then; that was what Kearney wanted. His hand began to close on the weapon, then stiffened out suddenly. Something, he thought, had touched his fingers—something cold. He could not move them, nor could he move his feet. He stood rigid, staring down at the revolver, conscious of utter paralysis of effort and of a creeping ice chill. At last he spoke.

"So that isn't it!" he exclaimed. "You don't want that. It would be letting me off too easily. I see."

He tossed the revolver back into the still open drawer, and began to pace the floor. Until dawn came he walked back and forth, back and forth; and, close behind him, pressing forward against his shoulder at times, the Thing paced with him, step, by step.

The next day Belden applied for, and was granted, six months' sick leave; and two weeks later he sailed for France. He had been told of a doctor in Paris, a world-famous specialist in diseases of the nerves.

He would go to him and tell him his story, from start to finish.

He did so, and the physician, who had an excellent, command of English, listened to him with interest and sympathy.

"But, naturally, you understand what it is!" he exclaimed when the young man had finished.

"Of course. Nerves," replied Belden tersely.

"Exactly. Hold fast to that, and we can keep these runaway horses of yours—how do you say it?—in the middle of the road, and avoid a smash."

He monologued long and learnedly, and Belden, by listening with close attention, succeeded in grasping about half of what he said. But the concluding words were very clear.

"It rests wholly with you, my friend," the specialist declared. "It is for you to decide whether you will conquer this, or let it drive you mad."

Belden smiled grimly. He knew that very well.

"And remember, the longer it lasts, the harder it will be to overcome."

Belden's smile faded. He knew that, too.

"What's the prescription?" he demanded sombrely.

"Courage and time; and, again, *courage*."

"Time hasn't helped so far," muttered the patient. "I've grown worse from the start."

The physician nodded.

"Because you remained in the place where the thing happened. That was a mistake. You should have left it at once."

"But the Thing has followed me—I mean, I have the same symptoms here."

"They will pass—*if you do not fear them*."

The doctor gave the last words very slowly, and eye to eye.

Belden set his teeth and straightened his shoulders.

"I'll do my best," he said quietly.

"Good! You shall come with me to my place in the country, where I go for the summer. I take with me a few patients only, and my family. We will give you what you need—an absolute change of environment, a new life."

Belden liked his doctor, and when he reached the country place in Touraine he liked that, too. He liked the charm and novelty of French domestic and social life, and the beauty of the valley of the Loire. Most of all, he liked the daughter of the specialist, a charming girl of eighteen just graduated from a convent in Tours, and with a singing voice whose beauty made his heart, turn over.

At first he treated her as if she were the young sister he had always longed for but never had. Then, almost unconsciously, he developed, a deeper interest in her, and he ended by falling in love with the thoroughness and abandon that characterised all he did. In his life he had had a few sentimental affairs, which, looked back upon now in the blaze of this wonderful revelation, he diagnosed scornfully as "puppy loves." This experience was altogether different, and he began his wooing with the impetuosity and magnetism that had made him one of the best-liked officers in the Army.

Daily he walked or drove for hours with Victoire, properly chaperoned by her mother or the maiden aunt who was an almost speechless appendage of the household. And each evening Victoire sang for him, played to him, and improved his French until she was banished to her room at ten o'clock.

In the fullest sense of the words, Belden was leading a new life, and as the weeks passed he made a discovery. The Thing was disappearing. It no longer followed him upstairs. For a week or ten days at a time he did not hear it in his room, and when he did it seemed to move about feebly, like a Thing whose vitality was gone.

When, three months later, he was pronounced cured, he promptly asked Dr. Sequard for his daughter's hand. The physician hesitated.

"I will be frank with you, my friend," he then said quietly. "Personally, I like you. Your family and your profession are excellent. That you have an independent income and can support your wife in comfort is most satisfactory. But, candidly, I would ask a better nervous system in the husband of my daughter."

Belden stared at him uncomprehendingly, as one who listens to babble in a strange tongue.

"But, good heavens," he cried, "I'm as right as rain now! I never had a 'nerve' in my life till six months ago, and I never expect to have one again. Why, I've almost forgotten that I ever had any."

Dr. Sequard studied him.

"The fear of the Thing is no longer with you, then—not in the least degree?" he asked curiously.

The young man laughed and flushed.

"Why, of course not." he cried. "I can't even understand why I let it worry me at all. I'm ashamed of myself. It seems so absurd."

Dr. Sequard's face cleared.

"If it already appears absurd, then the cure is assured," he smiled. "And, monsieur"—he drew his heels together and bowed with a Frenchman's formal courtesy—"it will give me pleasure to accept you as my son-in-law."

Lieutenant Belden and his bride had a three months' honeymoon—a glorious one. Then they sailed for home, and the young man reported for duty to his commanding officer in November, on the last day of his leave.

"I have good news for you, lieutenant," smiled "the Old Man," after their greetings were over. "The regiment's ordered to Egypt—Cairo. That will be a congenial home for a charming French bride, who certainly should not be buried in a frontier post. Eh?"

Belden was delighted. He rejoiced in the broader and more interesting life that awaited her in the East. On their arrival at the post he had taken her to his old quarters, intending to remain there only a week or two, until he could find more suitable ones; but now it seemed useless to change, as the big move East was to be made in December. He settled into the routine of his military life, and worked hard to make up for lost time; and he was preparing a report in his old room late one night while his wife chatted with some women guests in the living-room below, when, for the first time in many months, he heard a movement in the corner—Kearney's corner.

For a moment he did not recognise it, but looked up expecting to see a fallen newspaper rustle in a draught or possibly under the movements of a frightened mouse. There was nothing on the floor, however, and as he stared, puzzled for an instant, he heard the sounds of footsteps in the room. His heart dropped a beat.

"So," he said dully. "You're at it again, are you?"

There seemed no doubt that the Thing was at it. He felt it come near and press up against his shoulder. The perspiration broke out upon his forehead.

"Heavens!" he cried. "Don't make me go through *that* again!"

Was it only a few months ago he had told Dr. Sequard that this obsession was "absurd"? It had seemed so then. Now, in a single moment, it had reduced him to a condition of craven terror. Yes; he was afraid—afraid, though the one sure cure for his malady was courage.

A laugh came up to him—Victoire's laugh. In the lower hall she was saying good-bye to her callers. In another moment she would be upstairs, with him, in the room with the Thing. Would she hear it? Certainly not, for it was not really there. But she would see her husband trembling. She would realise that he was afraid of some-thing, she would discover the truth; and thus, through him, she, too, would come under the terrible dominion of the Thing.

At the thought a sudden fierce fury shook Belden, followed as suddenly by a cool and deadly calm. The Thing had tortured him and he had borne it. But that it should now threaten to torture, through him, the woman he loved—that it should lay a blight on her youth and wreck her happiness, oh, no, that simply could not be allowed! He had borne it. *She should not*! And his courage stiffened and hardened under the decision like molten steel that is suddenly chilled. He had married a girl—almost a child. She had given up for him her country and her family. Her dependence on him was absolute, and he would prove worthy. He would kick the obsession of Kearney dead out of his life, and hers as promptly as he would have kicked Kearney alive and drunk out of her bedroom.

Suddenly he realised that the noise in the room had stopped; the sense of an unseen presence had vanished. He was free; he was master of himself. He was a man in every inch of him—a man never again (he knew it in that moment with absolute conviction) to be afraid. Courage alone, even if he had had enough of it, might not have won his fight. But courage and love together—these two irresistible forces could conquer anything. Already they had banished from his life the-devil of nerves and the greater devil of fear—and she who was Love's handmaiden now stood facing him in the doorway, returning his triumphant smile.

WHEN SPIRITS STEAL

Philippa Forest

In the years immediately after the First World War there was a surge of interest in spiritualism, a natural desire by those who had lost loved ones to find some way to make contact again. The magazines catered for this need in various ways, sometimes with articles by the great and the good—more often than not by Sir Arthur Conan Doyle or Sir Oliver Lodge—arguing that it is possible to contact the dead, and sometimes with stories of spiritualism or the occult. Pearson's Magazine ran several of these, including the "Borderland" series by Philippa Forest. The series began in the March 1920 issue with "The Seven Fires" which introduced Peter Carwell, a successful businessman who trades in Oriental fare, along with his "Watson", an artist called Wilton. The story concerned a house seriously affected by spontaneous combustion. The series ended with "A Satyr Who Stole a Bride", about nature spirits, in the June 1920 issue.

Philippa Forest was the alter ego of journalist Marion Holmes (1867–1943) who was very active in the women's suffrage movement. She had helped found the Margate Pioneer Society in 1897 with the aims of educating women in the law and to promote equality. Later settling in Croydon, she became president of the local branch of the Women's Social and Political Union and joined the National Executive of the Women's Freedom League. In 1907 she was sentenced to two weeks in Holloway prison for taking part in a protest march at the House of Commons. She remained active in the movement right through to after the First World War, chairing meetings and writing plays performed at suffrage events.

Meanwhile, as Philippa Forest she explored her interest in spiritualism and astrology. Her own psychic experiences began when she was seven. Whilst playing with another girl in an old shed in Yorkshire she had a premonition of something swinging above her. A week or two later a man hanged himself there.

There were not enough Peter Carwell stories to make up a complete book and, as a result, they have been forgotten—until now.

B OTH CARWELL AND I ALWAYS AVOID THE MEMORY OF THIS incident, for, unlike most of the problems we have faced together, it ended in a hopeless situation. And yet—I don't know! If we could get Mary's version of it, perhaps—but I am beginning my story at the wrong end.

It began at the end of a long August day's tramp in Somerset. Carwell and I were on a holiday tour. I had been over the ground before, and was obsessed by the memory of an inn that I knew was somewhere "just round the corner." I could not remember the name, or anything about it, except that it was a "perfect picture"—latticed windows, a swinging sign, thatched roof, an overshadowing oak-tree, and a duck-pond!

"Add a rapacious landlady and impossible beds; I know those inns!" said Carwell, disgruntledly. "If we don't strike it within the next ten minutes I, at any rate, shall go back to Redthorne. We've covered a good twenty miles to-day, and I'm at the end of my tether. Your legs are a generation younger than mine, remember, Wilton."

A rustic turned the corner of the lane at that moment and I hailed him.

"Aw—you du mean 'The Green Dragon' at Chigley 'Ighfield," he said, after he had ruminated for a while. "Goa to the end o' this ro-aad, and bear tu your right for a matter of 'alf a mile or zoa, an' you'll strike it zurely."

Which we did; and even Carwell admitted that it was all my fancy had painted it—outside anyway.

And within ten minutes we were joyfully acknowledging that the inside was worthy of the picturesque exterior. It is true the huge feather beds in the rooms to which we were shown for a much needed "wash and brush-up" did not look exactly the kind of resting places one would have chosen for a hot August night, but—as I pointed out to Carwell—spring mattresses would have been as great an anachronism in those dark low-ceilinged rooms as electric light in a hermit's cave.

"We've gone back to the days of Dickens, and judging from the delicious aroma that is coming up from the kitchen, we are going to be treated to the welcome and good cheer that he gave us to understand was always on tap in his days. Ham, my dear chap," I sniffed rapturously, "ham—and eggs—and home-made bread—and jam—or I've missed my guess!"

The landlady matched her wares very happily, we found. She was a broad-shouldered, deep-bosomed woman, with smooth dark hair and kindly twinkling eyes, and her solicitude that we should make a "real good tea" made that succulent meal like a school-boy's homecoming feast. When at last we declared ourselves absolutely unable to accommodate another drop or crumb, she asked how long we should be staying.

"If it depends on *me* it will be for the rest of our lives!" I answered enthusiastically.

A slow rumble of laughter came from her ample white-bibbed chest.

"Well na-ow, that's good hearin', I'm zure!" she drawled. "It du show you've relished your food praper—an' you du both look the better for it, I will zay. Mary, you can come in an' clear. The gentlemen are goin' to have a smoke na-ow."

Mary came in on her words and began heaping together the remains of the meal.

She interested me from the first; I don't know why, exactly, for there was nothing in the least physically attractive about her. A short, rather stout girl of about twenty, with wispy fair hair, and big blue eyes that flickered nervously in a face of yellowish pallor, the only beauty she had lay in her hands, which were small and remarkably well-shaped, though roughened with work. But there was something about her—something behind those frightened, childish eyes— that appealed to me. And to Carwell also, judging from the quick, interested glance he shot at her as soon as she entered. It was not intelligence; far from it. She was rather stupid indeed, as we soon discovered, and so nervous that she could not touch anything in the way of china without making it rattle like castanets. It was rather an ingratiating air of—well, the only word that I can think of to describe it is "motherliness," incongruous though it seems consider- ing our respective ages—that wrapped you round in an atmosphere of goodwill.

We hadn't been there two days before we found that there was no need to wonder whether you might ask Mary for a cup of tea, or anything else, in unauthorised hours. She would beam as if you had done her a favour, instead of asked one; and though half the tea might be spilt in the saucer by her jerking hands, what you did get would be piping hot and strong. It was the same with her waiting at table. She would drop, or spill, or rattle, nearly everything she touched, but the plates she handed would be thoroughly clean, and the silver bright and shining, and everything at just the right degree of heat.

We realised we were on velvet the very first day, and the next morning I wired for my painting kit, and announced my intention of finishing my holiday there.

"And if you know when you're well off you'll do the same, Peter," I advised. "You'll find a 'barrow,' or a Druid's altar, or cave, or something of the sort to play with, if you look about, I'm sure. I noticed a very promising looking mound in a field this morning."

"Probably last winter's turnips," he commented lazily. "But that's all right. I'll stay as long as this weather lasts. I can always put in time happily with a rod and fly, even if I catch nothing."

I was not in the least surprised to find that Mary quickly developed a devotion for Carwell. He has an extraordinarily soothing effect on highly strung nerves, and his kindness and consideration are as proverbial amongst his friends as his unique knowledge and experience are amongst students of occultism.

"I'd like to hear the story of that girl's childhood," he said, one evening after she had brought in the after-dinner coffee. "She has either been badly frightened, or—"

He stopped as Mrs. Raplin came in to know if the meal we had just eaten had been satisfactory and served "praper an' hot."

"It was as near perfection in every respect as a meal has any business to be," answered Carwell. "You have a treasure in that girl, Mrs. Raplin. Her only fault is her nervousness. Was she ever in an accident, or badly frightened as a child, do you know?"

"No—not as I ever 'eard on, an' I should a-done if she had been, for she's my own niece, an' I've knowed her ever since she was no bigger than that—" she indicated a minute something that could have gone into one of the pewter pots that decorated the sideboard. "But she's allus been a frightened gormy—terrified of her own shadder, as the sayin' is. I dunno as whether her 'abit of—'Ere, John! I wants you! Doan't you be in sich a hurry, na-ow! 'Tain't half-past *yet!*"

She darted to the door with lumbering agility to intercept the ostler, who was making rapid preparations for departure. I speculated idly for a few minutes on what Mary's "habit" could be, but Carwell seemed disinclined to pursue the subject, so it soon dropped.

I do not know whether my constant contact with Carwell as a Borderland expert at that time quickened such psychic faculties as I possessed or not, but it is certain that that night—a fateful night as it turned out to be for at least one of the inmates of The Green Dragon—I was restless and disturbed. It may have been the atmospheric conditions, of course, for it was abominably hot and still, with the oppression that comes before a thunderstorm. I tossed and turned, and finally got up, slipped into a few clothes and leant out of the window for a breath of refreshing air.

There must have been a strong breeze up above for a bank of thick low-lying clouds was racing up from the south, and blotting out the waning moon, which hung low down in the sky like a huge golden plate, out of which a giant had taken a greedy bite. There had been a sharp shower earlier in the evening, but it was evident we were in for something more drastic now. A deep warning rumble came from overhead, and the leaves of the oak-tree gave a mysterious rustle, as if the hidden lives within it were gathering closer together for protection. A few heavy drops fell with an audible patter into the pools that had been left by the previous shower, and I stretched out farther to let them fall on my bared neck and hands. As I did so I saw a figure slip across the road and disappear round the corner of the house. The next minute the storm burst with a terrific crash, which seemed to release a spring somewhere in the clouds, for immediately afterwards the rain came down in a solid sheet.

The sight of the quickly swamped windowsill reminded me that I had left a canvas near the open window of the coffee-room. It would be spoilt if it got wet, as it certainly would if it were not moved.

I had reached the top of the stairs on my way to the rescue when the sound of soft padding footsteps coming from the direction of the kitchen made me pause. The Green Dragon was invariably sunk in slumber by eleven o'clock at the latest.

Who could be prowling about at this hour? I peered into the darkness below and saw a short figure disentangle itself from the shadows and begin to ascend the stairs.

"Who is there?" I said sharply.

There was no answer but the soft pad of feet. I clung to the rail at the stairhead feeling decidedly "nervy," and the next minute the figure brushed past me. As it did so it gave a little nervous cough, and I bent over the rail in a fit of silent laughter at my own expense. It was Mary!

She crept noiselessly down the corridor in the direction of her room, and I waited until I heard the faint click of a closing door. Then I went down, retrieved my canvas, and returning, undressed and was soon fast asleep, in spite of the inferno the storm was creating a few feet above my head.

"You look tired this morning," I said to her when she entered the coffee-room with breakfast the next morning, "and no wonder!"

She gave a startled gasp and the dish of bacon and eggs nearly slipped from her hands. I fielded it just in time and set it on the table.

"I—what do you mean, sir?"

I shook my head portentously.

"Half-past twelve when you came in last night. Shocking hours you do keep, Mary, to be sure!"

It never occurred to me that I should scare her with my chaff. Nocturnal adventures of the kind one would instinctively associate with some girls somehow never entered one's mind in connection with Mary. If I thought about it at all I thought she had been paying a late visit to friends or relatives in the village a couple of miles away. It gave me a genuine shock when her sickly face turned a deep distressed crimson.

"*Me?*" she gasped breathlessly. "I was in my bed by ten last night an' I never stirred till six this mornin'—that I'll swear on the Bible!" Then she buried her face in her hands and burst into a fit of low choking sobbing that made me feel a perfect brute.

"Oh! for goodness sake don't do that, Mary—my dear good girl, *don't!*" I implored in acute distress.

"I—I never—that I'll swear—"

"Of course you didn't! I was only joking," I lied hastily. "For pity's sake stop! Here's Mr. Carwell coming. He'll punch my head if he knows I've upset you, and serve me right too! Do stop, there's a good girl. I was only chaffing—really."

She stopped crying as suddenly as she had begun, and stared absent-mindedly at the table for a minute or two. Then she gave a sigh that seemed to come from the very soles of her clumsy boots, and superfluously set the salt-cellar straight.

"I'm sorry I been so silly, sir," she said in a trembling voice, "but you scairt—what's that?"

Carwell entered as a noisy clatter of hoofs outside came to a jarring stop. John had ridden up on a lumbering cart horse, and thrown himself off with an urgent shout of "Missis! Missis! Mary! Where are ye? Here be news an' no mistaake! That old villain Hodgson 'ave been found murdered in his bed—smothered, or strangled, or summat!"

There was a shrill cry from Mrs. Raplin and a clamour of voices all asking questions at once. Carwell and I went to the window but before we had caught more than a momentary glimpse of the excited group round the door a dull thud in the room recalled our attention. Mary had fallen in a dead faint to the floor.

*

For some reason that I did not attempt to define, I was not surprised to see her walking slowly across the fields towards us that afternoon. I was painting, and Carwell was idly pitching pebbles and tufts of grass into the river. We had been talking in a desultory fashion of Quilter's latest scoop on 'Change and his ingenuous pride in his newly-arrived son.

By mutual consent we had avoided any mention of the events of the morning. We had both stayed behind until Mary "came to," as Mrs. Raplin phrased it, and the look of furtive terror in her face when she regained consciousness, coupled with the agitation she had shown at my knowledge of last night's escapade, had caused me a vague uneasiness. Thoughts—too indeterminate to be called suspicions—were buzzing and stinging all the time just below my active consciousness with the maddening persistence of a gadfly, but I steadily refused to recognise them.

Carwell was uneasy, too, I could see, though he gave little indication of it beyond a slight restlessness. He was evidently expecting her, for when she appeared he said, "She's coming, then—that's right!" in a relieved tone.

I was horrified at the dead whiteness of her face and the indigo shadows under her eyes when she came to a stop before us.

"Here, sit down," I said, pushing my camp-stool in her direction; "you look ghastly tired."

She seated herself without a word and folded her hands in her lap like a weary child. Her eyes were fixed on Carwell. He returned her gaze steadily.

"Tell me all about it," he said gently.

"That's what I come for. I shall go ravin' mad if I don't—though I dunno what you'll think of me—but I'm past carin', anyway."

Suddenly she turned to me.

"What made you say that this mornin', sir? You wasn't jokin', I know. What made you say it?"

I hesitated a moment; then I told her. After all, in the state she was in, a shock—if it proved one—might be beneficial rather than otherwise. She nodded her head slowly as I finished.

"I remember comin' in an' the rain comin' down all of a sudden like a waterspout. I just got under cover in time. But I didn't hear no one speak."

"You were walking in your sleep," interjected Carwell authoritatively.

"Yes, sir." She looked at him blankly for a minute; then her cheeks flushed and she clasped and unclasped her hands with feverish intensity. Suddenly the floodgates of speech were unlocked.

"I done it ever since I was a child, but I thought as how I was growin' out of it. Oh, nobody'll ever know what I gone through all my life! I dunno if God made me like this, but, if He did, he must have had a powerful spite agen me for summut or another! When I was nothin' but a tiny kiddie I used to see faces an' 'ear voices no one else could see or 'ear, and they scairt the wits out o' me almost. An' once, for a year or two, it was just—hell!

"Everybody thought I was possessed by the Devil, an' I don't wonder. They chivvied me away as if I'd got plague, or smallpox, or summut. I couldn't play wi' the others; no one wouldn't let me mind their babies—an' I loved doin' that" (oh, poor Mary, how well I could imagine that!), "an' everybody but me mother an' one or two others 'ud jeer at me an' call me a witch—"

"But why?" I interrupted indignantly.

"'Cause things 'appened when I was there. Pictures would fall from the walls, an' the crocks jump off the tables an' smash themselves on the floor, an' stones 'ud fly through the winders... An' then some clever men comed down from London an' watched me… Oh, I wished I was dead many a time when I was a kiddie! 'Twasn't as if I *wanted* to do it, or as if I got anythin' by it. I didn't. I just wanted to be like the others, an' play an' laugh, and look after the little uns an' when I went to bed—go to sleep. But I was tormented wi' dreams—beastly, horrible dreams!—an' I had to be tied to the bed-post 'cause I used to wander about the 'ouse… It got a bit better as I got older, an' I was hopin' I was growin' out of it… but last night I dreamt agen—oh, my God!"

She hid her face in her hands and shuddered violently.

Carwell clasped one of her wrists with firm steady fingers, and after a minute she looked up and resumed her pitiful monologue.

"I'd gone to bed pretty tired out, an' I was soon asleep. It seemed a long time after, but I suppose it couldn't 'a' been so very long, that a whisper woke me. 'Get up,' it said, 'an' go to him.' An' I got up an' dressed, knowin' I was dreamin' all the time, if you can under-stand. I knew that if anyone 'eard me stirrin' I should be stopped, so I moved so quiet as a mouse, 'cause I felt if I couldn't go I should die… Presently I was out an' walkin' down the road. 'Twas only then I knew where I had to go, an' who *he* was—an' I knew, too, who 'twas that was guidin' me…

"You never 'eard of Hodgson, of course, sir, but everybody about here knows him well enough. A surly, cruel beast, who led his wife a dog's life right up to the day of her death a few months back. 'Twas believed he'd tried to get rid of her several times after she come into a bit o' money from a cousin, p'raps he did kill her in the end, an' when he fell off a hay-cart which went over 'im and lamed 'im a while ago, 'twas very few felt any pity. Served 'im right, they all said, an' some declared as well as how they believed *she'd* 'ad a hand in it… An' though poor folks is mostly ready to see a neighbour through any trouble, he'd 'a' fared badly if a niece hadn't come to look after 'im. He lived in that cottage the other side o' the wood there—near the stone quarry—a lonesome place enough, an' out o' the main track... Well, it was *him* I had to go to..."

"There was a light shinin' in the winder, an' he called out 'Come in, whoever ye are.' when I knocked at the door. He laughed when I comed in an' stood before 'im. Heaven knows what he thought I'd come for—but it 'ud be beastly enough if born in his mind, I'd swear to that!"

She paused, and the painful flush in her sallow cheeks burned deeper.

"Was he alone? Where was the niece?" asked Carwell.

"Gone 'ome for the night. She don't stay after nine o'clock. She'd evidently gone earlier last night an' left him to cook his own supper, for a little table wi' a basin an' some flour an' milk was by the side o' the bed, an' a tiny paraffin stove was flarin' an' makin' the place smell worse than usual—an' that's bad enough, for that Ellen is a dirty feckless drabbit, as everyone knows.

"Well, I shut the door an' stepped up to the bedside. He'd upset whatever it was he was tryin' to make, an' some of the flour an' milk had trickled on to the floor.

"'Shall I get some supper for you?' I asked, an' he laughed agen in his disgustin' way.

"'Zure yu can, an' I'll pay yu for it wi' a kiss—if that's what yu be wantin''—an' he added somethin' else that I can't remember—only when he said it I knew all at once what it was I had to do...

"I mixed him some flour porridge an' made a bit of toast at the fire, an' then I put it on a tray an' took it to him. He'd been layin' quiet while I was getting it ready, an' I saw why when I went up to the bed an' looked at him. He was scared—scared to death of *me!* He lay on his back wi' his eyes glarin' an' his mouth dropped open.

"'Who be yu?' he says in a hoarse whisper. 'What be yu goin' to do? When yu comed in yu looked like Mary Amherst up at The Green Dragon, but now you're like—Susan? You got a young face, but your eyes are like hers, an' your 'ands—look at 'em—what yu done to 'em? Them's not the 'ands of a young maid! They're old, an' big, an' wrinkled, like Susan's! What be yu going' to do?'

"He began on a whisper, but he ended up on a dretful shriek, an' shrinked back in the bed up agen the wall, pushin' out at me all the time wi' his 'ands... I took the tray away agen, an' as I did so I looked at my 'ands—an' he was right. They was not the 'ands of a young maid, smooth an' small as they are now.'

She held them out in front of her, and regarded them curiously for a moment, then she twisted them again in that feverish, restless clasp. Neither Carwell nor I spoke. The horror of her story had turned me cold and numb. I knew what was coming, and I would have given almost anything I possessed to stop her—but I couldn't.

"They was knotted an' big an' strong—strong as a man's, I felt— an' I was glad. I never hated anything so much in my life as I hated that whimperin' crouchin' thing on that bed... I picked up a cushion that was layin' on a chair, went back to the bed agen an' bent over him.

"'Susan!' he screamed, 'Susan—don't.—I niver meant no harm to yu, Susan!'

"'That's the last lie you'll tell in this world, Dick Hodgson!' says I... An it was." She stopped abruptly.

I looked at the painting kit lying about me on the grass, at the placid river and group of trembling alder trees, and wondered if I were not in the grip of a horrible dream, as Mary Amherst had been the night before.

"And then you woke up?" asked Carwell.

"I never woke till six this mornin'. I told Mr. Wilton that—didn't I, sir?—when I took the breakfast in. No, after he was... still... I come out, shut the door, an' come home. An' Mr. Wilton saw me go upstairs, he says."

Carwell sat perfectly quiet. I gathered my wits together with an effort. *Something* had to be said to comfort the poor girl, and if it meant my forswearing myself—well, it did, that was all.

"Don't take any notice of what I said, Mary," I began. "I saw someone come upstairs, it is true, but I don't know that it was you. How should I? It was very dark. I only guessed, and stupidly chaffed you on that assumption. You had a horrible dream, but it *was* only a dream."

I flung an indignantly imploring glance at Carwell. Why didn't he explain to her that she had been the victim of an extraordinary instance of thought transference, or witnessed the scene in her astral body, or something? He could make it clear and plausible—didn't I know it? But he sat there with his eyes broodingly fixed on the river and said nothing. So I recklessly plunged in.

"It was an unusually vivid dream, that was all," I repeated. "Your mind, which is like a photographic plate ready to receive impressions, simply recorded the thoughts and feelings of the person who committed the crime, and in your sleep you translated them into your personal experiences—thought you were doing it yourself, you know. That's what happened, isn't it, Carwell? I've had the same kind of dreams myself," I invented glibly, "and they seemed so real that I was not sure when I woke whether they had actually happened or not. I remember once I dreamt I was at a fire—"

"Yes, sir," said Mary simply, "only, when I looked at my house shoes this mornin' they was all muddy, an'—an' underneath the mud when I scraped it off there was a cakin' of flour..."

A nervous tremor suddenly shook her from head to foot.

"Will they hang me for it, do you think, Mr. Carwell, sir? I never meant—I—why, I wouldn't 'urt so much as a kitten—"

She began to sob helplessly.

"They certainly will not hang you, Mary. Even our muddle-headed juries would have to listen to the men I'd bring—oh! don't cry like that, you poor child—you poor child! You are no more guilty really than I am, or Mr. Wilton. You were just a blind instrument in the hands of something infinitely stronger than yourself"—his voice trailed off into silence. After all his first instinct had been right. Scientific explanations could bring no balm to a soul in agony.

Before she left us he made her promise that she would speak to no one else on the matter. She gave the required assurance readily enough, but it was evident she was not thinking much about it. A fit of dreamy lassitude had succeeded her feverish outburst and she spoke and moved like a dazed child.

Carwell looked after her pitifully as she walked slowly away.

"I suppose rigid upholders of the letter of the law would say we were compounding a felony, Wilton. But are you prepared to fling that poor bewildered soul on the tender mercies—well, of course I knew! I don't think any suspicion is likely to fall on her; the only clue would be her footprints leading from the cottage, and the heavy rain will have washed those away. But we will stay until after the inquest, and—should the need unhappily arise—I shall ask to be allowed to speak on her behalf."

"What would you say? That she was possessed by the spirit of the dead man's wife, and executed a delayed vengeance on him at her bidding? My dear Peter, do you *really* see a British jury giving serious consideration to that plea?"

"I'm afraid I don't, in spite of what I said to the girl just now, and yet it is the truth."

"Did you suspect from the first that she was mediumistic?"

"Yes, she bears all the marks of it. And I've been expecting a crisis of some kind for the last few days—those flickering, frightened eyes of hers gave her away. Of course I had no idea it would take the terrible form it has done, but when she fainted after hearing the news this morning I felt sure that she knew something about it."

"I hope the others won't suspect anything from that faint!"

"There's not much fear of that. Luckily for Mary her reputation as a 'frightened gormy, terrified of her own shadder' will protect her."

I began slowly putting my kit together. The light was perfect, but I had no heart for work just then. And yet I dreaded going back to the inn. Should I be able to watch Mary's little jerking hands performing kindly offices for us again without remembering that they had held a cushion firmly and ruthlessly down over a twitching, terrified face until it was—still? Heaven knows I pitied her from the depths of my heart, but I did not want to see her again until the horror had dimmed a little. It was no use dreaming of flight, however. Carwell had said we must stay for a few days longer, and that settled the matter.

"Do you think her hands really did change as she says?" I asked as I wiped my brushes perfunctorily. "It was a gruesome detail that I should think would be beyond anyone's powers of invention—let alone that poor unhappy girl's."

"I've no doubt they did—to her and that wretched terror-stricken man, anyway. Suggestion could make any of us see cabbages as kings if we were brought sufficiently under its sway."

Fortunately we were not called upon to do anything. The verdict at the inquest was "Murder by some person or persons unknown," and not so much as a whisper arose that connected Mary with the crime.

The following day we left, and about a week afterwards I had a long letter from Mrs. Raplin, telling me she was sending on some handkerchiefs I had left behind. After this she added:

"You will be sorry to hear as how we have lost our poor Mary. She either slipped into the river by accident when she was walking in her sleep, a habit she's had since she was scarce more than a baby, or drownded herself a-purpose last night, and her poor corpse was bringed home at midnight."

And that is why I said at the beginning that if we could have Mary's version perhaps we should find that she did not consider it a "hopeless situation." In the next world, at least, one must believe that the scales of Justice swing true.

THE HOUSE OF THE BLACK EVIL

Eric Purves

When John Reed Wade, the editor of Pearson's Magazine, *ran the following story in the May 1929 issue, he announced it as "One of the most original mystery stories ever written." In fact, so taken was he with the story that it received a major advance billing in the previous issue and the cover illustration, with artwork by Kenneth Inns. It portrayed the mystified postman staring through the letter-box into impenetrable darkness, the scene which opens the story.*

Yet, original though the story is, and full of atmosphere, to my knowledge it has never been reprinted. What's more, I'm not even sure its author wrote anything else. It's certainly not a name I've come across elsewhere and I can't find it in any index or archive. So perhaps Purves was a genuine one-hit wonder.

T HE PECULIAR BEHAVIOUR OF THE POSTMAN, AT THE TOP OF the steps, again called my attention to that dismal and forbidding house. That usually discreet official was actually kneeling on one knee and peering through the letter-slot, his letter-bag a shapeless lump on the doorstep.

I hesitated for a moment at the foot of the steps, but it was none of my business; a letter had probably stuck. Anyway, that postman was a good fellow, with whom I had had many cheerful conversations; if he chose to do unusual things why should I interfere?

I made as if to go on, though reluctantly, for that shuttered, gaunt, ill-favoured house fascinated me always, when the postman, standing up, turned and saw me. At once, in the strangest agitation, he called me by name, urgently and yet, as it were, in a distraction, and not looking at me, but stepping back and surveying the whole house hastily and anxiously.

Let me confess. I obeyed his summons indeed, but in what a confusion of dread, curiosity and amazement! Imagine then, my feelings when, on my joining him on the top step, that postman said nothing, gave no greeting, made no movement save to gaze at me with troubled eyes of fear, and to point at the letter-slot with a hand which shook.

I forced myself to kneel as he had done, to lift the flap and to peer through the slot. There was nothing there, only a black darkness.

★

Furious at the trick he had played upon me, I rose angrily to my feet to confront the postman. At once, however, observing my evident anger, he spoke.

"No, sir; no, sir," he said, "there is no letter-box; that's the hall you are looking into. And it's black—black dark. And the letters, sir, they disappear!"

I gazed at him. I had a moment in which I thought he was crazy, a moment in which I thought he was drunk; but no, this man was sane and sober, but terribly afraid. I did not so much as begin to understand him, however. Suddenly, without any apology, he pulled my morning paper from under my arm, thrust it, folded lengthwise, into my hand and said, with a sort of gasp:

"Shove it in, sir, shove it in and *watch* it!"

This was incomprehensible. Again I knelt. I put the paper to the slot, and as I did so he cried:

"Slowly!"

And I thrust it in slowly.

How shall I describe what happened? There was the door, there the letter-flap in the clear unshadowed light of bright but hazy morning. There was the wide black oblong of the letter-slot cut by the printed white of a folded *Times*. Now, when you thrust a paper into a hole you can see it go in. There is a part outside and a part, still visible, inside; shadowed maybe, but visible all the same. But as I pushed in that newspaper it disappeared. There was the part outside, then the line of the letter box, then—nothing, blackness!

Amazed, I hastily withdrew the paper; at once it reappeared. For a second I hesitated; then suddenly all my fear dropped from me, and with a little laugh I thrust my fingers into the slot, confident that they would encounter some strip of black cloth put there against the draught. There was nothing.

"No, sir," said the postman; "I've felt again and again; this has been like this for days; there's nothing there. Them letters simply disappears—disappears into blackness. 'Tisn't right, sir; there's something too much like magic about it. And where are the people of the house, sir? Never opened, never unshuttered; but the police men on the beat say they believe there's people in there, and certainly it's a live address, for I've brought a lot of letters here!"

While he spoke I had been thrusting my own hand into the slot. Believe me although there was nothing tangible to explain it, my hand also, like the newspaper was cut off sharply from sight across the line of the door.

The inexplicable is always fearful. All my dread returned, and was increased a hundredfold as I looked up at the postman.

My own house was on the opposite side of the square, and it happened that I had observed the arrival of the effects of the people whom I presumed to be the present occupiers. At all events I had observed this house with some curiosity for several weeks, for whereas before the furniture came it had stood confessedly empty, its unshuttered windows, void of blinds, revealing the empty, barren rooms, since that date, every window had been closely shuttered I had never seen any sign of life; no smoke from chimney, nor waiting milk bottle at any hour. Once before I had seen letters delivered; and now this extraordinary puzzle.

Upon a common impulse, and silently wondering, the postman and I went together down the steps. I was not surprised when, without a word, my companion hitched up his bag and strode rapidly away upon his round. He knew I was a man of leisure; he knew that at once I should begin to probe the matter to the bottom; he knew that, whatever I might find out, I should not leave him uninformed.

While I stood with my back to the house something of my dread left me. I could think more clearly. At once it was obvious that nothing could be cleared up without getting into the house. Accordingly I re-mounted the steps and pulled the bell.

At once, as if I had pulled the handle of a shower bath, the full chilling flood of unreasoning terrors descended upon me. I heard the clang of the distant bell. Sheer terror held me motionless. Nothing whatever happened.

At last, after what seemed an eternity, the cheerful whistle of an errand-boy passing in the road below broke the spell. I did not ring again. Instead, with an abruptly formed resolve, I set off to seek the house agent's office.

It happened that I not only knew who the agent was, but also that he was a good friend of mine. Once more among the busy streets I laughed at my fears, and it was almost shamefacedly that I greeted my friend. He was obviously exceedingly excited and interested by my story.

He told me that he had been much concerned about this house and its occupants. It had been taken, very abruptly and with but the briefest consideration, by a "rather overwhelming lady, a foreigner," who had paid a quarter's rent in advance, arranged about water, gas, electricity and the like, moved in two days later, and (so far as my friend knew, and my own observation only confirmed the impression) had never again been seen, nor any of her household. Steevens (my friend) had been disturbed, very naturally, by this odd circumstance alone.

"Is the woman dead?" he said. "I had begun to think it possible; but even were it so I do not see that we are any nearer to an explanation of your side of the mystery."

★

After some talk we determined to seek legal advice and, if necessary, to make entry into the house. He promised to ring me up as soon as a decision was reached; he also promised, upon my request, that my friend the postman should, if possible, be allowed to be present were an entry to be made.

There is no need to recapitulate the steps taken by Steevens in the course of the next few hours; enough that I had just lit my pipe after lunch when he rang me up and asked me to come round to his office at once.

I arrived in company with the last few of a not unimposing assembly. In all there were, besides Steevens and myself, Holt, the postman, now in mufti and shyly standing at attention, as it were, in the corner by the door; little Meadows, the ironmonger from his shop below Steevens' office; Crosby, the lawyer who attended to most of Steevens' business; and finally, their big bodies blocking most of the light, a large policeman and an equally large detective, in mufti, whose not unintelligent face was surmounted (designedly?) by the commonest and stupidest of bowler hats.

Steevens quickly made us all acquainted, and briefly recapitulated all the points of the problem as we knew it.

The only new information he had to give me, resulting from his inquiries since our consultation in the morning, was that the lady who had taken the house in the square was a notable, or rather a notorious, occultist—"spiritualist" if you like, but the better sort of spiritualist would have nothing to do with her.

"However," said Steevens, "do not let us waste time in details which can be left till later, but let us go straight to the house." It was in the silence of men who brace themselves to meet the unknown that we tramped down the stairs.

In the street I walked with Crosby. He questioned me, as he had previously questioned Holt, about the letter-box. I had thought that perhaps to his comfortable common-sense the whole thing would appear an absurdity; that probably he was coming with us mainly in the hope of finding cause for indulgence, at our discomfited expense, in that ponderous guffawing laughter of his. Instead I found him anxious and troubled, and, as he listened to my story, I could see his face darken with the shadow of the same fear and dread which was shared by Holt and by me.

As we turned into the Square another silence fell among us. What were we approaching? Three weeks had passed since that house had been entered.

At the foot of the steps we hesitated. Then Steevens and little Meadows, the locksmith, went up first.

Steevens rang the bell with a hand which trembled. We all listened, with intent expressions as of men who strain to hear the first note of an expected passing bell. Twice and three times he rang, but none replied. Then he motioned Meadows to the door (for Steevens had no duplicate key) that he might pick the lock.

A few stragglers in the square were brusquely sent about their business by the constable; but it was a quiet place—few came that way, and we were not likely to be troubled with a crowd. For myself, I confess that had it been in a busier street I should probably have laughed at the fears which now truly held me in so firm a grip that I felt a chill cold about me and a weakness of the knees.

For several leaden-footed minutes Meadows worked at the lock. Then came the definite scrape of the turning mechanism. An instant later Meadows, twisting the handle, gave the gentlest of pushes to the heavy door. It moved sufficiently to show that the bolts had not been shot. Then he moved aside.

★

At once, with a rather white face and with obvious reluctance, Steevens put up his hand and thrust the door forward and open.

The result was as simple in its awfulness as it is difficult to describe. There before our amazed, uncomprehending eyes that massive door swung inwards, and as it swung was swallowed up and disappeared in an impenetrable black darkness that filled the vacant doorway exactly as black oil would fill a tank. Where the door had been, that is to say, was now a clear-cut plane of blackness, definite as if it had been cut out of marble, so sharp that the very hinges of the in-swung door were cut in two, half visible, the inner half engulfed; and yet that black wall was *simply* black. No gleam, no hint of reflected light came from its dead blankness. Nothing like it has ever been seen before.

Black paper, black cloth, black paint, all these clearly define them-selves by gleams and reflections. A black hole shades from light into the inner obscurity. Here one can say no more than this—outside was light; inside—the boundary clearly marked as where the door had been—was darkness, abrupt, absolute, inexplicable and terrible.

We stood amazed and awed, gazing at that strange thing.

Then suddenly Holt, the postman, did a brave thing. I do not doubt that he was prompted to it simply because, without explana-tion, investigation at the least, this thing was too terrible to be borne; but the action all the same was as brave as anything could be.

Stepping forward he crossed that fearsome threshold and was instantly swallowed up. It was as if he had walked right through some impalpable black door. He disappeared completely, though we could still hear him. He took a step or two, then, with a low, shuddering gasp and a scrambling shuffle, he suddenly reappeared, stepping backwards, stumbling at the lintel and collapsing among us all, wet with clammy sweat and shaking violently from head to foot, so as some mighty engine could scarce vibrate more fiercely. In a few moments, however, he was enough recovered to speak to us:

"Oh, I can't tell you! Black, black dark! At once, at once; like being smothered—the hall-mat under your feet and the sounds from outside, and nothing whatever to see but the dark the minute you pass that door."

"Was there any peculiar smell, or smoke, a gas, a feeling, *anything*?" I asked.

"No, sir, nothing at all. If it had been at night, a dark night, I don't think you'd have noticed anything. It's just plunging in out of the blessed day that is so horrible."

At this the detective spoke up.

"Come, sir, we shall learn nothing this way. Into that house we must go, and into that house I am going."

So saying he stepped in, and disappeared; at once, stirred by his words and determination, we crowded after him, all except Meadows and Holt, who made no move even to approach the door.

The sensation was just as Holt had described it. But already something of the first horror had worn off. As I stepped in I spoke aloud:

"Steevens, where are you?"

"Here," he replied, out of the dark, and took me by the arm.

Once we had overcome the shock of so suddenly and inexplicably leaving the light of day it was no worse than moving round in a strange house in dark of night.

We stepped cautiously forward into the hall, and, guiding each other by voice and hand-grasp, gathered in a little group at the foot of what could be felt to be the stair.

Suddenly there was a little click, and then an exclamation of irritation.

"Torch won't light," said the detective.

I heard some movements, and then the scrape of a match—no light. Another, and another. There was quite a little fusillade of the sputters of striking matches from several of the party; then a quick exclamation from Crosby.

"What is it?" said Steevens.

"Match burnt my fingers," said Crosby. "I held it to make sure it would light properly; the flame burnt me, but I never saw a spot of light."

At once (the sounds revealed) we all tried the experiment. One by one we reported matches burnt down to our fingers; there was no trace of light! Quite suddenly, with a horribleness made inconceivably more horrible in that impenetrable dark, Crosby's nerve gave way.

"Darkness!" he cried, "weeping and gnashing of teeth!" And with a horrible shuffling he took two steps and then fell headlong over something. Moving carefully towards him, feeling with hands and feet, we felt him on the floor, where he lay muttering: "A horror of great darkness! Oh, God! Let there be light!"

While we felt about there, horrorstricken and rapidly approaching poor Crosby's broken condition ourselves, we were startled by a sudden exclamation:

"Where are you, gentlemen? What's happening?"

For a moment none replied. Then Steevens cried:

"Is that you, Holt? Where are you?"

Holt and Meadows both answered:

"Here, outside!" and then there was a sound of footsteps, and (it sounded) in they both came, Holt saying: "We heard a fall. Are you all right?"

The detective's voice was heard explaining; then he said:

"Mr. Crosby, sir, pull yourself together. Will you listen to me? I have an idea of what we ought to do."

Crosby made a gasping effort.

"I'm sorry," he said; "strange affair, nerve went, better now," and he seemed to be picking himself up.

Then Grainer, the detective, said: "Gentlemen, I've been told this house was taken by a spiritualist: This must be some spooky hanky-panky. Don't let us get foolishly alarmed. Let us search the house, which we have come to do, from top to bottom; even if we can see nothing, if we make a careful plan we can search thoroughly enough by feeling. Mr. Steevens, sir, you know the house; what is there on this floor?"

Steevens hesitated an instant. One could almost hear him pulling himself together.

"Er—thank you, Grainer," he said; "that is very sensible. So far as I can remember, there is this hall, a dining-room, a drawing-room and a morning-room opening off it, and a baize door at the back of the stairs which leads to the kitchens."

"Listen, then, everybody!" we heard Grainer reply. "Fall back gradually, all of you, till you reach the walls of the hall." There ensued a minute of shuffling, and a few half-whispered exclamations, as each of us, feeling an increase of nervousness from the added sense of isolation, found his place around the walls.

"Now," said Grainer, "let us each find a door, a window, all the objects we can find in our immediate vicinity."

In this manner we made as thorough a search of the hall as was possible, announcing our discoveries, in response to Grainer's continual questioning.

The constable, who was next to me, reported a window. At the same moment I ran my head with some violence against the still wide-open door, and, explaining, I was directed to shut it, lest some passer-by should think to investigate a doorway apparently hung with a jet-black curtain, as doubtless it would appear from the pavement.

Having done so I heard Grainer cross the floor to the constable, and there came the ring of curtains along the rod, then the clatter of the shutters, and finally, the whirr of a spring blind run up. No light appeared.

"Can you find the catch of the window?" said Grainer.

"Here it is," from the constable; and then the sneck of the latch, and the rattle of the opened window. Still no light; but quite suddenly, from outside, a horrified exclamation in a young man's voice:

"Good Lord! Bob, look at that window. There's a living arm sticking out of the middle of it, cut off short!"

"What an extraordinary thing," came the reply. "But I suppose it's some trick. Hi! You in there, what d'you mean by frightening people with your silly jugglery go away and do it somewhere else. It's enough to frighten anybody out of their wits."

To my surprise Grainer made no reply to this save to pull down the window again.

I have, often-wondered what those two young fellows—I am guessing at them by their voices—can have thought as they went on across the Square! As for us within that black and silent house, I think that nothing could have so emphasised the terrible strangeness of our situation.

Grainer, who had, with his official manner and solid common-sense, taken charge of the investigation by the tacit consent of us all, allowed us no time, however, to give way to our fears. Under his direction we made a weird, difficult, but thorough search of the whole of the ground floor. As far as was discoverable in that pitch darkness there was nothing unusual there—simply the ordinary furnishings and equipment of an average middle-class home.

We then mounted the stair and searched the upper landing. Steevens informed us that there were no attics; when we had searched this upper floor we should have searched the whole.

How strange it was, the seven of us, crawling gropingly on hands and knees, stretching out timid hands into the terrible dark, suddenly and terrifyingly encountering some all-too-much-expected body, only to discover that it was that of one of our number.

To search through a house wherein one more than half expects to come upon a corpse is a fearsome enough task at any time. To do so in absolute darkness, and with the cause of that added horror still all unexplained, was one of the most terrifying experiences that can be imagined.

Fortunately our suspense was now, by a little, curtailed, for we discovered all the doors on this upper landing locked, with the keys outside, save one—the door of the room which, said Steevens, was usually used by the mistress of the house as her boudoir, and had probably been so used by the present mistress.

Anxiously we felt our way in. What should we find? Had the lady left the house? Would she be found in this room? Had this fearsome darkness come to overwhelm her, horribly, terrifyingly, so that she had fled from it in such a fear as to have left house and town in panic, telling none of her departure?

I am not one who is sensitive to those delicate sensations and impressions which are called psychic. "Atmosphere" has but little effect upon me. Yet so exalted was my nervous condition by the strain of this evil dark that I distinctly felt an added horror, a creeping "scunner" as we entered that room; and it took all my self-restraint to refrain from a yelp of terror when, a moment later, poor Steevens uttered a sort of shuddering groan (rather than a cry) of discovery.

I was feeling along the jamb of the door at the moment, and as Steevens uttered his exclamation my hand closed on the electric switch and pressed it down. No light resulted—by now we were used to this—but I left the switch on, and moved forward with the others towards Steevens.

"Keep back a moment!" he said. "I've found something, some-body—yes, a man—sitting in a chair—here—here." We felt towards him. My hand encountered a shoulder.

"Here?" I said, feeling it motionless and strangely cold beneath the cloth, but:

"No, here," said Steevens' voice a foot or two away, and an instant later his hand came groping towards me, found me, was identified, and guided by me towards the shoulder I had touched.

"It is another," he whispered dreadfully. I will not try to describe the stages, second by awestruck second, of our discovery. It is too tense, too horrible to attempt. Indeed, the shuddering mind halts and refuses to remember that which it first received with so deep a shock.

It is enough to say that we found there, seated in the cold silence of that dreadful dark, colder, yet more silent themselves in the darker dreadfulness of death, six human bodies—three men, three women—seated about a round table as men and women sit who try the spirits in séance.

Their outstretched hands rested on the table, little fingers linked to those of their neighbours'; while at one place we found a figure which we took to be that of the medium, seated on a chair which was deeper and more comfortable than the others, its eyes blindfolded (as if ever blindfold could be imagined darker than the blackness in which *we* moved), and with its head and trunk crumpled forward as if in the trance usual to the spirit-intermediary.

One by one each of us investigated every one of that dreadful circle. Suddenly Grainer, whose voice sounded from beside the medium, startled us by exclaiming:

"Which of you have felt this blindfold chap? Did he seem to you dead-cold?"

Without waiting for reply (though *we* waited tense as bowstrings, still as marble, horribly expectant), he was heard making rapid motions... Almost one could see him; laying back that figure from its chair on to the floor, feeling for a pulse, gently loosening clothing. There was a cork-noise and a bubble of liquid as Grainer's flask came into requisition, a rhythmic movement...

Suddenly, fearsomely, through the dark I *saw*, high up and across the room, two huge and horrible mis-shapen eyes, red, enormous, lurid, the eyes of a monster. My hair crept; my skin twitched with terror, ran with a cold and clammy sweat; my throat, strangled with fear, uttered an involuntary choking cry!

"Eyes!" it said, and my hand pointed as though the rest could see.

I heard chattering teeth and my own chattered; my heart pounded and thumped so fiercely that in a moment I seemed to hear no other sound than the dreadful drums of the marching regiment of the eternal spheres.

A cry, croaking, cackling, *laughing* cry, and Crosby's voice:

"See, see, not eyes! It isn't eyes at all; it's the electric lights"; and even as he said it we knew it to be true, and everything was happening at once. Grainer was grunting with satisfaction, and the light was growing, blessed, blessed light, and we could see each other again, with white, drawn faces; and there is Grainer on the floor, a figure stretched beside him; he is dropping brandy into the mouth with a wonderful calm, matter-of-fact care, and look! the eyes are opening...

And all the while the light grows. The figure sighs with returning life, the eyes open wide, and at once the lights blaze out, the room is bright with light, and the constable is pulling the curtains, opening the window, letting in the day. And there are our horror-struck selves, there on the floor the emaciated figure of a pale young man, and there seated at the table five still bodies, white and cadaverous, with the indubitable stamp of death.

Late that evening we gathered at Crosby's house, the same little company, and a police-surgeon in addition. We were ushered into a large bedroom where Grey, the medium, was lying. The doctor reported him as much stronger and quite able to tell his story. In view of the inquest to be held on the morrow into the deaths of those two men and three women now lying in the grim house in the Square it was urgent that the main threads of the strange affair should be gathered at once.

I will not attempt to give at full length the question and answer, the gasping repetitions of that strange investigation. If this should do something to remove the cloud of horror wherewith, for all of us who sat there listening, it was invested, that is all to the good, for, indeed, the tale itself was weird beyond imagining. I will simply give the outlines of the tale.

It seems that Grey had been for some years a friend of Madame Seulon (the tenant of the "house of darkness"), and had frequently helped her in her psychic researches. To these her husband had given a disapproval which grew at last into an open breach, so that, leaving him, Madame travelled about into various places, making inquiries into ghost stories, haunted houses, and other mysteries in many places. Her separation from her husband had the worst effect upon her, for now, without restraint, she gave herself up to the blackest art, the most evil mystery.

A short while previously the sudden death of one of her companions, during séance, had caused some scandal, so that in taking and in moving into the house in the Square, Madame had used some secrecy, and, indeed, had determined at first—until she had completed a certain investigation—to engage no servants, to bring in an ample supply of provisions, and to shut herself away from all the world. This done, she then communicated with some of her closest spiritualistic friends and also with Grey.

When these arrived she explained to them the theory she had formed. She had found—indeed, it is well known—that all things strange and evil *fear the light*. Thirsting for knowledge, longing for power, Madame had often held her séances in darkness absolute; but always as the strange border-land of the spirit world was passed some light appeared. Evilly lurid it might often be, angry red, foul purple; dread elemental things appeared, wrapped in the sulphurous flames of the pit, glaucous eyes would glare, and livid flashes glimmer in the baleful dark.

Now it occurred to Madame that manifestations of the most potent order might be brought forth if, in some whole-willed company such as that which she had gathered the Powers that rule the spirit world should be asked to make a darkness absolute, a darkness not of this world only, but of that Other also.

Grey was frightened. This was necromancy of a very dangerous sort! But he was over-persuaded, and on a certain night nearly a fortnight before this tale was told the séance began.

Now, it must be explained that mediums vary greatly. Some are almost indifferent to all that happens, even though it is through their help. Some have no memory of anything occurring from the moment that first they pass into a state of trance until they are reawakened. Some retain a sort of semi-consciousness all the while.

Grey, it seems, held an intermediate place, being subject to two states of trance, a lighter and a deeper. In the lighter trance, while he retained a memory of what was happening, yet he was quite without volition of his own, and communication with the Spirit World through his mediumship was complete and quite unhampered by his semi-consciousness. In the deeper trance he was completely "absent," as it were in a temporary death, and, on being awakened, had no memory of anything occurring during that degree of trance.

On this occasion the company being assembled as usual at a round table, Grey went almost at once into his lighter "spirit sleep." At once (he says) the" control" with whom Madame was in the habit of holding communication, took possession of him. This was no good spirit, but some vicious and depraved monster, against whom Madame had been warned again and again, but vainly.

At once Madame put her request—that there should be a darkness complete and absolute, "both in this house," said Madame, "and in the Spirit World immediately about us."

The request was acceded to, having been received with the most horrible and gleeful laughter both by the control and by that evil company which was with him on the spirit side.

"And at once," said Grey," that strange, dim spirit-light of which I am always conscious, no matter how darkened the room may be, for, indeed, it is a light not of this world, went suddenly out, and the livid eyes of the ghostly company about me disappeared.

"And then—oh! then the most fearsome things at once began," cried Grey; "screamings and angry raging, the sounds of some most violent conflict. Voices there were, evil, fierce voices, horrid with the joy of battle; soft, kindly voices of their adversaries fighting for ourselves and our souls, grown hissing, breathless, and heavy with strife as they struggled bravely for the mastery, baffled and thwarted though they were by the cruel darkness wherein evil ever finds itself at home, while good, robbed of its natural, pure light, fights blindly and fearfully against an unfair odds.

"It seemed as if space itself rocked with the battle.

"Suddenly, trembling, terrified and small, I heard close by me five new voices, weak, strange, out-crying as it were like drowning kittens.

"I recognised them; they were the voices of my companions."

What had happened?

"Some fearful and compelling power had surely reft those shuddering souls out of their bodies and hurled them, trembling, into that Stygian battleground. Already, then, the powers beneficent were losing hold?

"And I? I was alone in all this conflict; neither in this world was I, nor in the Spirit World, but rapt away from both in my state of semi-trance. It would seem that I was safe; but what, oh! what horrible thing had happened to Madame and her companions?"

At this stage, it seems, Grey was so terrified that he did a very unusual thing. By the very potency of his terror he succeeded in overcoming, voluntarily, his trance, and in returning suddenly into his own body seated at that mystical table. Here all was silent (in this world), for he had left behind the clamour of the struggle which was going on about him in the world of spirits. Silent it was and dark.

With a terrified effort the medium spoke to his companions. There was no reply, no word, no breath, no sigh, no movement even.

Weak from the trance, poor Grey could scarcely move, and yet at length he summoned up sufficient force to sit up and to stretch forth a hand shaking with the most appalling fear into the darkness. One by one he sought and found his companions, one by one he felt under his hand the chill of five corpses already cold.

How long his trance had lasted, what had happened in that dreadful room, he knew not. And as he sat there, palsied with terror, suddenly, fierce and loud, and uttered by what agency he knew not, nor would ever know, a mighty voice rang through that room of death, speaking to him in urgent command:

"Sleep!" it cried. "Sleep deeply! These are the Dead! the Dead! Sleep on in darkness, till the Living bid thee wake!"

At this command the medium sank at once into the deepest trance—until the Living bade him wake."

What had happened, what happened then, what horrors passed about that house of dreadful dark, who shall say?

It is a terrible thing to meddle with the Powers of Darkness; it is a terrible thing to defy, with impious rashness, the laws which have been given for our quietude and peace.

The next day, in a dreary and forbidding court-house, the windows loud with the angry tumult of a gale and cold, spattering rain, the inquest was held upon those five dead bodies.

No trace of wound or poison had they, and no sign of any ill sufficient to be the cause of death.

Long and earnest was the inquiry; long and difficult the jury's consultation. Nor is it a wonder that, returning with awed and sombre faces, and having sought permission from the coroner (which, in the amazing circumstances, he gave), they declared it to be their will that the verdict in each case (and here their foreman's voice fell low and shuddering as that of one who speaks of awful doom) should be:

"Slain by the Wrath of God."

THE WOMAN IN THE VEIL

E. F. Benson

E. F. Benson (1867–1940) certainly needs no introduction. He was one of the pre-eminent writers of ghost stories in the first half of the twentieth century with five collections published during his lifetime and many compilations made since. He was a son of the Archbishop of Canterbury, Edward White Benson, and two of his brothers also became known for their stories of the supernatural, A. C. Benson (who also wrote the words to "Land of Hope and Glory") and R. H. Benson. Between 1998 and 2005 Jack Adrian assembled five volumes of Benson's weird tales which purported to be complete.

I was astonished, therefore, to discover the following story, which surprisingly was not included in either Benson's Spook Stories *(1928) or* More Spook Stories *(1934) and somehow escaped inclusion in Adrian's otherwise complete set. It was published in* The Evening News *for 26 June 1928. Over the years most major short-story writers appeared in the paper, usually with reprinted stories but occasionally with new ones. Benson appeared there just twice during his life time, and the second of those was a reprint, but the first was the following, written specially for the paper.*

I T WAS A JOYFUL SPECTACLE, AS THE GREAT TRAIN ROARED WEST-
wards, to watch the clearing of the skies which in London for the
last week had dripped with chilly relentless rain. Before we reached
the first halt at Exeter the floor of compact grey clouds had been
rent in a dozen places, and gleams of sunshine lay in golden patches
over the landscape: swiftly after that the rags of vapour which hung
on to the heavens were shrivelled and consumed in that genial fire,
and by the time we struck the coast near Dawlish the radiance of
the May afternoon poured down brilliantly on a sea of peacock blues
and greens on the rich red earth of the cliffs.

Soon we clanked across the Saltash bridge, and after a delectable
travel through the beech-woods sown with bluebells, and passages
over spider-web viaducts slung above the tree-tops of the gashed valleys below, came to a station of soft-sounding Cornish name, where
I had to change for the branch line to Poltreath.

Here the country became of a more austere aspect, and of a
brisker air, for a westerly breeze was blowing, laden with the salt
freshness of the Atlantic, and on an evening of unclouded splendour
I got out at the little town that clustered steeply on the sides of a
dip in the uplands. Half a mile of huddled streets brought me on to
the open downs on the edge of which stood the square, grey-stoned
Beach Hotel for which I was bound.

Like every proper Londoner, I took advantage of all possible reasons for flying from the town which I adored so deeply, and two such,
irresistible in their combination, had just presented themselves. One
was that I had some work to do which required a week of seclusion

and serious spade-work; the other that painters were proposing to make my house uninhabitable for some days: a remote hotel was, therefore, a desirable refuge.

By chance I had seen in weather reports that Poltreath was enjoying insolently long hours of sunshine, and since I had pleasant recollections of that coast generally, but had never seen the place itself, that was a reason the more for now doing so.

Somewhere in the darker pools of my mind was the knowledge that I had heard of Poltreath quite lately in some special connection, but, though I had been intermittently fishing for it all day, I could not arrive at it. Perhaps I had seen a picture of it in some illustrated paper, perhaps there had been a wreck on its coast, perhaps somebody had gone round its golf links in wholly incredible figures. My knowledge seemed to me to be of this class, merely of an incident with which I was in no way concerned, but which had just caught, though not held, my attention. But what that incident connected with it was, I had no idea.

It was impossible to imagine a more delightfully situated lodging for one who loved sea and sun and was in need of solitude. The big grey hotel, once clearly a country house, was planted four-square close to the edge of the cliffs that tumbled steeply down to the beach: on one side of it was scooped a broad sandy bay; in front, and on the other side, a fringe of sharp-toothed rock bordered the sea. Round it were spread the maritime downs, short-turfed and starred with pink clusters of thrift, across which the coast road ran north and south; before it was spread the Atlantic.

Bleak and desolate it might indeed be when the gales of winter boomed from the south-west, and the few trees that grew about it, dwarfed in height, and bent landwards with crooked trunks and oblique branches, showed that such winds were prevalent. But this evening only the lightest of airs streamed in from the sea, and the water far out across the sands was scarcely rimmed with white.

The air was of the most exhilarating vintage, provocative of activity both in mind and in body, and looking at sun-steeped sea and the smooth-turfed golf-links that lay along the bay, I regretted that the most of my activity would be concerned to exercise itself with a pen plunged in ink instead of shoulders in the sea, and with delvings for words rather than golf-balls.

But quickly I made with myself a bargain which the most scrupulous conscience would approve. My mornings should be long and studious; so, too, my evenings; I vowed that every night after dinner I would settle down for a solid three hours of work. That would make a full day of industry, and thus from lunchtime to dinner I should be free to enjoy the sands and sun and sea of Poltreath.

I inaugurated that dutiful programme at once, and, till dinner, scrambled about the rocks below the hotel, recapturing again the magic that lurks in rock-pools, those entrancing lakes of clearest water, fringed with sea-weed, the home of sideways-scuttling crabs and strawberry-like anemones of the sea. Never have I seen such ranges of rocks as here, such fruitful pools, such sequestered little beaches of sand tucked away in valleys guarded by mussel-covered crags, exposed now at the ebb of the tide.

Then came dinner in a sparsely-populated dining-room, for the sea-side season was not yet in full swing, and after that I went to my sitting-room for the other branch of my programme. This was on the ground-floor, a small slip of a place opening out of that apartment known to hotels and house-agents as "the lounge," where a wireless apparatus, to my deep satisfaction, was telling us, even as the sun, near its setting over the sea, poured light and warmth on us, that rain had been incessant all day in London, and was likely to continue… Then with a profound sense of rectitude I turned my back on the window and sat down to work.

Daylight faded, and without drawing my blind I switched on the lights. As a reward of my industry I had got absorbed in my tale, and when after an unestimated interval I heard a clock in the lounge outside strike a lengthy hour I was astonished to find that it was already midnight. That was full measure of my work, and I dropped my pen and wheeled round in my chair to look at the night. Tranquil it was and brilliant: a moon, a day from the full, blazed whitely on the expanse of the sea, turning it to a sheet of twinkling silver; for foreground there was a narrow strip of downland and then the edge of the cliff. Close outside my windows ran a broad gravel walk.

I suddenly became aware that there was standing on it, not more than a couple of yards distant, the figure of a woman dressed in a long coat, with a motor-veil tied around her head. She was looking into the windows of the lounge, and thus was almost directly in full face to me, but her face was in shadow, and I could not see it at all distinctly.

She seemed to me to have very large or very prominent eyes, her mouth drooped open, and she was very dark of complexion, But the lights, and even more the shadows of moonlight, are very confusing: pink and topaz, black and red, brown and purple are indistinguishable in it. But certainly this middle-aged lady, with pronounced features, was dark…And then her presence there and her strange immobility struck me as odd, as startling even. I was sure she had not been at dinner: what then was she doing just outside the hotel? Then the very natural explanation occurred to me that she had arrived just now by car, and, like myself, was enjoying this rare spectacle of sea and moonshine.

I pulled down my blind, quenched the light, and went out into the lounge on my way bedwards. It was already empty, with only a solitary light burning, and at the far end of it was the night-porter, locking and bolting the front door. He had just finished with this when I came to the foot of the staircase, and he offered me the accommodation of the lift. And then it occurred to me that he had locked out this motoring lady.

"Surely you're locking someone out," I said. "Hasn't a lady in a motor just arrived?"

"No, sir; no arrival," he said.

The memory of that figure looking in at the window of the lounge began to interest me.

"But I saw a woman on the path just outside my window two minutes ago," I said.

He looked at me, a little puzzled, a little bored, but with some glint of interest (was it?) of unease.

"Can't be anyone from here," he said. "No one's gone out since I came on duty, and none's arrived. Some visitor from Poltreath, sir; there's a right of way all along the cliffs."

I bade him goodnight and went upstairs. From the open gallery of the floors above I saw that he had gone to the window at the end of the lounge and was looking out.

Alas for the sunny serenity of Poltreath! During the night I heard the wind awake, and in the morning a gale laden with rain was battering on my panes. Yet that made my industries but the easier, for who would want to be abroad in this tempest? But after lunch the rain ceased and, tiring of the house, I set forth along the coast-road northward.

The wind was tremendous on the upland, and it was a relief, after a mile of buffeting, to dip into a valley, where the force of it was cut off by a headland seawards. There was a very vale of Avilion: copses lined the road, thick with primroses and blue-bells and birdsong, but soon it began to mount again and at the corner just ahead of me I saw from the gestures of the struggling tress that I should emerge into the full blast. I said to myself that I would just walk to that point and then turn homewards.

I came to this corner, and then quite suddenly I found I knew the place, not from having been here before, but from some picture which I had seen quite recently: there was a steep spur of rock, a sharp angle in the road and a glimpse of the sea. At that the solution of what had intermittently puzzled me the day before was manifest. It was just here, at this very corner, that a week before there had appeared in some illustrated paper the picture of a motor-car standing empty in the road and with a rush of retarded recollection the whole memory linked itself up.

Miss Alice Trellings, that iron-willed and ruthless explorer of unknown lands, had been staying at Bude, and had set out alone one evening after dinner to drive to Poltreath where she had engaged rooms at the Beach Hotel. She had never appeared there, nor had she been seen since, but at this corner had been found her motor, facing not towards Poltreath, but in the direction from which she had come. Before now she had suffered more than one attack of loss of memory, due to a sunstroke while crossing the Arabian desert, and the theory of the police had been that, feeling the approach of some such seizure, she had turned back, and then, at its onset, left the car.

It was known that she was wearing a string of very valuable pearls, but it was difficult to imagine that a thief had boarded the car while in motion, had killed her and had disposed of the body. Loss of memory and identity, while seeking the place where she was known, was a far more probable theory.

So there was the memory I had been fishing for; it was a certain satisfaction to have caught and landed it, but its connection with Poltreath was of the most shadowy, and thinking no more about it, I pressed my way homewards. Already the sea had risen angrily under the violence of the gale, and was whitened with breaking wave-crests, while the great rollers were riding in, pounding at the rocky coast; the spouts of foam rose high in the air, and, blown landwards by the wind, hissed as they fell on the grass above the cliffs. I had scarcely got into shelter of the hotel, when again the rain began to stream against the window of my room.

With the close of the day, the hurly-burly redoubled: squalls descended on the house with squeals and thunderings, making the solid walls to quake under their grip, and the rain was flung in solid sheets against the panes. But my work prospered, and after dinner I became immersed in it, heedless of the passage of the hours, and at length, yawning and suddenly aware of fatigue and uneasiness, I again heard the clock in the lounge strike midnight. The wind seemed to have somewhat abated, though still the rain fell heavily, and I pushed aside the blind to look out.

The moon, full to-night, though totally obscured behind the wrack of clouds, made a twilight in which I could clearly see the huge spouting of the waves above the black edge of the cliff, and there again on the path outside my window, beaten on by the rain and blown on by the gale, stood the figure I has seen the night before.

Her long coat, I noticed, hung straight and undisturbed by the wind, the edge of her motor-veil reposed quietly on her shoulders, as if the wild fury of the storm was powerless to touch that dire tranquillity. After a moment she moved slowly away, disappearing towards the corner of the hotel, round which lay the front door.

I let the blind drop, and stood there with some icy horror of the spirit closing round me, for I knew, not by the ocular evidence alone of that windless isolation in the storm, but by some interior sense, that I had looked upon a visitor from that dim region beyond time and space, which is invested with our terror of death and of the kingdom of its mute citizens.

But mixed with that horror was an overwhelming curiosity. Whose was the spirit, I asked myself, which stood tranquil in this cauldron of the winds, and which on some dread errand of her own had clothed herself again in the sheath of mortality, and to whom was her errand, and how would she accomplish it? Where, too, had she gone now and where would she reappear again?...All this, churning though my conscience, mingled with my terror, stiffening into a certain courage. The terror was there all the while ready to freeze me, but curiosity controlled it.

The lounge, dimly lit, looked to me at first to be empty; then I saw that the hall-porter was sitting in a chair at the foot of the staircase, asleep. There was no occasion for me to disturb him, and I had already set foot on the bottom step for my ascent, when there came on the front door two raps, distinct, but not loud. Instantly, with a further qualm of fright, my mind suggested that the knocker at this late hour was she whom I had seen on the walk outside. Yet how absurd a notion; here, no doubt, was some expected guest arriving late...And then I saw that the porter had awoke and was listening.

"Someone has arrived," I said. "There's someone knocking…"

He shook his head.

"No one expected to-night, sir," he said. "That's but the wind rattling the shutters."

Even as he spoke the two raps were repeated, and on the heels of them came the faint tingle of an electric-bell.

"And is that the wind ringing the bell?" I asked. "A strange thing! I tell you, there's someone outside."

He stood there a moment, evidently on the strain, and then pulled himself together.

"I seemed to hear the bell, too," he said. "I'll see who it can be, though I think it was only some bell on the landing upstairs."

He turned up the light just inside the door, then drawing back the bolts, threw it open. The illumination streamed strongly out, and standing with him on the threshold, I saw that there was no one there. A space of gravel for some yards in front was clearly lit, round it the wet and roaring darkness I felt sure no one could have hidden himself, so short was the interval between the summons and the opening of the door, but now, to make assurance surer, the porter switched on the light outside the porch, and for fifty yards in every direction the lawn and the gravel-sweep sprang into brightness.

"'Twas just a bell from the landing, sir," he said, "and the rattle of the wind."

Certainly that seemed likely, yet even while this demonstration of the empty night shone round me I felt that invisibly, but somewhere close at hand was the presence that had manifested itself on the other side of the hotel three minutes before. Just the porter quenched the light outside, and in the darkness something pushed by between him and me.

"What was that?" I rapped out, and turning, saw in the lit hall behind, shadowy and wavering of outline, the figure which I had twice seen already. Even as I looked it grew clearer and more solid, and there, with face turned towards us, and eyes directed not on to me but my companion, stood the woman in cloak and motor-veil. The eyes protruded, the mouth gaped, as if starving for air, the face was flushed with a mottled purple. Round this death-mask of one strangled was wound the pink motor-veil, through which I saw the sheen of notable pearls clasping the neck...

It was in some such catalepsy as belongs to nightmare that I stood staring at this head of horror, and then I heard close beside me a gasp and a hoarse, whispered exclamation.

"O God! O Christ!" it said, and the man who stood by me crouched and stole away out of sight into the tumultuous darkness. The phantom moved: it came forward, passed through the glass screen that shielded the door, and followed.

Now fear, like all other pains of body and mind, defeats itself as an instrument for anguish, because when it has reached a certain point some sort of numbness succeeds, just as to the tortured body on the rack comes the failure of the nerves to register pain any more. Thus it was not with any semblance of courage now but with unconcern that I in my turn followed that strangled image of wrath and retaliation.

Into the roar of the tempest we passed, and now borne to me on the wind there came from somewhere ahead thin squeals as of mere animal terror, not human. There just in front were the cliffs with the background of the whitened sea and the curtain of spray, and for one second I caught sight of the fleeing figure of the doomed man outlined against them. His hands shot up in one supreme gesture of despair and then vanished. Vanished also now was his pursuer, and, what was more, the sense of his pursuer. The terror cleared off from my mind like a frosty breath, and I knew only that a man, human like myself, had fallen over the cliff's edge.

I crawled to the top of it, and by the dim moonlight that pierced the clouds I could see some thirty feet below the sheer brink, the man lying huddled on the showers of spray that spurted from the rocks just beyond. It seemed impossible to reach him without assistance, and even if I had managed to climb down without disaster there was nothing I could do.

Accordingly I ran back to the hotel, pealing on the bell at the entrance, and in the bureau I found a switch labelled "Emergency." I pressed my finger and held it there till I heard the creak of the lift and the thud of footsteps on the stairs. Then ropes were fetched and blankets in which could be lifted that which we should find below, and a couple of men, one a doctor who was staying in the hotel and myself, were lowered. Under his direction we slung the body in a hammock of blankets and waited there till those above on the cliff had conveyed their burden into the hotel. The man had stirred; he had groaned as we adjusted the rough transport, and seeing me beside him he had signed to me to come close and had whispered: "Close here; in a rock-pool, full of seaweed."

He died during the night, leaving that legacy of half-a-dozen words, and next morning I found a way down to that sandy inlet where he had fallen. Close to it was a very big rock-pool hidden away in a labyrinth of slippery ledges and masked with the podded growth of the sea. But at one point the thick harvest of brown tendrils strangely bulged out of the water, and among them I saw some pink tissue as of a silk veil.

I convinced myself of what lay below, and went back to the hotel to give my information. In the interval they had searched among the effects of the dead man for the purpose of telegraphing to his relatives, and at the bottom of his trunk, which was pushed under his bed, was a string of pearls.

Now any complete reconstruction of my story is necessarily a matter of guess-work, while the circumstances, as related above, which led to the solution of the disappearance of Miss Alice Trellings would no doubt be laughed to scorn by any jury of sensible Englishmen. Yet they were very oddly confirmed by the inquest held over her swollen body which I had seen pushing up the seaweed of that rock-pool, and it was established that she had met her death not by drowning, but by strangulation.

Again, the night-porter knew that the corpse lay there, for the last words he spoke were to say that there was something in the rock-pool close at hand, while the pearls found in his trunk, which were proved to be those of the murdered woman and to have been worn by her on the last evening of her life, were sufficient to complete the chain of evidence as to the identity of the murderer. But all these disclosures were due to an apparition in which no sensible man could possibly believe...

For the rest we are obliged to fall back on conjecture as to the actual place and manner of the crime, but such conjecture, if it fits the facts, is bounded within very narrow limits.

The murderer was certainly on duty on the night when the crime was committed, and since the strangled body was found in the place indicated by him close to the Beach Hotel, it would follow that Miss Trellings arrived at Poltreath, was admitted, and strangled by the porter who possessed himself of her pearls. He then carried the body down to the beach and hid it under the thick curtain of seaweed in that sequestered pool, difficult of access, about which he whispered to me.

He had then to dispose of her motor-car, which, of course, must not be found near the hotel, and this he apparently drove to that bend in the road where it was found next day, and, leaving it pointing in the direction from which Miss Trellings had come, walked back to the Beach Hotel.

A better device whether arrived at haphazardly or by subtle calculation, could scarcely have been planned, for it put the police on an entirely wrong scent, and led them to suppose that Miss Trellings had abandoned her idea of going to Poltreath, and had turned again in the direction of Bude. That she had suffered before from loss of memory gave them an additional wrong clue as to her disappearance.

But of the phantom itself which I personally saw twice on the gravel walk alongside my windows and of its third and avenging appearance when the murderer saw it also, I have no explanation to offer. It seems a terrible fate for the actual spirit of the dead that it must haunt (unless of its own free will) the scene of its corporeal death, though there is a justice, no less terrible, that it should be the means of vengeance.

Even without that ghostly interference, human justice, slower-footed, would probably have overtaken the murderer, but I can imagine no fear of the gallows, no ticking away of the hours of his last night on earth, so awful for the condemned as that pursuit of him through the night of gale and tempest which elicited those squeals of animal terror.

Nor again can I come to any conclusion as to *how* the apparition of vengeance made itself visible to mortal eyes, whether it was the image of the woman in cloak and motor-veil which was transferred from the mind of the murderer to me, so that I visualised something that had no objective existence, or whether some glimpse into the unseen coming first to me and subsequently to him, revealed not a subjective impression, but the manifestation of a living spirit angry and intent on vengeance. If so, we can only hope that it is at rest now in that world which lies so closely round us hidden by the merciful veil which sometimes is momentarily lifted.

THE TREASURE OF THE TOMBS

F. Britten Austin

Frederick Britten Austin (1885–1941) was a prolific contributor to the magazines in the years between the First and Second World Wars, particularly to The Strand, *which ran his series featuring the detective Quentin Quayne. Were it not for the inclusion of the Quayne story "Diamond Cut Diamond" in Dorothy L. Sayers's massive compilation* Great Short Stories of Detection, Mystery and Horror—Second Series, *published in 1931 and frequently reprinted in various truncated forms, I'm sure Austin's name would be totally forgotten. Hardly anything else by him has been anthologised, although his early story, "The Strange Case of Mr. Todmorden", originally published in* The Magpie *in December 1913, was included in* The Evening Standard Book of Strange Stories *in 1934. The fiction editor at* The Evening Standard *clearly liked Austin's work as the newspaper reprinted other stories from his collections* Battlewrack *(1917),* According to Orders *(1918) and* On the Borderland *(1922), this last containing most of his weird tales.*

He sold several stories to magazines before the War, plus his novel The Shaping of Lavinia *(1911), whilst he worked as a clerk in the London Stock Exchange but on the day War was declared he signed up for the London Rifle Brigade. He served with the British Expeditionary Force and Royal Army Service Corps throughout the First World War, rising to the rank of Captain. He used his military knowledge in many stories. A Saga of the Sword (1928), traced the history of warfare in fictional form,* A Saga of the Sea *(1929), likewise retold early naval exploration* and battles and The Red Flag (1932) looked at the power of the people through the centuries.

Yet, after Austin's death in March 1941 of a "seizure", aged only 55, his work went out of print and his name sank into oblivion. He deserves a better fate. There remain plenty of stories amongst his magazine writings to allow for a good quality collection of strange stories and mysteries. Here's one, from the January 1921 Strand, which would seem ideally suited to Indiana Jones.

I F EVER A MAN WAS EMPHATICALLY AND ARTICULATELY THANKFUL that the war was over and that he could return to the comfortable if humdrum ways of peace, that man was myself. The contrast of my quiet, cool office in London town after three years of the heat, dust, and flies of Mesopotamia was inexpressibly grateful to me. And although my military service, thanks to my job on the staff, was certainly not only far more interesting but accompanied by infinitely less hardship than the experiences of most of my comrades, I told myself, as once more I took my seat in my mahogany and red morocco private room, that I had had enough adventure for a life-time. Nothing would induce me—I remember my father's nod of satisfaction as I said it; he felt that he could safely resign the management of the business into my hands—nothing would induce me, short of extreme national danger, to quit the solid comfort of three meals a day and the club at the end of it for that fallacious lure of the unexplored horizon which had thrown so strong a spell over me when I had volunteered at the beginning of the war. And I believed myself. I did not even feel the pull, as did so many of those who fought in the war, of those old battlefields of France and Belgium, so familiar to me in 1915. Sometimes, it is true, I thought, of a few of my old comrades and speculated on what had happened to them, but I kept in touch with none. The war faded into a dream-memory, remote from actuality.

Remote though it was, nevertheless when one day my clerk tapped at the door and brought in two cards, inscribed respectively Richard Franks and Henry Jefferson, I had an instant vision of two dirty, haggard flying-officers standing before me in my map-hung office in the old palace at Mosul. Their machine had crashed whilst on reconnaissance over the mountain-range of the Jebel Abjad, and they had escaped to our lines only after miraculous and hair-raising adventures sufficient to fill a book. My report of the valuable information they had brought back had contributed not a little to their promotion. I smiled at the memory of the two cool-headed young daredevils, who had narrated their thrilling experiences as though they were the most ordinary thing in the world.

"Show them in," I said, as I rose from my seat to welcome them.

I recognised at once, despite the disguise of their civilian clothes, the two young men who came rather diffidently into my room. Obviously they were awed by the unfamiliar surroundings of commerce.

"Good morning, Major," said Franks, a tall, thin young fellow with an aquiline nose on a determined face oddly out of keeping with his nervous manner. One would never have imagined that, single-handed, in what he called a "dog-fight," he had brought down three German machines attached to the Turkish army.

"'Morning, Major," ventured Jefferson, sententiously, evidently not less nervous. He was younger than Franks—not more than twenty-two or three, a mere boy, fair-haired and blue-eyed, the typical stripling who, in thousands, manned and fought England's air-fleets during the war. I noticed that, despite the prejudices of his kind, he carried a somewhat bulky brown-paper parcel.

"Good morning, both of you," I responded heartily, genuinely gratified by their visit. They brought into my work-a-day office a touch of the past which seemed pleasantly romantic in the retrospect. "Glad to see you! Sit down." They subsided rather sheepishly into the nearest chairs. I held out my cigarette-case. "What's the news? Anything I can do for you?"

They helped themselves to cigarettes and then looked at each other in embarrassment, each evidently hoping the other would take upon himself the task of opening their business.

Finally they both spoke at once.

"The fact is. Major—"

"We want you to lend us three thousand pounds!"

They both stopped. Franks frowned at Jefferson in deprecation of this bluntly undiplomatic approach.

I laughed.

"Three thousand pounds! That's a tall order, young gentlemen." I felt old enough to be their father, and had some difficulty in keeping my countenance as I looked at their deadly-serious young faces. "What do you want with three thousand pounds?"

There was another pause of embarrassed silence, and then Jefferson nudged his senior.

"*You* tell him, Dicky!" he said, in a hoarse whisper. "You can explain things."

Dicky Franks flushed and his brow corrugated for a moment of concentrated thought. Then he dived a hand into his breast-pocket and fished out a map which I recognised at once as of Army origin. In fact, as he unfolded it, it proved to be our old staff map of the Mosul area. The young fellow looked up at me and cleared his throat.

"You remember, Major, that Jefferson and I crashed one day in the Jebel Abjad—in 1918?"

I smiled.

"Perfectly. If my memory is not amiss," I got both you harum-scarum young devils a decoration for that—not to mention another pip."

Franks nodded acquiescence, his face grave.

"You did. Major. Well—" he hesitated, fumbling for an opening—"the fact is we didn't tell you quite the true story about that stunt—" He paused, moistening his lips in his nervousness.

"What do you mean?" I asked. I am afraid there was a sharp severity in my voice. I had an unpleasant vision of having been made a fool of, of having recommended these two young devils on an utterly fictitious story. It flashed into my mind that they had come to me, conscience-stricken, to confess. "Didn't you crash way back in the Jebel Abjad as you said you did?"

Franks's smile relieved me.

"Oh, yes, we crashed right enough, Major—but not exactly as we said we did. All we told you was true. Only we left some of it out."

Young Jefferson wagged his head in emphatic corroboration.

"That's it. Major. There's some of it we didn't want to tell just then. And we've come to tell you now."

Franks threw a glance admonitory of caution towards his companion.

"Yes," he said, a certain reluctance in his voice, as though afraid to give himself away too quickly. "We want to tell you the whole story, Major—but first I—we—want you to promise that whatever happens you won't mention a word of it to anyone else. That's only fair, isn't it, Harry?" He turned to young Jefferson for support.

"We know we can trust you, Major," interjected Jefferson.

"Of course you can!" I said, seating myself again in my chair and lighting my own cigarette. "I'll keep your confidence, whatever it is. Fire away—and cut out the 'Major'! I'm a civilian, and my name's Ogilvy." My smile was intended to put both of them at their ease.

Franks took up his story, reassured.

"Well, Major—sorry—Mr. Ogilvy," he smiled at his automatic slip—"we came down twice on that stunt in the Jebel Abjad—"

"Twice?" I queried, in surprise." You only mentioned once in your report to me."

"I know, Major—Mr. Ogilvy," said Franks. "That's the point. It's the other time we've come to tell you about now."

"Go ahead," I said." I'm listening."

"Well, the details of that flight don't matter," he resumed, playing nervously with the open map on his knees as he spoke. "You remember we'd got a roving commission over the Jebel Abjad—reconnaissance to see if old Johnny Turk had tucked himself away in any of the valleys. It was top-hole weather for observation—clear as possible—but we flew all the morning without a sign of the Turk.

"We circled round to the north-west for a bit before making for home, and searched up and down the cracks of those mountains pretty thoroughly. Suddenly we saw all round us one of those big ugly thunderstorms which spring up from nowhere in no time among the mountains. It was a rotten place to be caught in. We were about the middle of the range and following a valley, the machine a thousand feet or so below the summits on both sides. I put her nose up at once—and just as we were climbing out of the hole we were in, the confounded old bus missed fire! The engine stopped dead. Just the sort of thing that would happen, of course, in a thunderstorm on top of a mountain range!

I saw the barograph needle switch round as we dropped—and I tell you I thought it was all up with us. We were already once more below the summit of the mountain on our left. The valley bottom was boulders. Suddenly I saw that a broad ledge projected from the flank of the mountain, a terrace two or three hundred yards wide. It was almost below us as I spotted it—an unobstructed stretch of smooth rock. I made for it instinctively—there was no time to think—the second flash of lightning flickered all over the machine. I put her down to it, and just as the rain came down on us in bucketfuls we touched and taxied along the ledge. I swerved round to get her head to wind against the gust that blew back from the mountain-side, and pulled her up by a miracle.

"We jumped out, lightning blazing all round us and rain coming down like a thousand waterfalls. It seemed a pretty hopeless place for shelter—and shelter at that minute was worth our next leave, and that's saying something in Mespot. Suddenly, straight ahead of us, I spotted the mouth of a cave. We both dashed for it like rabbits to a hole.

"It was a cave all right, and there we were, sheltered from the storm, with the lightning playing all over our machine outside. Our chances of ever getting back again looked pretty slim at that moment, I don't mind admitting. If the old bus was struck we hadn't an earthly of ever getting down from that mountain. We looked at each other in the lightning flashes, and we both got the idea to explore the cave to take our minds off the unpleasant possibilities outside.

"It was a big lofty hole, that cave, and the first thing that hit both of us was that its sides had been smoothed by human hands. The chisel marks were still visible. That was surprising enough, for the place seemed absolutely inaccessible. Of course, it occurred to both of us that if people had taken the trouble to climb up here to smooth the walls of a cave they must have had some pretty good reason for doing so. We'd both got electric torches in our tunics and we set out to find that reason.

"It didn't take us long. Twenty or thirty yards inside that cave were three enormous tombs—sarcophagi, don't you call them?—supported on pedestals of squared stone. They were carved all over with figures and covered with roof-like slabs of solid rock. At least, two of them were. We saw at once that we weren't the first to discover those tombs. Someone had been there before us. The slab on the nearest one had been prised off sideways—and underneath the edge of it was a skeleton with an iron bar alongside. Evidently, just as he had got the slab off, it had fallen on him and killed him.

"I tell you we felt pretty excited as we climbed up the pedestal and flashed our torches inside that tomb. The original occupant was still there all right—at least, bits of his skeleton were. But that wasn't what interested us. There were heaps of broken ornaments and things round that skeleton, and the body rested on a bed of what we first thought were neat little bricks. Look!" He extracted a small bar from his pocket and handed it to me. "What do you make of that?"

I took it curiously. It was heavy yellow metal.

"By Jove!" I exclaimed. "This is solid gold!" I turned it over in my fingers and saw upon one of its small ends an embossed oval cartouche filled with hieroglyphic figures. "You've come across the burial treasure of some old Assyrian king, my lads!" I am naturally of an unenthusiastic temperament, but I utterly failed to control the excitement which leaped up in me.

"What an extraordinary adventure!"

Franks nodded gravely.

"What do you reckon that is worth?" he asked.

I balanced it in my hand. It weighed very nearly a couple of pounds.

"About a hundred and fifty pounds sterling, I should say," I hazarded.

"Then, Major—Mr. Ogilvy—there's a hundred and fifty thousand pounds' worth of gold in that tomb alone! We counted the top layer of bricks, and there were about two hundred—and we estimated that there were at least five layers of them. They're all the same size. Jefferson here has another."

Young Jefferson pulled out a gold brick from his pocket also. It was identical with the first. I put them side by side on my desk.

"I suppose you stuffed your pockets full?" I said, highly interested and a little envious.

"Lucky young beggars!"

The pair of them looked sheepishly at each other. Then Franks laughed.

"Well—to tell the truth, Major—all of a sudden we both got wind up. A most horrible moaning sound came from somewhere out of the darkness of that cave. It was most uncanny, especially with that skeleton pinned under the slab. We didn't stop to think. We both cut and ran for the entrance, scared out of our lives. All we got was the one brick each we had slipped into our pockets and a lump of stone broken off the slab which Jefferson was holding when we heard the noise."

Jefferson undid his parcel.

"Here it is," he said, passing it over to me. Part of a winged bull remained on the fragment, which was incised with characters unknown to me but obviously of great antiquity.

"What happened next?" I asked.

"Well—the storm had ceased. It was bright sunshine outside and neither of us felt like going into that dark cave again. Our nerves were all to pieces. We tinkered up the old engine—it was only a choked jet—and took off from that ledge just as quick as might be."

"You left the treasure?" I did not conceal my surprise.

Jefferson laughed boyishly.

"I guess you would have left it too, just then, Major," he said. That infernal moan was no joke—I know I turned over pretty queer inside me when I heard it. It seemed to go right through you. Ugh!"

he shuddered. I suppose we were a bit tuned up just then," he added, in self-apology. "We'd had a near shave before we got on that ledge."

"Go on," I said, nodding my appreciation of their feelings. "What next?"

That's all. You know the rest of it," said Franks. "Just as we were getting clear of the mountain the engine gave out again and we crashed properly. Everything else happened just as we reported it."

"And the gold is still there?"

"So far as we know. We never had a chance to go back." Franks got up from his seat, came across to my desk, and spread out the map. He put his finger on an inked cross in the middle of the brown intricacy of the mountain-ranges. It looked a most inaccessible spot. "Here's the place!" he said. "Think of it! Pretty nearly half a million pounds' worth of solid gold waiting for us! Worth trying for, isn't it, Major?"

"You are assuming that the other tombs also contain an equivalent amount," I said, damping down his enthusiasm in an effort to control sudden wild fancies of my own. "And you don't realise the difficulties. The place could only be reached by a long and most dangerous expedition. All that country is worse than ever since the Armistice. It is inhabited by wild Kurds who would make a virtue of cutting your throats. Besides, from your description, it would be no easy mountaineering feat to climb up to that ledge."

"Next door to impossible, I should say," agreed Franks, cheerfully. "I can't imagine how the poor devil who was crushed under the slab ever got there—or how they put the tombs there, for that matter. Perhaps there has been a landslide since. No man could climb to that ledge now, that's certain."

"Then how do you propose to get there?" I asked.

The two young men smiled at each other in amusement at my simplicity.

"By aeroplane, of course!" they said, in one breath.

"So that's why you want my three thousand pounds?" My smile was not so cynical as I intended it to be. The fascination of the thing had already got a greater hold over me than I realised.

It was. Breathlessly, both of them speaking at once, they informed me that they had found the ideal machine—an ex-Army bomber designed to carry four tons of explosives and fitted for a flight to India that had been given up at the last moment. It had a saloon in which we—they included me in the expedition with an amazingly calm assumption of my assent—could sleep comfortably and get our meals. It would lift easily the cargo of gold—three tons they reckoned it to be—and had a petrol capacity sufficient for the journey. They offered me a third share of the treasure if I would finance the expedition. Apparently, also, they had set their hearts upon my accompanying them.

"Not so fast," I protested. "I've got a business I can't leave."

"You take holidays sometimes, don't you?" countered Franks. "We shall be back again inside a fortnight."

The upshot of it all was that, when at the end of an hour they left me, they carried off with them my cheque for two thousand pounds for the immediate purchase of that aeroplane, and I—definitely committed to what in solitude I now saw to be a mad adventure—sat in my chair, puffing at my pipe, and staring at the mysterious inscription incised upon the slab of stone. Of course, it conveyed nothing to me, but I could not help a considerable curiosity as to its meaning. I felt rather grimly that at least it would be satisfying to know whose tomb it was that we were proposing to rifle.

It occurred to me to take it up to the Assyrian Department of the British Museum, and then a happier thought followed upon the heels of the first. McPherson at the club! If anyone could decipher that inscription, it would be old Mac! He had devoted the best part of his life to Assyrian archæology. I wrapped up that slab of stone in Jefferson's brown paper, and five minutes later I was in a taxi on my way to the club.

McPherson was there sure enough. I went straight to my point and, without telling him how this fragment came into my hands, I opened my parcel and asked him if he could decipher the inscription. He took it with the eager interest of the man of science presented with a new specimen, pored it over as he twisted it in his hands, nodded his head vigorously.

"A very interesting piece, Mr. Ogilvy!" he said. "Most interesting! The British Museum would be real glad of it. Where did you get it?"

"Never mind where I got it," I replied. "Can you read the inscription?"

"Easily, man! Easily!" he said." There is no difficulty whatever about it. It is mutilated—incomplete, of course. But what is there is plain as print! It is in the usual cuneiform character—the middle Assyrian variety. I should say it dates from about 1500 B.C."

"Interpret, O Sage!" said I.

He adjusted his spectacles and, following the nail-shaped characters from left to right with his finger, translated as follows:—

"I, Sarchon, King of Kings, son of Nimrot, King of Kings, lying in this tomb, say, Come not to open this tomb. He who shall remove the stone that covers me shall die and in the grave find not repose, neither shall the sun shine upon him nor his kindred know his fate.' That's all," said McPherson, looking up at me through his spectacles.

"The inscription is broken at that point."

"You read it like a book!" I said, in admiration.

"Pooh!" he replied. "'Tis easy enough. It presents no points of difficulty. There are hundreds of inscriptions like that. This happens to be a king's, that's all. The interest is in the name of the monarch. Otherwise it is quite commonplace."

I thought of the skeleton lying pinned under the slab in that dark cave.

"*Is it?*" I said, with an emphasis which made him look curiously at me.

He gave me an odd smile.

"Be careful how you go digging about in those tombs, young man," he said.

Unwilling to expose myself to the inquiries obviously on the tip of his tongue, I made an excuse to cut short the conversation. But, as I went out of the club, I felt that my enthusiasm for the adventure had considerably evaporated. I could not help seeing that confounded skeleton with the iron bar beside him.

II

I will not here dwell upon the details of our preparations for the flight. Suffice it that within a week Franks and Jefferson had flown the aeroplane over to the grounds of the country place near London which I had recently purchased. In the absence of a hangar, firmly secured tarpaulins protected it at once from the weather and the curiosity of the local inhabitants. So far as my unskilled eye could judge, it was a beautiful machine, eminently suited for our purpose. She carried fuel enough in her tanks for a fifty-hour flight, and more could be stowed in the interior. Her water-tank contained two hundred gallons of that vital necessity in the desert. There was ample storage capacity for all the provisions we should require. The two young men were in ecstasies of enthusiasm over her, but I confess that, novice as I was in this form of travel, it was with considerable awe that I stood under the vast spread of her wings and looked up to the cabin which was to carry us, high above the clouds, those thousands of miles to the mountains beyond the Mesopotamian desert which seemed, here in this English countryside, fantastically unreal in their remoteness.

But during the next two weeks there was little time for brooding. The die was cast. I could not decently turn back if I would, and I will confess that sometimes the fascination of our adventure gripped me as strongly as it did the two young pilots. We kept our project as quiet as possible. Those official inquiries which could not be avoided we satisfied with the story of an independent flight to India.

Our route was mapped out in easy stages—six hundred and fifty miles to Marseilles for the first day, six hundred to Messina, eight hundred to Alexandria. Thence, pushing boldly to the north-east, we might, by starting at dawn, make the final one thousand three hundred miles to our destination in one flight if circumstances were favourable. If not, we could come down in the desert for one night. Franks and Jefferson, of course, proposed to fly the machine in alternate shifts. My *rôle* was that of cook and steward. Naturally, in view of possible trouble with the desert tribes, should we descend among them, we provided ourselves with arms and ammunition, in addition to the implements necessary for breaking open the other tombs.

At last all was ready. I shall never forget the thrill with which, in the fresh brightness of an English summer morning, I saw the great machine, stripped of her last coverings, poised on the greensward in waiting for the start. Franks was already at his post in the pilot's seat, and first one, then the other of her engines whirred in a deep-toned roar as he tested them, flattening the grass in the wind under the propellers. Jefferson was clambering over the wings in a final examination of every stay and strut. I climbed up the ladder into the interior. My butler, gloomy in disapproval of these newfangled contraptions, but dutifully resolved to be with me until the last moment, pulled away the ladder and shouted "Good-bye, sir," in a tone strongly suggestive of an eternal farewell. I saw him dodge back out of the wind of the accelerated propellers. "Right away!" shouted Jefferson, cheerfully, clambering from the wing into the interior.

The engines leaped to a synchronised deafening roar. Through the windows I saw the grass flit past, drop away from us. The trees around my house sank suddenly—we were up! House and trees twirled away from us as we climbed in a long sweep over the foreshortened figure of the butler waving his valedictions. They reappeared again, far below us, tiny like toys. Then they slipped back out of vision, left behind. We roared over a patchwork of miniature fields, bound—it was almost inconceivable—over distant lands and seas for the vast spaces of the desert and those long-talked-of mountains which loomed, like a mirage in my imagination, beyond its yellow immensity.

III

Mosul, white among its verdure, on the nearer bank of the blue Tigris forking about its islands, showed up ahead of us. On the other side of the stream, plainly discernible, were the mounds which covered all that remained of the glory of ancient Nineveh—the city where perhaps, thirty-five centuries ago, had been hammered into shape those gold bricks which had lured us all the way from the heart of a distant Empire greater even than that which here had once been the ultimate of human grandeur. Franks and Jefferson grinned at each other as they glanced down at the white mosque and took a bearing over the confused mass of wooded foothills to the north and east of Mosul towards a stupendous snow-clad peak—the Judi Dagh, I remembered its name—which towered in the distance above the endless chaos of sternly rugged mountains stretching far and wide and reaching back, to the limits of vision, into the recesses of Persia. I stood behind the two lads in the pilot-chamber, straining my eyes towards our destination. In which of those cleft gorges was hollowed the tomb of the three kings on their lofty terrace?

We sped onwards. Beyond the first range of mountains a valley dipped itself into a bowl of green where white houses twinkled among the trees—Amadiyah! We soared over it, swung to the north-west and then to the west, towards another wilderness of hills. Our pilots were following their original course. A silence as of death seemed to brood over this sterile desolation of crag and boulder. The roar of our engines re-echoed from it with an alien sound as we dipped below the summits in scrutiny of one valley after another.

Suddenly Jefferson pointed ahead of us, one hand clutching at the shoulder of his comrade seated at the controls. "There it is!"

I looked, with a thrill of excitement. There in front of us, a thousand feet or more below the summit of the mountain, but thousands of feet above the bed of the sombre ravine which dropped away from it in a sheer precipice, was a long, broad terrace, obviously artificial. We swung round above it, commenced a cautious descent. It would be no joke to be caught in a sudden air-flurry in such a place. The roar of the engines ceased suddenly. An uncanny silence enveloped us with their cessation. None of us spoke. I could feel my heart beating in my breast. Our nose went down and the rock rushed up towards us, became a wall upon our left hand. Below us that smooth terrace, larger and larger with every second, rose and broadened. The engines started again in a quick brief roar which reverberated endlessly after they were abruptly stilled. We swung round towards the mountain, touched and skimmed across the ledge at an angle, slowed with a quick turn perpendicular to the wall of rock, stopped less than a hundred feet away from it. We had arrived!

Like three eager schoolboys we tumbled out of the machine, ran along the face of the rock. At first glance I noticed what my companions, too preoccupied with the storm, had failed to observe upon their first visit. The precipice which towered above us was a picture-gallery of ancient Assyrian art. Great winged bulls, eagle-headed human figures of colossal size, in flat relief, dominated an endless succession of sculptured scenes, comparatively miniature, depicting the wars and conquests of a vanished empire.

A shout from Franks, in advance of us, told that he had found the entrance to the cave. A pair of vast human-headed bulls arched their wings above its opening. The three of us stopped at the portal. A sudden awe came over us as we peered into its obscurity, a feeling of an indefinable presence that pervaded the atmosphere.

"Listen!" whispered Franks, clutching at my arm.

From the interior came a long weird moan that swelled and died away. We sprang back, a primitive terror quick upon us. Then, as silence once more fell upon that lonely terrace, we crept forward again to the entrance.

A little wind stirred into whorls the dust about our feet as we stood under the archway of those mighty wings. Once more the weird moan issued drearily from the cave. My faculties, heightened with excitement, leaped, to an association of ideas.

"All right!" I cried to my companions. "All right! It's nothing to be afraid of!"

Those cunning old artificers, of a piece with those who had contrived the statue of Memnon in Egypt, had hollowed that rock to such acoustic properties that a breath of wind blowing into it resounded magnified, as from a trumpet, in that mysterious moan so eminently calculated to unnerve the least superstitious. I explained it to the two lads.

"All very well," said Franks, "but I propose we go back to the old bus and have a meal before we risk ourselves in here. We've got plenty of time. We shall feel all the stronger after we've filled up. What do you say, Harry?"

"I think so too," said Jefferson. "We've got to have a meal anyway. And personally I want to make the fewest possible visits to the inside of this cave and get finished with it as soon as may be. It may be only the wind, of course. But I don't like it, all the same. Besides, we must go back for the crowbars."

It was well that we did so. Eager as we were to discover the entrance to the cave, we had forgotten to fasten down the aeroplane in any way. As we approached it, we noticed that it seemed farther from the rock wall than we had left it. A moment later a gust of wind, reflected from that sculptured surface, moved it perceptibly towards the sheer gulf a few hundred yards behind it. Dicky Franks shamed us both with his instant presence of mind. While we stared aghast, he darted forward to the machine, swung himself up over the lower wing into the pilot-compartment, started the engines. He taxied her gently back, and Jefferson and myself made her fast with ropes to projecting points of the rock.

The young man's face was white as he dropped out of the machine and rejoined us.

"They're trying to kill us!" he said, hoarsely, his voice unsteady with a genuine fear.

"Nonsense, Dicky!" I replied. "It was just the wind."

He turned upon me.

"This wind about here is too confoundedly intelligent for my liking!" he said. "I tell you, I've got a feeling—"

"Keep it to yourself, then, my lad!" I said, sharply. "You'll be giving us all cold feet in a minute with your sickly imaginations. We have not flown over three thousand miles to this cave to be put off now with superstitious fancies."

"The Major's right, Dicky," said Jefferson. "We made up our minds to come back for that gold, and here we are. Let's get on with it. We'll have a bite of food first—and then to work!"

Franks remained silent. I could see that he was badly shaken. However, as all three of us sat in the saloon about our meal he recovered his cheerfulness.

"We shall have to make a camp of it, Major," he said." For to-night at least. We can't shift three tons of gold between now and dark."

"Three tons!" murmured young Jefferson. "Ye gods! Three tons of gold—think of it! It's got to be a full-sized ghost that will scare me off three tons of gold!"

Dicky frowned, but made no comment.

"Yes, we shall certainly have to stay for the night," I agreed. "But we'll get as much as possible on board while the day lasts."

"By all means," said Dicky. "I'm ready as soon as you are. I propose that we start first with the tomb that's already opened." He hesitated a moment, as though half-ashamed of what was in his mind." By the way, Major—have you got the copy of that inscription on you?" His attempt at a casual voice was not very successful.

I looked at him, reproof in my eyes. But he was not to be diverted.

"Let me have a look at it, will you?" he said.

I could not very well refuse. I took from my pocket the sheet of paper on which I had jotted down my memory of McPherson's reading of that ominous inscription, and handed it to him.

"'I, Sarchon, King of Kings, son of Nimrot, King of Kings, lying in this tomb, say: Come not to open this tomb. He who shall remove the stone that covers me shall die and in the grave find not repose, neither shall the sun shine upon him nor his kindred know his fate.'" The threat as he read it out, calm though was his voice, sounded peculiarly awesome in the presence of those ineffably placid stone monsters visible through the windows of the saloon. Their very silence seemed eloquent. Dicky looked up from the paper.

"Do you think, Major, that—just supposing, for example, there were anything in this—I don't say for a moment there is—but just supposing—do you think that the curse is fulfilled so far as the first tomb is concerned? I've been thinking about that skeleton under the slab. If that poor devil paid the penalty—it only says 'uncovering the tomb,' you know—then we ought to be pretty safe in taking the treasure from it. What do you think? We might find so much there that we should not want to disturb the others."

"Shut up, Dicky!" said Jefferson. "You are giving me the creeps."

He was giving me the creeps, too. This kind of talk had to be stopped at once. A solitude such as was so profound about us was not the place to indulge in fanciful speculations.

"By all means let us clear the opened tomb first," I said, with a happy achievement of cool imperturbability. "But I should like to get one of the others open before nightfall. This ledge is apparently not a very safe place for the machine and we do not want to stay a moment longer than is necessary. If a wind-storm sprang up while we are here, it would be extremely awkward, to say the least of it. The cool air from the mountains sometimes blows with hurricane force in its rush to fill the place of the heated atmosphere of the desert-plains, you know." I was determined to be ready with a rational explanation of everything that did or might happen.

Jefferson sprang up from his seat.

"Let's get to work, Major! Come on, Dicky! I bet you I get in first with a chunk of rock at any old ghost that shows himself—loser pays for a dinner at the Savoy when we get back!" He laughed in youthful high spirits. "Come on, you fellows! This way to the pirate's hoard! Where are the old money-boxes?"

I was grateful to him for his boisterous jocularity. Dicky actually smiled as we both rose from the table. A few minutes later, the aeroplane firmly secured behind us, we were on our way to the cave, carrying between us two ammunition-chests with rope-handles—Jefferson's "money-boxes"—which we had brought for the conveyance of the treasure.

After our good lunch, fortified as it had been by a bottle of the best, the dark entrance to the cave no longer looked so forbidding. We ignored the great human-headed bulls as we marched in, Jefferson chanting, in humorous defiance of our past fancies, the refrain of Stevenson's "Treasure Island":—

> "Fifteen men on the dead man's chest,
> Drink and the devil had done for the rest.
> Yo-ho-ho! for a bottle of rum!

This way to the pirate's hoard, my hearties! Personally-conducted tours under the guidance of expert British officers! Inclusive terms, authentic skeletons provided! Everybody free to help themselves. You pays your money and you takes your choice! Yo-ho-ho! for a bottle of rum! This way to the pirate's treasure!"

Franks interrupted his comrade's seriocomic declamation.

"Shut up, Harry!" he said, irritably. "Don't make a jest of it! After all—" He did not finish his thought. I knew he had our treasure-hunting predecessor in his mind.

That long weird moan came again from the interior of the cave. We ignored it resolutely, switching on our flash-lamps as we advanced into the chill gloom.

"Very clever the way those old fellows arranged the acoustics of this place," I said, with an affectation of indifference not quite in correspondence with my feelings. "Did you notice that puff of wind?" I told myself that I shuddered only at the cold of this sunless place.

"Wind, was it?" said Franks, in a strange voice.

We went on in silence until we reached the first tomb. There, just as the two lads had described it, was the slab aslant from it to the ground—and underneath it that fleshless skeleton with the iron bar by his side.

We gave but a cursory glance either to that luckless relic or to the undoubtedly interesting carvings upon the exterior of the sarcophagus. The glamour of its imagined contents, now after so long journeying almost at our touch, dazzled us to all but instant possession. I understand now that madness of the goldlust of which I have read in tales of the early diggings. I think we would then and there have killed anyone who stood between us and the treasure. I was startled at the expression of my comrades' faces as I saw them in the circle of light from my torch. They were no longer boys. Fever glittered in their eyes. They looked like old men, lean and covetous. The metamorphosis shocked me in the instant of attention which I gave to it. Without a word, but with a concentrated intensity of action, the three of us clambered up the pedestal of the tomb. The long dreary moan reiterated from the black interior of the cave fell this time upon deaf or heedless ears. An apparition itself would have been unnoticed in our excitement.

We switched our torches into the sarcophagus. The uneasy fear at the back of our minds, which none of us had dared to express, was instantly dispelled. The light was reflected in a dull glint from the metallic bed on which reposed a few crumbled fragments of bones and cerecloths. The treasure was still there! Two only of the close-packed bricks of gold were missing.

"Hooray!" shouted Jefferson, his voice reverberating uncannily under the vault of the cave. "The old gentleman has saved it for us! Now, my hearties!" He reached down an eager hand, pulled up a brick. "Once aboard the lugger and the treasure's ours!"

"One of us had better get down and pack it into the boxes," I said. "The other two will hand the stuff down to him."

"I'll pack it," responded Franks, obviously keeping himself under stern control. I noticed that he looked up apprehensively as once more that sinister moan seemed to breathe past our ears. He sprang down to the floor of the cave, took the golden bars we passed to him, packed them neatly into the boxes.

We all worked silently, but with a curious instinctive haste, as though we were menaced by interruption. Nothing stirred, however, not even a resting bat, in that cave lost among the mountain solitudes. Our vague fears dropped from us as we worked without any interference, visible or invisible. Jefferson even began to whistle.

The two boxes filled, the three of us—Dicky, as the strongest, in the middle—staggered with them back to the aeroplane. Their weight was surprising. Everything was perfectly normal as we returned to the machine. She had not shifted in the least.

We climbed on board and stowed away the chests in the cargo-hold. As we leaped down again, with two empty ones for the next load, I noticed that the sun was already sinking behind the higher crests of the chaos of mountains around us.

"We sha'n't do more than clear this tomb before nightfall," I said, rather anxiously. "And we shall have to hurry to do that." I did not relish the prospect of passing two nights on this dangerous ledge.

We hastened back to the cave and worked with a will. Journey after journey we made, heavy laden, to the aeroplane. Layer after layer of gold bricks was exposed and packed away in the chests. There was more of it than we expected. Instead of five layers there were seven. (I might have guessed that they would be in a sacred number.) It was already pitch-black night when, utterly wearied, we staggered with the last load to our now familiar home. The light left shining through its saloon-windows welcomed us with a pleasant suggestion of comfort and security. Those last trips in the gathering darkness had been decidedly eerie.

We were all in the best of spirits, however, as we sat round our evening meal in the saloon and toasted our good luck with another bottle. The three of us went to gloat over the stack of treasure-chests in the baggage-hold between the wings. Jefferson, characteristically, expressed a doubt whether the space would contain the spoil to be obtained from the other tombs.

"We'll tuck it away somewhere, never fear!" I said, cheerfully. "We'll start work at dawn to-morrow and get clear away before dark! My lads," I added, turning to them, "do you quite realise how rich we are? It seems fantastic to me."

"To me too," agreed Franks, seriously. "We won't talk about it till we get it safely home. And, by the way, I'll have another look at those tethering-ropes. This would be a nasty spot if it came on to blow during the night."

So saying, he jumped out into the darkness. In a few minutes he returned, quite reassured.

"Nothing short of a gale can shift us," he said. "But I'm going to switch on the headlights all the same. An accident in the dark would be no joke."

He went forward and a moment later the terrace was suffused with a reflected radiance from where the two great circles illumined the stiff placidity of those grotesque monsters carved upon the cliff.

We all turned in to our berths, thoroughly exhausted, and in a few minutes were all asleep.

How long I slept I do not know. I was awakened from a confused nightmare of affrighting Assyrian figures that pelted me with gold as I sat in the dining-room of the Savoy Hotel and filled the air with a rushing tumult in which the cream-and-gold pillars of that firmly-established hostelry swayed and rocked as though in an earthquake. It seemed to me that the entire hotel was slipping, slipping, slipping, with an awful grating noise, into a bottomless gulf that had opened for its reception. My consciousness struggled through the welter of dream-phantasms that overlaid it, came to full perception with a shock of wild alarm.

The aeroplane was lifting, slipping, bumping, now pulled up short by a rope, now jerking away in a sudden release, rising and falling from side to side, in a gale of wind that howled among the mountains with the fury of a hurricane. Torrents of rain hammered and drummed upon the canvas roof overhead. Through the saloon windows I had a sudden glimpse of that sculptured rock-face illumined in a blinding jag of lightning. An appalling crash of thunder drowned my voice as I shouted to my companions.

But they were awake. The saloon started into illumination as Jefferson, springing to his feet, switched on the lights. Franks was making for the door to the pilot-compartment, lurching as he went as though in the cabin of a tempest-tossed yacht at moorings.

"We shall be adrift in a moment!" I heard him shout as he disappeared through the door. I guessed his purpose instantly. He was going to start the engines.

Another moment and, with a sharp crack in the midst of that tumult of wind and rain and thunder-coupled lightning, the last rope parted. The machine lifted on her beam. I heard her wing scraping along the terrace as we slid. Instinctively I clutched for support, vain though it was, at a stanchion of my bunk. In another instant we should be over the precipice.

Even as I agonised for the cessation of the scraping sound, I heard the welcome roar of the engines starting into life. Good old Franks! I could imagine him, desperately battling, at the controls. My relief lasted not a second—with a sickening suddenness we dropped, backwards, in an awful vertical descent. The machine swayed violently as she tried to right herself. The engines re-echoed thunderously from the black gulf I glimpsed through the windows, leaped to spasms of their fullest power, yet futile, I was only too conscious, in the fury of that hurricane.

Then ensued a desperate battle for life. It was useless to think of rejoining Franks at the pilot-wheel; I could have been of no assistance even had it been possible. As it was, I had to cling for dear life to prevent myself being thrown through the canvas roof. But Jefferson had vanished, had managed somehow to go to the help of his comrade. I was alone in that saloon which lurched and twirled, bumped and pitched and rolled, fell and rose again at every variety of angle. The wind assailed her with a frenzy of sledge-hammer blows. I wondered how long she could hold together. The headlights were still on. Through the windows I could see them now making white circles on the rock-face, now shooting their beams endlessly, without a target, into the infinite blackness of the night. The engines raved and roared as, struggling with the brutal buffetings of the gale, they strove to pull us up out of this pit among the mountains into the rock-free regions of the upper air.

There was perhaps a minute of suspense, and then the disaster for which I held my breath happened with a vicious suddenness. Caught in a terrific blast of wind that whirled against the precipice, the machine was flung right over, upside down. A hail of small loose objects in the cabin leaped up about my head as, clinging desperately to the support wrenching in my hand, I felt my feet break through the roof. Simultaneously, I heard a clatter and a crash, loud above the uproar of the gale. The boxes of gold—loose amidships in their compartment—had smashed through the roof on to which they had been flung! As I realised it—visualised our hard-won treasure hurtling into the black gulf below—I had a last glimpse, upside down though I was, of the entrance to the cave, its winged guardians vividly illumined in a lightning flash of peculiarly intense brilliancy.

It was perhaps imagination, but I thought I heard a scream of unearthly triumph mingling with the wild howling of the wind. No theory of cunning acoustics was plausible just then.

But I had no mind, in that dreadful crisis, to bemoan the loss of our treasure. At any moment our lives might be extinguished. Hope of survival was a mockery I did not entertain for an instant. Yet the engines still roared against the fury of the gale and still we kept, despite our inverted position, a purchase on the air. Rocking violently from side to side, the miracle happened. A sudden dive nose-down and we returned, in a sickening swoop, to right-side up. I extricated my legs from the torn canvas of the roof, dropped them to the floor. I had a mental glimpse, warm with gratitude, of Franks dauntlessly sticking to his controls, fighting with every ounce of his strength and amazing skill. "Good lad!" I shouted, though I knew he could not hear.

A moment later and we were dashed violently against the face of the rock. I heard the planes on one side crack and break. It was all over! The next instant we were descending in long circling sweeps at an acute angle. The engines still roared intermittently. I looked, following the beams of our downward headlights, into a bottomless gulf whose walls rushed round giddily in our spiral fall. I saw suddenly great boulders directly beneath us, expanding like bladders in quick inflation. Our nose came up suddenly—sideways. There was a terrific shock—blackness.

It was three weary, tattered, half-starving men—shaken still with the miracle of their escape—who dragged themselves four days later into Mosul. They left behind them, in that gloomy valley, not only a wrecked aeroplane but those golden bars which had rained down from a night of fury into some unknown gulf. As they had picked themselves up, bruised and battered, in the dawn slowly brightening to their returning consciousness, and groped for a way out again to the haunts of men, they had not dared to look up to that terrace where, inaccessible to the boldest mountaineer, those carven winged monsters guarded the treasure of the tombs.

STORY SOURCES

All of the stories in this anthology are in the public domain. The following are listed in order of first publication.

Reynolds, Mary, "A Futile Ghost", *Crampton's Magazine*, February 1899.

Mee, Huan, "Phantom Death", *Cassell's Magazine*, March 1900.

Thorne, Guy, "A Regent of Love Rhymes", *The Lady's Realm*, December 1905.

Philips, Austin, "The Missing Word", *Pall Mall Magazine*, November 1907.

Norris, Elsie, "The Mystery of the Gables", *Yes or No*, 20 June 1908.

Barr, James, "The Soul of Maddalina Tonelli", *The Red Magazine*, December 1909.

Scott, Firth, "The Wraith of the Rapier", *The Red Magazine*, 15 January 1911.

Edwards, Jack, "Haunted!", *The Weekly Tale Teller* #83, 3 December 1910.

Brebner, Percy J., "Our Strange Traveller", *The Weekly Tale Teller* #105, 6 May 1911.

Xavier, Francis, "Amid the Trees", *The Weekly Tale Teller* #110, 10 June 1911.

Schultze, Mary, "The River's Edge", *The Weekly Tale Teller* #188, 7 December 1912.

Deakin, Lumley, "Ghosts", *The New Magazine*, October 1914.

Jordan, Elizabeth, "Kearney", *The Premier Magazine*, April 1917.

Wright, Hugh E. "On the Embankment", *The Blue Magazine*, September 1919.

Forest, Philippa, "When Spirits Steal", *Pearson's Magazine*, May 1920.

Austin, F. Britten, "The Treasure of the Tombs", *Strand Magazine*, January 1921.

Benson, E. F. "The Woman in the Veil", *London Evening News*, 26 June 1928.

Purves, Eric, "The House of the Black Evil", *Pearson's Magazine*, May 1929.

BRITISH LIBRARY TALES OF THE WEIRD

*Haunted Houses: Two
Novels by Charlotte Riddell*
Edited by Andrew Smith

*From the Depths & Other
Strange Tales of the Sea*
Edited by Mike Ashley

*Mortal Echoes:
Encounters with the End*
Edited by Greg Buzwell

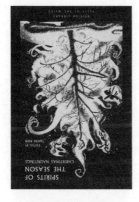

*Spirits of the Season:
Christmas Hauntings*
Edited by Tanya Kirk

British Library Tales of the Weird collects a thrilling array of uncanny story-telling, from the realms of gothic, supernatural and horror fiction. With stories ranging from the 19th century to the present day, this series revives long-lost material from the Library's vaults to thrill again alongside beloved classics of the weird fiction genre.

Martin Limón
(South Korea)
Jade Lady Burning
Slicky Boys
Buddha's Money
The Door to Bitterness
The Wandering Ghost
G.I. Bones
Mr. Kill
The Joy Brigade
Nightmare Range
The Iron Sickle
The Ville Rat
Ping-Pong Heart
The Nine-Tailed Fox

Ed Lin
(Taiwan)
Ghost Month
Incensed

Peter Lovesey
(England)
The Circle
The Headhunters
False Inspector Dew
Rough Cider
On the Edge
The Reaper

(Bath, England)
The Last Detective
Diamond Solitaire
The Summons
Bloodhounds
Upon a Dark Night
The Vault
Diamond Dust
The House Sitter
The Secret Hangman
Skeleton Hill
Stagestruck
Cop to Corpse
The Tooth Tattoo
The Stone Wife
Down Among the Dead Men
Another One Goes Tonight

(London, England)
Wobble to Death
The Detective Wore Silk Drawers
Abracadaver
Mad Hatter's Holiday
The Tick of Death
A Case of Spirits
Swing, Swing Together
Waxwork

Jassy Mackenzie
(South Africa)
Random Violence
Stolen Lives

Jassy Mackenzie cont.
The Fallen
Pale Horses
Bad Seeds

Francine Mathews
(Nantucket)
Death in the Off-Season
Death in Rough Water
Death in a Mood Indigo
Death in a Cold Hard Light
Death on Nantucket

Seichō Matsumoto
(Japan)
Inspector Imanishi Investigates

Magdalen Nabb
(Italy)
Death of an Englishman
Death of a Dutchman
Death in Springtime
Death in Autumn
The Marshal and the Murderer
The Marshal and the Madwoman
The Marshal's Own Case
The Marshal Makes His Report
The Marshal at the Villa Torrini
Property of Blood
Some Bitter Taste
The Innocent
Vita Nuova
The Monster of Florence

Fuminori Nakamura
(Japan)
The Thief
Evil and the Mask
Last Winter, We Parted
The Kingdom
The Boy in the Earth

Stuart Neville
(Northern Ireland)
The Ghosts of Belfast
Collusion
Stolen Souls
The Final Silence
Those We Left Behind
So Say the Fallen

(Dublin)
Ratlines

Kwei Quartey
(Ghana)
Murder at Cape Three Points
Gold of Our Fathers

Qiu Xiaolong
(China)
Death of a Red Heroine
A Loyal Character Dancer
When Red Is Black

John Straley
(Alaska)
The Woman Who Married a Bear
The Curious Eat Themselves
The Big Both Ways
Cold Storage, Alaska

Akimitsu Takagi
(Japan)
The Tattoo Murder Case
Honeymoon to Nowhere
The Informer

Helene Tursten
(Sweden)
Detective Inspector Huss
The Torso
The Glass Devil
Night Rounds
The Golden Calf
The Fire Dance
The Beige Man
The Treacherous Net
Who Watcheth

Janwillem van de Wetering
(Holland)
Outsider in Amsterdam
Tumbleweed
The Corpse on the Dike
Death of a Hawker
The Japanese Corpse
The Blond Baboon
The Maine Massacre
The Mind-Murders
The Streetbird
The Rattle-Rat
Hard Rain
Just a Corpse at Twilight
Hollow-Eyed Angel
The Perfidious Parrot
The Sergeant's Cat: Collected Stories

Timothy Williams
(Guadeloupe)
Another Sun
The Honest Folk of Guadeloupe

(Italy)
Converging Parallels
The Puppeteer
Persona Non Grata
Black August
Big Italy
The Second Day
of the Renaissance

Jacqueline Winspear
(1920s England)
Maisie Dobbs
Birds of a Feather